All of Nothing

VANIA RHEAULT

 Created with Vellum

*For the women who have to fight every day for what they need for
themselves and their families.
Never stop fighting.*

One

She wasn't coming.

Jaxon Brooks leaned against the cool church wall, the murmur of the wedding guests carrying to him down the hallway. He hid in a small room, that, judging by the posters on the walls, was used as a space for Sunday School for younger children.

"Jesus is always with you!" proclaimed one bright poster attached to a cork board with pushpins.

Jax never felt more alone than he did at that moment.

No, that wasn't true.

The organist began to repeat the song he and his fiancée had chosen as the hymn that would be played while the ushers led the wedding guests to their seats.

It was the fifth time the song repeated, and his wedding guests knew something was amiss. No one would still be arriving at this late time; the ceremony should have started twenty minutes ago.

The joy in the atmosphere began to slip away and was replaced with uncertainty and confusion.

Jax pulled a flask out of the inside pocket of his tux and took a long swig. He needed to face facts. His bride-to-be abandoned him, and he needed to stop the wedding and send everyone home.

His parents would be devastated. They'd been so happy their lonely son finally found someone to share his life with.

Unaware the room was occupied, a black-haired woman pushed a vacuum cleaner with squeaky wheels through the door. She stepped back when she noticed him, fear shooting through her eyes, her gaze locking onto his flask.

"What are you doing?" Jax barked. His muscles, tight with stress, loosened at the chance to lash out. "Surely you don't expect to vacuum now. There's a wedding starting soon. Everyone will hear it."

It gave him no satisfaction when she paled. She gripped the vacuum's handle until her knuckles turned white. "I, I'm late, and I—"

"I don't care. Do you expect the bride and groom to say their vows over the growling of an ancient vacuum cleaner?"

Tears sprang to her eyes, and for just a moment, Jax felt a pang of remorse. It quickly faded. He was miserable; why shouldn't she be as well?

Nothing had gone right for him in sixteen years.

He narrowed his eyes, calculating her measurements.

Tears spilled down her cheeks, mascara smearing under her eyes. She was short, too slim, her collarbone visible beneath her worn and stained t-shirt, but he could work with that. Her feet, clad in tennis shoes, looked too small to fit Gwen's pumps, but if the dress hid her feet, she needn't wear any shoes at all.

The cleaning lady wasn't entirely unattractive, though the pitch black color of her hair washed out her complexion and the pink and blue cotton candy stripes near the ends looked ridiculous. Her t-shirt hid, or tried to hide, a pair of small, perky breasts. Ragged jeans with holes in the knees encased delicate hips and thin thighs.

No one would believe he'd marry someone like her, or if they did, they'd think perhaps he was finally lightening up a little.

Not that it mattered what people thought.

He only needed her for as long as it took to say, "I do," accept congratulations, and then he'd drop her in the nearest gutter where she came from.

"Marry me."

~

Raven Grey could smell the whiskey from the doorway even though he leaned against the far wall in the corner of the room.

She hadn't meant to walk in on him, hadn't meant to see anyone. It was supposed to be her job to clean the small church before the ceremony scheduled that day, but she'd overslept.

Her cheeks flamed with embarrassment. She wanted to finish and leave. But of course, he was right, she shouldn't even be here. She should have been long gone.

She licked her lips, her mouth watering. What she wouldn't give for a taste of that whiskey in his flask.

God, she needed a drink.

Of anything.

"What—what do you mean?"

"My fiancée walked out on me. I have no bride. Stand in for her, and I'll give you whatever you want."

His eyes pinned her to the industrial carpeting that covered the floor.

Raven lifted her chin, wiping away her tears. "I'm not surprised."

Bullies were no strangers to her. She dealt with them every day. Only, this one . . . this one could complain to her social worker and get her fired. It'd been a long time since she held a steady job, and the placement agency made it clear they wouldn't tolerate any fuck-ups.

The man wearing the impeccable tux tilted his head in acknowledgement. "I thought I found someone who could tolerate my . . . aloofness. But it appears I was mistaken."

Raven sniffed. "Is that what being an asshole is called these days?"

He ran his hand through his short-cropped blond hair and slid the flask into his jacket pocket. Straightening his gold cuff links, he murmured, "I do not think you are in a position to judge me."

If looks could kill, she'd be deader than Old Vic who'd frozen to death last winter when all the shelters filled and he'd been left on the street. Alone.

Raven trembled in the tennis shoes given to her by organization that helped women get back on their feet. They donated gently used clothes and helped women like her with their résumés. Not that her résumé contained much, but if she didn't keep this job, she'd need it to look for something else.

How could she stand in for a bride? For the type of woman who would marry a man like him? Even hidden in the shadows of the Sunday School room, the man oozed money. Maybe it wouldn't matter if she was let go. Not if he paid her, and she could use the cash to buy some decent clothes and maybe another stint in a rehab center.

She took the chance. "I'll do it if you pay me."

"Of course you will." He sneered. "Gwen was marrying me for my money, but in the end, my house, bank accounts, and social status weren't enough for her to put up with me. I don't know if that makes me respect her more or less. I'll give you all the cash I have in my wallet." He pulled out a black leather billfold out of the inside of his tux's jacket. Slowly, he counted the bills.

Raven swallowed. She hadn't seen so much cash in one place in a long time.

"Two thousand dollars. Take it or leave it."

She'd be a fool not to take it. But she wouldn't let him cheat her out of it. She knew his type. Users. Every last one. "Pay me first."

He scoffed. "You can hardly tell me what to do. You'll do this my way, or I'll speak to the pastor and explain his janitor thought she would add to my ceremony by vacuuming up broken Goldfish crackers. He may not appreciate it when I tell him if that would have happened, I would have discontinued my generous donations that no doubt fund his parsonage."

Getting mixed up with this man was a bad idea. Her stomach churned, and it wasn't because of the bottle of wine she'd drank last night.

She tried to suck in a breath, but fear clogged her throat. She was trying so hard this time. One little mistake could bring her whole recovery down like a house of cards.

She believed everything he said.

One word from him and she'd be out on her ass, and everything she gained these past couple months would be gone.

"What do you want me to do?"

Victory flashed in his eyes, and the predatory look that covered his face made Raven sweat. Her fight or flight response kicked in, adrenaline pumping through her veins. He looked like every man she'd ever come across in the street, pegging her as an easy victim.

Sometimes she was, and sometimes she wasn't.

Today she was.

And he knew it.

"Leave everything to me."

Jax slipped his phone out of his pocket. He had several texts from his mother and brother asking if Gwen was all right and what was happening.

Jax texted Erik. *Gwen bailed, just as you said she would. But I have a replacement. Meet me in Gwen's changing room.*

"Come on," he said, pushing away from the wall. "I'll show you where to get dressed."

The woman, girl really—she looked young but had a travel weary look to her—stepped back.

"How do you expect anyone to believe this? Are you trying to tell me not one person at your wedding has ever met this woman?

You didn't have a rehearsal dinner? She didn't have a bridal shower?"

Jax crossed the room in two long strides, and he grabbed her arm, the bones under his fingers prominent under his touch. The girl was skinny to the point of malnourished.

Junkie.

He gritted his teeth. He knew where his two thousand would go.

Up her nose.

Erik was walking down the dark hallway when Jax pulled Gwen's stand-in out of the Sunday School room.

"Cover her face with the veil when you dress her," he said, nodding toward his brother. "No one will know the difference."

"What sort of messed up plan is this?" Erik snapped. "Cancel the wedding so we can go home."

Before the cleaning lady had walked into the room, Jax expected to do just that. He had no other choice. Send everyone home, have his personal assistant return the crystal, the china, the vases, and art Gwen had chosen for their registry.

Jax pushed the pale waif toward Erik. "She'll do. We just need to get through the ceremony."

Erik shook his head. "It's never that simple."

"It's easier than canceling and having to explain to everyone why Gwen left me. I'll figure something out after the ceremony."

"This is insane. There's no way you can pull this off."

"Can you bring her to Gwen's changing room or not? The dress and everything she'll need was delivered last night. I'll go into the sanctuary and let everyone know."

"Know *what*? That you bought off some . . ." Erik swept his eyes from the woman's head down to her feet. "Homeless girl? I have to say, this is a new low, even for you. Do you even know her name? What's your name, love?"

"R—"

"Her name is Gwen," Jax snapped, cutting off the woman whose stare bounced between the two of them as if she watched a tennis match on TV, trying desperately to keep her eye on the ball. Her color came back and she was no longer shaking or crying, but it would take some work for her to look like a bride. Too bad there wasn't anyone who could help her with that. They'd planned the wedding on the small side, and Gwen's maid of honor, her only bridesmaid, hadn't shown up. That was his first clue things weren't going to go according to plan. "Let's just make this easy on everyone, shall we?"

He turned on his heel and strode down the hallway toward the sanctuary, where the organist started once again playing the song, for God knows how many times in a row.

Jax didn't trust Erik to help "Gwen" dress for the ceremony. Erik was more apt to help her find a taxi and send her as far from the church as he could, just as quickly as possible.

But he counted on the girl.

He counted on the girl's greed to make her put on the dress and walk down the aisle.

He'd been wrong about Gwen, but he wasn't wrong about this street urchin.

She needed money, and Jax wasn't above using that to his advantage.

~

"You don't have to do this," Erik said, leading Raven down the empty hallway.

He had no idea what she could and couldn't do. Raven wanted to tell him so, but it wasn't any of his business, and besides, what was the point? She was in it now, and there wasn't anything she could do about it.

"Yes, I do."

"No, you don't. Just keep walking and go out the back door. I'll make up something to tell Jax."

"Jax?"

Erik pushed a light-colored wooden door open. Sunlight

streamed through the dirty glass of a large picture window where a dress hung on a hanger framed by white panes. The rays of light illuminated the white gown and the satin and lace shimmered.

"That's my brother's name. Jaxon Brooks."

Raven crossed the room and reached out to touch the dress, skimming her fingertips over the smooth satin. She expected Erik to tell her not to touch it—to keep her grubby fingers off the fine material—but all he did was sit in a chair and pull out a package of cigarettes.

He offered the rumpled plastic pack to her, a brown filter peeking out from the hole in the top.

"No, thanks." She wasn't a smoker; she preferred to spend what little money she came upon on booze. Now if Erik had offered her a flask . . . but no. Raven had to remember why she was doing this.

With an unlit cigarette between his lips, Erik stood and pulled the hanger off the window fixture. "Better get this on," he mumbled around the smoke. "Now that Jax has a way out, he'll want this over and done with. If you're sure you're going through with this, you better hurry up and strip."

Raven's heart leapt into her throat. The last time she'd been told to strip she'd been looking for work and had stumbled into a stripper joint. The owner wouldn't hire her until he saw "the goods."

The gig gave her some pocket money—little had she known the owner would skim most of her wages before he paid her—and it hadn't been enough to get back on her feet. It was just another unsuccessful attempt in a long string to turn her life around.

"W-what?" she whispered, the sound of her voice barely coming out of her mouth. What would Erik do to her before she dressed? Rape her? Force her to give him a blowjob? They were alone in this back room, and he outweighed her by a good hundred pounds. It would be nothing for him to overpower her, take her on the couch, his hand pushing her head into the cushion to drown out her screams.

"You can't put the dress on if you're still in your clothes. Gwen's maid of honor didn't show up, so I'm all you've got to get this dress fastened. If you're that modest, I can turn around, but love, you don't have anything I haven't seen before."

What he said could have been taken as an insult, but the spark of mischief in Erik's eyes calmed Raven's racing heart.

He was teasing her.

She wasn't used to a man being friendly with her. Well, not friendly just to be friends. She knew what "friendly" meant. It meant a man would do anything to get into her panties, and if his charm didn't work, he'd move on to force. Those were the kinds of men in her life, except for Axel.

Erik jutted out his arm to pull the sleeve away from his wrist. Revealing a gold watch, he said, "We better get moving."

"Okay." She undressed and tried not to feel self-conscious. The shelters she'd stayed at didn't condone communal sleeping areas, and she only undressed in front of other women, but Erik acted like he really didn't care what she looked like under her clothes.

The design of the dress allowed her to keep her ill-fitting cream-colored bra on, for which she was thankful. While she didn't mind being clad in only her underthings in front of Erik, she didn't want him to see her boobs.

"What's my brother got on you, anyway?"

Her eyes shot to his in surprise. "What do you mean?"

Erik scoffed and gently nudged her, turning her around, giving him her back and the rows of pearl buttons that needed fastening.

The dress fit as if it had been made for her, and if she were the type to believe in fairy tales, she'd feel like Cinderella on her way to the ball.

But her life hadn't been a fairytale, not since she was fifteen, and she knew fairy godmothers didn't exist.

And Jaxon Brooks was no Prince Charming.

"My brother knows two ways to get what he wants: he'll

either blackmail or bribe someone to get it. He's a cold fish, and you might think that's a shitty thing to say about your own flesh and blood, but I can see him for what he is. He didn't always used to be like that, mind you, but it's hard to feel sorry for someone who acts like he does. He has his reasons, though. We all do."

Erik was right. She would never feel sorry for someone like Jax. Looks, money to spare. What could possibly have gone wrong in his life that couldn't be easily fixed with the resources someone like Jax had?

"It's why Gwen could leave him, you see."

Raven shivered as Erik's fingers trailed up her back, deftly doing the small pearl buttons as if he had a million times before. The dress hung heavily on her body, pounds of lace and satin, and she imagined Gwen, the mysterious Gwen who'd been able to get away, would have felt like the dress was an anchor, pulling her down, drowning her. "No, I don't."

"Gwen realized all the money in the world wasn't worth it if Jax couldn't love her. So, there goes the bribery. And, well, Jax didn't have anything on her, either, so he couldn't force her to stay. Is he blackmailing you, love? Or is he bribing you?"

"He's doing both."

The words slipped out before she could keep them inside her head, and she tensed, waiting for the slap she was sure would come. It was one thing for someone to say ill of their own family, but it was a different matter if someone agreed.

Erik didn't hit her, only laughed and turned her around. "An honest one." He tilted his head, and Raven flinched as the blond man scrutinized her. He looked like Jax, only . . . a softer version of the man, somehow. If she lived in a different world, she would have let herself be attracted to him. "It would be interesting, love, if he were to marry you for real. I think he'd have met his match."

"He's not my type."

Nodding gravely, he said, "He isn't anyone's." He tucked the unlit cigarette behind his ear. "Let's put that veil on you and get out of here. If the organist plays that song one more time, we're all going to go batshit crazy."

~

Jax stood at the front of the church, sweat sliding down his back as his guests stared at him, perplexed.

Erik and the girl were taking too long.

She all but drooled as he counted the money in front of her, but he could have underestimated Erik's dislike of his plan and maybe his brother sent her away to protect her after all.

But she looked scared enough when he threatened to report her to the pastor of the church, though he doubted the old man would have taken any action. The pastor didn't look like he cared much about anything. All this time while waiting for the ceremony to start, he'd been playing Candy Crush on his cell phone, not a care in the world.

It'd taken all of Jax's strength not to grab the phone off the podium and fling it through the stained glass window. He could have taken Jesus out, right between the eyes.

He was already going to hell, and the thought didn't bother him much.

Movement at the back of the sanctuary caught his eye, and Erik gave him the thumbs up. They were ready to start.

Jax blew a relieved breath through his mouth.

"She's ready," he murmured to the pastor.

"Good, good," the pastor said, clicking off his phone. He nodded to the organist who began to play the "Wedding March."

His mother, sitting in the front row with his father, melted into the pew in happiness.

His fake bride's beauty took him aback. Only twenty minutes ago she looked like a strung-out druggie, but this woman was radiant.

Erik erased any vibe of poverty the girl had given off.

Accompanied by his brother, she glided to the altar, her face full of apprehension, holding a bouquet in one hand, her other resting in the crook of his arm. If anyone asked why Erik gave "Gwen" away, he'd have nothing to say, and he hoped Erik thought of a good story. As it was, he wouldn't have forced her to walk the aisle alone with everyone staring at her. That was his brother's way.

Through the white veil, Erik kissed her on the cheek, and the woman smiled.

It faded when she turned to him.

He didn't know why it pissed him off, but it did.

He wasn't a monster, dammit. He had a heart. Feelings.

Once.

"We are gathered here today to . . ." Jax tuned out the pastor.

Fortunately, the service he and Gwen decided on was a short affair, and only fifteen minutes passed before they were saying their vows and he was slipping a band onto "Gwen's" finger.

She did the same for him with the ring he passed to her from his pocket.

Her small hands shook.

She was probably glad she wasn't going through with this for real, and he didn't blame her. He could barely look at himself in the mirror; how could he expect his wife to wake up to him for the rest of her life?

"You may now kiss your bride," the pastor said, closing the book that had guided him through the ceremony.

Jax fought not to lean away. Kiss her?

"Gwen" looked equally appalled.

But he had to kiss her. There wasn't a happily married man in all the world who didn't want to kiss his new wife in front of his family and friends.

He lifted the veil and took a moment to look at her, really look at her. Not just to pass her off as some gutter rat who somehow found her way inside the church.

Erik swept her hair away from her face, revealing delicate, arched eyebrows. Her skin was smooth and clear, though her eyes held a sadness and tiredness he carried with him, always. High cheekbones gave her a regal look, and her full lips sparkled with either spit or gloss. He wouldn't know until he kissed her.

Suddenly, that was all he wanted to do.

He pulled her into his arms, her frailty catching him off guard.

Jax covered her lips with his, swallowing her small gasp as he did so. After a moment, she was kissing him back, wrapping her arms around his neck.

He could be thankful she was a fine actress. He wouldn't have anyone questioning if their love and passion for each other were true. It would only be after the ceremony, after her disappearance, that the lies would start.

When the applause died and the tittering started, Jax lifted his head. His breath hooked in his lungs, and an erection strained his pants. That wasn't the reaction he'd expected to have, kissing this woman, this girl who would snort the two thousand he'd give her up her nose.

Disgusted, he kept his face passive as he turned to the congregation. "Keep your head down," he growled.

He dragged her down the aisle while his guests stood and clapped.

Staring at the floor, she stumbled as she tried to keep up, and he pulled her closer to him. He didn't want to slow down. He wanted to avoid the receiving line his mother would want to form, and Jax pulled her into the pastor's office located off the lobby in the front of the church.

As Jax caught his breath, Erik said behind him, "I started a rumor that Gwen didn't feel well, and you were bringing her right to the hotel. If she felt better, she'd come down for the reception."

"Thanks."

The woman cowered on a small loveseat in the corner of the office, shivering in a cloud of satin and lace, gripping Gwen's bouquet made of white calla lilies and baby's breath.

"We need a few moments with the pastor, then I will drive you wherever you need to go."

Erik dropped down onto the loveseat next to her and laid his arm along the top of the cushions. His brother, dressed in his best man tux, and "Gwen," in her dress, looked like the couple who had just gotten married.

Jax turned away.

He'd never find happiness like that.

In fact, Erik seemed so at ease with this woman, Jax wouldn't be surprised if his brother remained in contact with her.

"That was a beautiful ceremony," the pastor mumbled, narrowly missing the doorframe as he punched buttons on his phone. "We just need the marriage license signed, and then you are free to celebrate." He slipped a black folder from beneath his arm and spread out two pieces of paper.

The woman handed Erik her bouquet and stood next to him by the pastor's desk.

He whispered in her ear, "Don't sign your real—"

"Jax! Darling, the ceremony was wonderful! Just wonderful! Erik told me Gwen wasn't feeling well, so I won't take any of your time, but I just wanted to say congratulations and hopefully we'll see you at the hotel later."

Jax shielded the woman as she signed the paper, and he addressed his mother who was peering around the pastor's office door trying to make eye contact with his bride. "Thank you, Mother. I'll go down to the reception, of course, after I see Gwen to our room at the hotel."

"A terrible thing, to be sick on your wedding day!" his mother chirped. "But perhaps now that the ceremony is over the nerves will calm down a bit."

To Jax's relief, someone in the lobby called to her, and beaming happily, she shut the door, muting the murmur of the wedding guests.

Jax scrawled his name on the line next to hers.

"I can drive her home," Erik said, rising off the loveseat. He slicked his hands through his hair and pulled the cigarette from behind his ear, placing it between his lips.

"That isn't necessary," Jax snapped, annoyed. His brother didn't need to spend any more time with this woman, and the fact Erik wanted to angered him beyond all comprehension.

"Then at least help her out of the dress," Erik said, his voice smooth and low. "You were the one who got her into it."

Jax gritted his teeth.

"Good luck, love," Erik said, and kissed the woman on her temple.

"Thank you," she whispered, the blood draining from her face.

She stepped away, and the tense line of her shoulders relaxed ever so slightly with the space between them.

It wasn't a surprise he scared her. He frightened most people he met. If it wasn't his gruff demeanor, it was his cutthroat business attitude. And if it wasn't the unrelenting way he ran his business, it was his cold-heartedness in general that made most people stay away from him.

"Thank you, Pastor Clark," Jax said, shaking his hand. "I'll be getting Gwen to the hotel so she can rest."

"Good luck, you two," the pastor mumbled, once again staring at his phone, his thumbs flying across the screen.

Jax handed the woman her bouquet and guided her down the hallway, his palm resting on the nape of her neck.

Skittish, she shuffled along the carpeted corridor, her breath coming out in frantic gasps. "You don't have to help me. I can take the dress off myself, and now that the wedding is over, I can finish my job."

Anything to get away from him. While it made sense to leave her at the church, he wanted anyone loitering around the yard to see them climbing into the limo. "No. I'll help you change, then bring you home." He pushed the door open. As she stepped into the back room he said, "Come on. Let's get this dress off you."

～

Raven didn't want him anywhere near her. She wished Erik hadn't gone. Erik's explanations about Jax hadn't made her any more comfortable around him. He had an aura of mercilessness about him, like he'd never care about anyone or anything, ever.

But she wanted the two thousand dollars he'd promised her.

If he hadn't changed his mind.

His piercing hazel eyes pinned her in place. The color was evident now, with the way he stood in the sun that still shone through the window.

The harsh planes of his face were sharp, and his frown made her insides quake. Her stomach churned bile, and she swallowed against the sour taste in her mouth.

She stepped back.

He stepped two forward.

They danced until her back pressed against the window, and there was nowhere for her to go.

Jax grasped her shoulders and spun her around.

She fought tears and pressed her lips together to hold in her sobs. What was he going to do to her?

Erik hadn't hurt her, but Jax wasn't his brother. She was at his mercy, and there was no kindness in his touch.

She gripped the windowsill as she felt Jax's hands near her veil.

Her head swam due to lack of oxygen, yet she couldn't bring herself to drag in a breath. But all he did was pull the combs out of her hair and fling the veil onto the floor.

Under the sloppy updo Erik had helped her with, his fingertips skimmed her skin. He trailed his fingers down her neck, between her shoulder blades to where the small buttons started, and she tried with all her might to hold still, to not bring attention to herself.

She didn't want to be in her bra and panties in front of him.

He did each button with such agonized slowness, by the time

he'd done four, she could have sworn he was doing it to torture her.

Raven waited while he unfastened every single button. By the time he was finished, she craved a drink so badly, her hands shook against the window, the glass warm from the sun beating against it.

"Turn around," Jax ordered.

"N-no." She didn't want to face him, didn't want to look at him. She wanted him to leave, let her dress.

Let her go.

She didn't even care if he gave her the money now.

It wouldn't be worth it.

"Turn. Around."

His voice was deathly low, and afraid of the consequences ignoring him would bring, she slowly turned to face him, the satin of the wedding dress brushing against her ankles.

Reaching for a bravado she didn't feel, she spat, "What are you going to do, rape me?"

Jax grazed his fingers along her collarbone, down lower to her cleavage, his fingers brushing the sweetheart neckline of the dress. "No."

She could get through this if she had a drink. Just a few gulps. A guy like this, he'd have a premium whiskey in his flask. None of the cheap stuff she usually drank because she couldn't afford anything better. "I need a drink."

Then you can do what you want to me.

The words hung in the air, but she didn't say them aloud. If he was going to do something to her, it would be a hell of a lot easier to get through it buzzed.

She might not have finished high school, but she was smart.

Street smart.

She couldn't outrun him.

And resisting would make it that much worse.

Jax pulled the silver flask out of his pocket, unscrewed the cap, and handed it to her.

Tentatively, she took a small sip. The flask was almost full.

She took pull after pull of the whiskey, relishing the burn in her throat running down to her belly. The alcohol immediately went to her head, and she sagged against the window in relief. It'd been too long. Too long without a drink.

Too soon she emptied the flask, and her cheeks burned in shame.

She finished at least three fingers of whiskey, chugged them like they were Kool-Aid.

He took the flask without a word, the metal scraping against metal as he screwed the top onto the opening. A rustling of fabric as he slipped it back into his pocket.

"Do you feel better?"

The carpet was a burnt orangish brown, and she couldn't lift her eyes from the ugly color.

"Look at me."

She couldn't keep the tears at bay any longer, and they ran down her cheeks, dripped onto the dress's skirt. She couldn't bring herself to lift her head.

The alcohol, the giddy fizz in her bloodstream, battled with the self-loathing as it always did whenever she succumbed. The combination dueled in her foggy brain and despite the tears, she laughed, finally locking her gaze with his.

Jax brought his hand to her cheek, and she flinched, used to being slapped whenever a man decided to pay her face any attention. But he merely wiped the tears off her skin and ran his thumb along her jaw.

"Let me."

Raven laughed again. *Let him?* Let him what? What was he asking permission for?

The church was quiet, silence hung heavy in the room. The pastor was probably gone, all the wedding guests were on their way to the hotel for the reception. There wouldn't be anyone to help her if she said no.

Slowly, Jax ran his hand down her neck, cupping her throat.

He could choke her, simple as that. Choke her, crush her windpipe.

She'd been in this position before.

The look in his eyes wasn't violent, though, and she knew violence, knew cruelty.

No, the look in Jax's expression . . . she couldn't describe it, exactly.

But his hazel eyes lacked malice, lacked coldness.

Through her whiskey-filled mind, she realized it then. It wasn't a desire to hurt her. It was simply desire.

She hadn't seen it on a man's face, not like this. She'd witnessed desire in the form of jealousy, envy. That kind of desire mixed with hate, greed, and vehemence.

Jax just wanted her.

But he stood there, waiting.

Her heart hammered.

He was waiting for her to say no.

And she knew as sure as she knew the sun was shining outside that if she said no, he wouldn't touch her.

She licked her lips. He might not give her the money then, either.

And oh, she needed that money. Needed it to try again.

Her blood pulsed under his thumb still pressing into her neck.

Whispering, she said, "Do what you want."

His mouth crushed down onto hers.

He was out of his mind. Out of his mind with lust. Out of his mind with rage that he even wanted to touch her.

She'd captivated him from the moment she walked up the aisle, and he couldn't do anything but think about having her.

Jax didn't even know her name, and he was too far gone to care now. She tasted of the whiskey she downed, like a dying woman who'd finally found salvation. Unless she had a tolerance as high as his, she was drunk. He shouldn't be trusting her to tell him what he could do, but she said yes, and that's all his cock wanted to hear.

He tore his lips from hers and greedily kissed his way down her neck to the tops of her breasts. He lapped at her skin and smiled in satisfaction when she shivered.

Tugging the dress off her body, his lips followed, trailing down her stomach.

He slid her tattered panties over her hips and leaving the dress in a pool on the floor, hoisted her onto the window's ledge.

The dress made a convenient padding for his knees. He knelt, and he spread her thighs apart, surprised she groomed herself in that way. He lowered his head and delicately licked her, running a finger along her opening, finding her wet, inviting.

"Jax," she panted and forked her fingers through his hair.

Spellbound by her musky scent, for a moment he wondered how she knew his name, but he pushed the insignificant thought aside, sliding his fingers into her.

The tip of his tongue focused on her clit, teasing her, and he brought her to climax, her muscles clenching around his fingers, cum dripping out of her.

He wanted his cock there now, and setting her on the floor, he growled, "Turn around."

She complied, using one of his forearms to steady herself as she still wore Gwen's white satin pumps.

Pressing her against the window that looked into the church's garden, he unzipped his dress pants and slid them down just enough to free his cock. He pushed inside her, not giving a fuck about birth control or sexually transmitted diseases. All he wanted was release.

They fit together as if God made them for each other, but as he fought for control, gripping her hips, he knew finding someone who would tolerate him for the rest of his life was a child's bedtime prayer at best.

His sandpaper to her silk, he came after several vicious thrusts, leaving a part of himself behind.

Bracing his hands against the window, he spooned her and fought for breath. "Did I hurt you?"

The standard question. He asked it every time. Not that he cared about the answer. All the women he'd ever screwed told him no anyway, and "Gwen" was no exception.

"Good. Get dressed. I'll have my driver drop you wherever you need to go."

He tucked his limp cock still oozing with cum into his briefs and zipped his pants.

She didn't turn around, and for that, he was grateful. He couldn't look into her eyes now.

He left her alone and closed the door behind him.

The buzz of the whiskey was gone.

Raven didn't feel any different than she always did when something like this happened.

Shame. Remorse. Guilt.

There was something about sex, something dirty when love wasn't involved, and her skin crawled.

The fact that he'd gotten her off, and *that way*, surprised her, perhaps softened those feelings. Such an intimate act, eating her out. He hadn't been rough with his fingers either, simply wanted to give her pleasure. At least, that's what she assumed, since he hadn't gone out of his way to be cruel, as he so very easily could have. She hadn't experienced civility in a long time.

She bent to the floor and searched for her panties in the puddle of satin. While she dressed, she half hoped he would leave her. Even if it meant she'd given herself to him for nothing. She didn't want to see him again.

He wasn't in the hallway waiting for her, and unbidden disappointment filled the pit in her stomach. In her mind, she already spent that two thousand dollars on rehab. New clothes.

Another chance.

She should have known not to trust someone like that.

Someone who already had it all and didn't care about the people he had to step on to get there.

She put the vacuum away after giving the Sunday School room a quick once-over. Jax might not have her fired, and it would behoove her to still try her best to keep her job at the small church.

When she let herself outside, a limo sat next to the curb, and Jax leaned against it, his ankles crossed, a frown puckering his lips.

"Get in."

The whiskey slithered in her gut.

He waited for her.

"Get in," he repeated, opening the limo's door.

She could run. He'd never chase after her. He'd let her go and never think about her again, but she slid across the black leather seat.

Tinted windows.

Raven pushed herself against the door, giving him space on the long bench.

"Where do you live?"

"What?" she asked, twisting to look at him.

There wasn't a strand of hair out of place, and his hazel eyes glued her to the seat with an impatient glare. His tux, though he just finished screwing her, remained immaculate. Even the flower pinned to his lapel that matched the bouquet she'd carried still looked fresh, untouched.

He looked like a model in a bridal catalogue.

Cold.

"The driver cannot drive unless he has some direction in which to go."

Raven had taken three buses to make it to the church from the part of the city where she could find a bed at night. Shelters, a dark corner of an abandoned building. A church pew. She kept what little she owned in a storage cabinet at her friend Elle's beauty salon. It was housed in one of the few remaining storefronts on Z Avenue, but she couldn't ask Jax to bring her there.

She'd never admit she didn't have a permanent place to stay.

She named a rundown plaza two miles from Elle's salon. It was close enough to Z Avenue she could find a place to sleep before the beds filled up, but far enough away Jax would never know her actual whereabouts.

With a curl to his lip, Jax repeated the address to the driver, who looked at them in the rearview mirror.

She sagged in relief when he didn't close the partition that separated driver from passenger.

The bus ride to that part of town took better than two hours. Raven had to change buses and wait through several stops to pick up more passengers, to make it to the church she cleaned three times a week, but the limo driver found the plaza in less than forty-five minutes.

Jax didn't say anything the entire way.

The limo idled at the curb, and he made it evident by the way he cleared his throat he wanted her gone.

"The money . . ." she tried timidly, afraid of what he would do.

He slid across the bench, leaned around her, and opened the door.

With a vicious shove, he pushed her out of the limo, and she fell to the ground, bashing her hip against the cracked and crumbling curb.

"What the hell?" she cried and kicked the limo's spotless wheel.

Tears of rage burned her eyes, but she wouldn't give him the satisfaction of seeing her cry again. She'd shown him weakness once, and that was once too many.

Jax pulled his wallet out of his pocket and ruffled through the cash.

He flung the wad of bills at her, and they fluttered in the wind.

Desperate not to lose one dollar, she scrambled on her hands and knees frantically chasing after the money as it blew down the sidewalk.

"Never try to find me. Ever. You'll never get one more penny out of me."

Jax slammed the limo's door shut, and as Raven clutched the last bill she managed to keep from flying away, the limo disappeared down the rundown city street.

She leaned against the chain-link fence that enclosed the plaza's parking lot.

Dandelions and burrs grew in with the sparse grass, and greasy pizza scents floated to her across the parking lot. Her stomach growled.

She still wore the plain gold band Jax slipped onto her finger during the ceremony.

In one last act of fury, she flung the gold ring into the street where it skittered across the road and stopped by a pile of fast food garbage.

He'd never even asked her name.

Two

Three Years Later

"What do you mean, I'm already married?"

Jax leaned back in his chair and angrily swiped at his forehead with the back of his hand.

"A . . . Pastor Arthur Clark . . . filed a marriage certificate on June 21, 2015 with your name on it. Are you saying this is incorrect?" a bored voice asked.

Fingernails clicking against a keyboard carried through the phone, and the *tap tap tap* grated on Jax's already frayed nerves.

"Yes, it's incorrect!" Jax said through clenched teeth. He needed to be polite to this woman or she would hang up on him, and then when he called back, he would have to wait on hold for another half an hour. "No, it's not incorrect. There was a wedding, but . . ." His words faded as the implication finally sank in. "Who was the bride?" he whispered.

Tap tap tap.

"It says here her name is Raven Grey. I have to admit, sir, it isn't often we have a groom who doesn't know who he married."

"It was a mistake."

He closed his eyes. He hadn't thought about the homeless

waif since he shoved her out of his limo in a cloud of cash and expletives. He'd been so appalled and ashamed he touched her in the church that all he could think about on the ride to that rundown plaza was getting rid of her just as quickly as he could.

He hadn't let the tears that gathered in her eyes, or the way she'd demeaned herself crawling after the bills like a little beggar girl as they blew along the cracked sidewalk, affect him.

There were reasons people called him heartless.

"Be that as it may, Mr. Brooks, a Raven Grey signed a marriage certificate that was filed by a Pastor Arthur Clark of Our Lord and Savior Baptist Church. Perhaps, since you didn't know you were married," Jax caught a hint of sarcasm in the woman's voice, "you could apply for an annulment. In most cases, annulments are more easily granted than getting a divorce, providing your situation qualifies."

Jax leaned forward. An annulment sounded faster.

Lucia would not be pleased with this recent turn of events, and he suppressed a sigh at the thought of the tantrum this information would cause.

An annulment would wipe out the entire marriage. As if it never existed.

"What are the circumstances for an annulment?" Jax asked, catching the eye of his brother, Erik, who lounged on his black leather couch with a cigarette dangling between his lips, and one dark blond eyebrow raised in question.

"One moment please," the woman said, tapping on the keyboard. "If either party married under duress . . ."

He'd been under duress all right, but he didn't think that was the kind she was referring to.

". . . If either party was mentally unable to consent to marriage, if either party was coerced by force, if either party was underaged, if either party lacked the physical capability to consummate the marriage . . ."

Jax sighed. If he wouldn't have put his hands on her, that would have been his ticket out of this mess.

"But, unfortunately, Mr. Brooks, the time limit has expired on an annulment. I am sorry to say that an annulment can only take place up to one year after the marriage, and three years have gone by. I apologize for thinking it was an option for you. I misspoke."

Of course she would get his hopes up, only to have his best option yanked away.

A divorce could get messy, but he assumed Raven wouldn't know what her entitlements were as he hadn't required her to sign a prenup. She would just sign on the dotted line as easily as she had the first time around.

Raven.

A peculiar name for a woman.

"Mr. Brooks? Are you still there?"

Jax jerked at the woman's voice. Now that the courthouse clerk was of no use to him, he'd forgotten about her. "Thank you for your time," he mumbled, and clicked off his phone, dropping it onto his desk like it turned into a fireball.

"What was that all about?" Erik asked, resting one ankle on his knee and nestling into the couch.

Jax wished he could be more like his brother. Erik had such an easy-going way about him, and women flocked to him. Even Raven had seen what a sincere and true person Erik was, and the scared little mouse actually appeared at ease in his presence.

So unlike when she was with him.

Most women treated Jax such as that—even Lucia remained wary and defensive, like prey stalked by a predator, lashing out in anxiety and anger—and that was after being in a relationship with him for two years.

"It appears Raven signed her real name to our marriage certificate, even though I distinctly remember telling her not to." She'd known it was all a sham. What in devil's hell made her sign her real name?

Erik clucked. "It was all such a whirlwind for her, to be sure. How did you expect her to do anything but? You put her on the spot that way, and then, if I recall, Mother came barging in for a look at the bride. You're lucky the girl had any wits about her at all, and that she didn't collapse in a glob of jelly on her way up the aisle."

Jax pinned his brother with a frosty stare. "Is that why you walked with her?"

Erik barely smiled. He was used to his brother's barbs. "I hardly think you have the right to look at me that way. In fact, you should thank me. For all you know, I was the only thing that made her stay."

Not the way she chased after that money.

He pushed away from his desk in disgust and poured himself a drink. He rather liked having the small bar in his office. It was a throwback to the old days where drinking had been a natural part of the work day. In his world, it still was. "I had that part of it covered."

"Oh, yes," Erik said drolly, also standing, slipping his cigarette behind an ear, tugging the hem of his suit jacket down, and smoothing the lapels. "She told me you were bribing *and* black-mailing her. Desperate times and desperate measures, I'm sure."

Jax handed him a low ball of scotch. "Why don't you just say what you want to say and get it over with. You've never been so pussy-footed before."

Erik took a sip of the scotch and regarded Jax over the rim of the crystal. After pausing for a lot longer than Jax would have given anyone else, Erik said, "I just think you could have given her a little more courtesy, that's all. You saw her. It was evident the kid was down on her luck. But did you cut her a break? No. You blackmailed her into helping you."

"It worked, didn't it? No one was the wiser."

It *had* worked, too. Jax had gone to the reception full of apologies. Gwen had fallen ill, he said, but everyone was welcome to stay for the dinner and for the monstrous chocolate ganache cake Gwen ordered. As a loving new husband, he would stay by his wife's side in case she needed anything.

What he'd actually done was go to the honeymoon suite and drink away his disappointment. He'd really given in to the hope Gwen was different, but she hadn't been. No woman in her right mind would marry a man with a heart of ice.

"You're missing the point." Erik set his glass on the bar, and again, dangled his unlit cigarette between his lips.

"The point is, I got what I wanted."

"Jax, the accident was years ago."

He pursed his lips. "How many times have I told you, don't talk about it."

"I think you need to start. Your life would be different if you could forgive yourself."

"I'm not having this conversation with you," he rasped.

Erik heaved a sigh. "What is your next step, then? You can't apply for a marriage license to marry Lucia if you're married to Raven."

He bit back a retort. Rarely did he appreciate the obvious pointed out to him. "Find her. Get her signature on divorce papers. She can sign her name easily enough."

"You could treat her like a person," Erik said, turning toward the door.

"So could you," Jax bit out, though the thought of Erik and Raven together made him grit his teeth.

With his hand on the doorknob, Erik said, "Maybe I will. Maybe I will."

Finding Raven was easier said than done, and Jax pounded his fists on his desk in frustration. A girl named Raven Grey attended a Timber Creek High School, and the grainy yearbook photo looked similar to the woman he unintentionally married, but there were no dates of graduation. She dropped off the school's website her junior year, when she would have been seventeen, and no hits on her using various search engines after that time.

The timeframe made bile rise in his throat, and Jax swallowed it back.

Three years after the accident.

To complicate matters further, Grey was a common last name, and the White Pages online filled several computer screens full of possible matches that could have been Raven's family.

He thought briefly of tracking down her social security number, but even if he had it, what good would it do? If the woman didn't have a credit card, or a bank account, if she didn't drive and didn't have a driver's license, having her number wouldn't help.

She didn't pay bills.

A search for a cell phone number hadn't popped.

No record of work.

Nothing.

Frowning, he searched the obituaries, but nothing for her surfaced there, either, and he sat back in his seat, stymied.

He'd married a ghost.

Only, she wasn't.

She was alive. He was married to her.

He needed a divorce.

There was only one thing he could do.

He dialed the first number at the top of the White Pages.

Jax rang the bell of a ranch style house in one of the older neighborhoods.

After making several calls over the course of several days, he struck gold with a Rozlyn and Philip Grey. He'd almost given up too, being they were near the end of the alphabet, but giving up wasn't his style and he'd pushed forward, finally rewarded for his tenacity.

The woman hadn't admitted she knew Raven, but the hesitancy in Rozlyn's voice was enough for him to know he finally found Raven's parents.

At least, he assumed they were her parents, though they very easily could have been her aunt and uncle.

I'll find out, whether they want me to or not.

A white curtain covering the huge picture window twitched, and he wondered what the person thought of him standing there on the weather-worn porch. He couldn't look more out of place if he tried. He'd dressed in his usual three-piece suit and slung on his long cashmere overcoat to ward off the chill.

Winter settled in to the point it was unpleasant to be outside.

Jax blew out a breath in irritation, and it turned white in the frozen air.

As he waited while the person decided whether or not to answer the door, he looked around. The residence was kept neat, the walks shoveled. The house appeared to have brand new siding on the outside, and the roof looked new as well. Whoever lived in this house took pride in its appearance, and he was curious why Raven would have family who lived like this while she . . . floundered.

She could have gotten back on her feet between the ceremony and now, though he thought it unlikely or more information about her would have surfaced during his search.

Finally, the front door cracked open, and a bottle-blonde woman with brown eyes peered at him through the screen door she did not bother to open. "Can I help you?"

The woman's eyes reminded him of Raven's, and he crowed to himself in victory. It didn't matter if this woman was Raven's mother, at least he had found some part of her family.

"I'm looking for Raven Grey," Jax said, hoping his firmness wouldn't earn him a door slammed in his face, but he knew of no other way to ask. His approach to all things was to be straightfor-ward. His lack of kid gloves had gotten him into trouble multiple times, such as marrying Raven in the first place, but it was his way.

"We don't know anyone by that name," the woman said, her eyes downcast in sadness, already shutting the door.

Jax could read misery. He knew it all too well.

He had to stop her from shutting him out.

"I'm looking for her because I'm her husband."

Jax stood in a living room devoid of any human touch. The room was neat and tidy just like the outside, but it wasn't what he would have expected from an older couple.

Pictures on the mantle.

Photos hanging on the walls. Books. Newspapers. Clutter.

There was nothing.

It made Jax uneasy because the empty feeling of their house echoed the feeling of his own.

"Do you take cream or sugar?" the woman asked, carrying a wooden tray laden with coffee and small cookies into the living room.

"Black's fine," Jax said, turning away from the window that overlooked a yard filled with snow.

The couple who sat on the couch were just as devoid of any humanness as the house itself. The only apparent indication they still had any spirit left was that the woman dyed her hair. She, at least, still cared about a little something, even if that something was a reluctance to go completely gray like her husband.

The man who sat on the sofa along with his wife looked just as gray as his last name implied, lifeless, without even a hint of spark in his eyes. His hair was the color of steel wool, and Jax guessed it must have been black at some point. He wore a gray cardigan with a dark gray pair of slacks.

"I don't know what makes you think we know Raven," the man said gruffly, handling a thick ceramic mug of coffee. "And if you're truly married to her, you should know better than we do where she is."

"Your wife's hesitation on the phone when I said Raven's name brought me here," Jax said, sitting on the edge of a chair, his hands cradling the mug Rozlyn gave him. He hadn't thought he'd been invited in for any significant amount of time, and he still wore his overcoat.

Now sweat was starting to run down his back, but he didn't want to imply this visit would take longer than necessary.

Get in, get the information, and get out.

"As for being married to her . . ." Jax swallowed. He was going to have to admit he'd been a prick. It wasn't something he was good at, and showing his true colors might do more harm than good, but it was a chance he was going to have to take.

"She was cleaning the church where I was to be married, and I have to be honest, my fiancée backed out on me. Raven looked like she needed money, and I . . . hired her . . . to be my fiancée's stand-in so I wouldn't lose face in front of my friends and family."

There was no need to go into the reasons why Gwen abandoned him. If he spoke with Philip or Rozlyn again, or if they got to know him in any capacity, they would find out soon enough.

Philip scoffed. "It sounds like one of those soaps you like to watch, Roz," he said, a scowl pulling down his mouth. "Then why are you looking for her?"

"Because she signed her real name on the marriage certificate. I'm about to . . . marry . . . and when I applied for our license, I was informed that my marriage to Raven was real. I need her to sign divorce papers."

This time it was Rozlyn who scoffed. "You rich people, thinking you can do whatever you want. We haven't spoken with Raven since she was seventeen. That's almost thirteen years, if you don't know how old she is," she sniped.

Apparently, he said the wrong thing after all, and Rozlyn's pointed glare told him visiting time was over.

Jax took the hint and stood, placing his mug on the tray, his coffee untouched.

"Then you have no idea where she is? I searched for her online and nothing popped."

"All I can tell you Mr. Brooks, is to remember how she looked. What did that tell you?" Philip Grey led Jax to the door and opened it wide in invitation to leave.

On the way to his car, his dress shoes crunching over the frozen snow, Jax thought about Raven's father's last words.

How *had* Raven looked?

Erik had seen it. Down on her luck.

Jax simply thought her a druggie, an alcoholic who would spend his money on drugs and booze. What if she was more than that? Instead of living in a rundown apartment in a poor section of town, maybe she didn't even have that.

He'd joked about it, in that couldn't-care-less-attitude he saved for most people, that the church janitor slept in a cardboard box under a bridge somewhere, but maybe she truly was . . . homeless.

"How are you going to go about that?"

Jax snarled. It wasn't like he hadn't thought about anything else since he left the Grey's residence. He glowered at his brother. "How would you?"

Later, after meeting her parents—and Jax still assumed they were her parents, though neither actually confirmed it—he seethed about that very thing in his study. A fire burned in the fireplace, and his housekeeper put a roast in the slow cooker that morning, the spicy scent of beef permeating the house. If he hadn't been so sick with the idea of telling Lucia they couldn't marry until he found his current "wife," the aroma would have made him crazy with hunger.

It was a cozy scene, all he needed was a dog sleeping at his feet.

Inside, Jax felt anything but cozy.

"This wouldn't be the first time I've done your dirty work for you."

"Why are you here again?" Jax asked, balling his hand into a fist under his desk. He loved his brother, he really did. Without Erik, he would never have come out the other side of the accident in one piece. Some would argue he hadn't, but without his brother, Jax would have been dead.

There wasn't any way to pretty up that truth.

Not that he didn't deserve everything and anything that would have come to him.

"Checking up on you—"

Jax growled.

"At Mom's request. She's at the same benefit as Lucia, remember? She knew you would be home alone tonight."

"I can be alone. I'm not five."

"Ah, but you still play with matches." Erik grinned, enjoying the verbal sparring.

"I'm not playing," Jax corrected, shutting his laptop. "I'm thinking of ways to track Raven down, if she really is homeless."

"That seems easy enough to me," Erik said, crossing his legs. He was dressed in an evening suit, a sign he would be leaving soon. A Friday night when Erik didn't have plans was almost unheard of, and it smoothed out Jax's temper.

He stretched. He'd been enjoying the peace and quiet of an empty house when Erik decided to play babysitter. It was his lucky evening the benefit tonight was a dinner and silent auction for a local domestic abuse crisis center.

Women only. Men were not welcome there.

"Do tell," Jax drawled.

"It's fucking colder than hell out there. Where do you think she's going to go? It's not like she can find a bench in a park or lay out a newspaper in an alley. Admittedly, summertime would be different, and you probably would have a harder time, but use your fucking brain. We're in the middle of a Minnesota winter."

Pouring a scotch at the bar in the back of the room, heat

burned Jax's neck.

Checking the homeless shelters should have been number one on his task list, and he should be thanking his lucky stars the average overnight temperature for February was fifteen to twenty below Fahrenheit. No one could be out in that kind of weather for any amount of time without the risk of dying from hypothermia.

"It's not like I haven't done anything. I found her parents. I've just had a lot on my mind, lately." Jax winced.

"Like the fact looking for Raven is a godsend because marrying Lucia is the last thing you need right now?"

That surprised him, and he met Erik's eyes over the rim of his glass. "Why do you say that?"

Erik rubbed his face, and a lock of dark blond hair flopped over his forehead. "You go after the same kind of woman. Lucia is Gwen all over again."

"That's not true. Gwen spent as little time with me as possible; she never fought with me like Lucia does." He hated arguing with his fiancée, and he always gave in just to make it stop. It was like fighting with a wolverine. Whoever tried came out bloody and mangled, and it was all for nothing. He never won.

"See? It *is* true. She's frightened of you, just like Gwen was."

"Obviously you've never been around when Lucia's thrown things at me because I've said or done something she disagrees with. That's not fear. Stupidity, maybe. But not fear."

He'd been livid when she destroyed an antique Chinese cloisonné vase worth over five thousand dollars. Cheap in comparison to some, but it still pissed him off. Her childish temper tantrum had been a waste of money, and all because he worked late. He hadn't known she'd made dinner plans for them.

"If you fought back just once—"

"I wouldn't. And Lucia knows I'll let her get away with anything," he said.

He'd never raised his hand to a woman. He'd never raised his voice. He'd never show any emotion at all. Calm. Cool. Collected.

Ice.

Except for one afternoon in a church when he couldn't keep his hands off a homeless stray, and he made her pay for his weakness.

Which brought him back to the conversation at hand.

Erik shifted in his seat. "All I'm saying is I see Lucia leaving you just as Gwen did. Your relationships are not based on love."

"And all *I'm* saying is that I'm not going to let looking for Raven delay me from marrying Lucia. Me loving her, or her loving me, is beside the point. Lucia's willing, and I'm ready. If I can't find Raven, then I'll see about getting a divorce in absentia. There has to be laws in place for spouses who go missing."

"Have it your way, little brother," Erik said, walking to the door of the library. "But mark my words, women want love, not credit cards. Lucia will turn into another Gwen, whether she's scared of you or not. She'll realize the prestige and wealth that comes with marrying you won't be enough."

"Gwen had her own money. She didn't need me."

Erik cocked his head, one foot in the hallway. "Is that why you chose Lucia, then? Because you think she won't take off like Gwen? Didn't get enough bribery when you dealt with Raven, huh?"

Jax was pouring another drink when Erik shut the door softly behind him.

If that's what had ended up happening, bribing Lucia to marry him, it hadn't been his intention.

They'd met at a benefit his mother dragged him to because his father couldn't go. Lucia had been the only woman with guts to approach him and begin a conversation. It hadn't been quite a year since Gwen abandoned him at the altar, but by then Jax had spun the whole ordeal into a sad story of neglect and desertion.

Lucia wanted to comfort him, and by the end of the night Jax asked her to marry him.

She said yes.

They had a two year engagement because his mother insisted

on it, saying he wasn't over what Gwen had done to him.

Which may or may not have been true. He'd buried his emotions so deep, even if Gwen had hurt him, he wouldn't have felt a thing.

He sat behind his desk and opened his laptop.

Lucia wouldn't be home until the early morning hours, more than likely going clubbing with her friends after the benefit or sneaking off to another man's bed.

He had time to research how many homeless shelters were in the city.

Then he would do what he needed to do.

Find Raven Grey.

It was like looking for a needle in a pile of needles. The homeless shelters were the way to go. Erik had been right. She had to escape the cold, but after visiting all the homeless shelters in the huge city, Jax still hadn't found her.

Apparently, there were still places Raven could hide.

"Maybe she made a friend, and she's bunking on a couch."

Across a rusted metal desk, Jax stared at the director of Heavenly Hands, the last homeless shelter he tried because it was located along the outskirts of the city. Anyone who needed the shelter's services would have to scrape up change for the city bus. At some point, Raven had been able to do so; the director knew her from the scant description he gave her.

His presence hadn't been welcome at most shelters in the city. Some were used as a refuge for domestic violence victims, and more than one director said they wouldn't give him information even if they had any. The look of dislike in their eyes spoke volumes—explicitly, they distrusted and hated men—and in a move of solidarity toward a woman they may not even have met, the female directors he spoke with kicked him out.

Another director at a different shelter took in his driver and

Mercedes through the dirty windows of the crumbling and rundown building and asked if this was some kind of *Pretty Woman* joke.

It did seem odd a man dressed in a suit and cashmere overcoat would be looking for a homeless woman, probably a junkie and alcoholic besides, but until the director's comment, he hadn't thought of Raven as a whore and with a twist of his lips, thought that he should have.

It could be why he was having a hard time finding her. She might be sleeping in the backroom of a strip club or living in one of the trashy downtown pay-by-the-month apartment buildings that had slowly started popping up when the new mayor was elected last year. Word was he looked the other way because it happened to be his favorite side activity.

That didn't have anything to do with Jax, he wouldn't judge another man's . . . hobby, except for the fact now he had a million other places to search.

Jax sighed.

He hadn't given Raven a thought after he kicked her out of the limo. Hadn't given one fuck if she would be okay or not.

He couldn't say he did now, either, except if she were safe and sleeping somewhere that wasn't a shelter, finding her just became a whole lot harder for him.

Son of a bitch.

Why yes, he *had* been called that on occasion.

He pulled a business card out of his breast pocket. He hadn't brought more than the usual supply, and this was his last one. If every director he talked to had taken one, he would have run out a long time ago.

"Can you at least call me if you see her?" he asked, knowing the answer.

The slim Black woman wearing jeans and a black shirt with the Heavenly Hands logo above her heart frowned. "I'm sorry, but if she shows up here, I won't be able to say. We have strict confidentiality rules. Some of these women are running from abusive husbands and boyfriends, and if we give out information all willy-nilly, we could be endangering *all* the women who stay here. All I can tell you is that I have seen her recently, and she was okay. As okay as a woman without a home can be."

She leaned back in her chair and narrowed her eyes.

Jax knew an accusing glare when one was aimed at him, and he took it as his cue to leave.

"Thanks, I appreciate it."

His words fell on deaf ears. The director was already picking up the phone and punching in numbers, dismissing him.

In the dim and dingy hallway, he shrugged into his coat, the lightbulb close to burning out. The women who stayed there tried to make it homey, but the peeling wallpaper and the smell of hotdogs negated anything pleasant they tried to do. Every space was used, and the shelter looked cramped and cluttered.

He walked past a living area where a couple of women were pretending to watch TV, instead eyeing him warily as he strode by. He offered them a smile that wasn't accepted.

He bristled.

What they saw on the outside was a man of privilege, looking for a woman he possibly used as a punching bag.

Not all men were assholes.

That he was wasn't anyone's business.

"Yo, mister."

Jax paused with his hand on the handle of the door leading outside.

A young Black boy wore black sweats and a stained NBA t-shirt two sizes too big. His wide brown eyes flashed with amusement, and his grin revealed white, even teeth. It didn't seem to bother him in the least he was spending the night in a homeless shelter.

"What's up?"

"I heard you talking to Miss Hayley. You want to find Raven."

Jax hunkered to his haunches. "Yeah, I do."

The boy's eyes grew concerned. "Are you gonna hurt her

when you find her? One time she came here, and she didn't look so good. Sometimes she plays checkers with me, but Mama wouldn't let me see her. She cried a lot. Mama said a mean man hurt her, and for me not to grow up like that."

Hurting Raven hadn't been on his radar, and with all his might, he tamped down the dread knowing someone had. Jax shook his head, honesty ringing in his voice. "No. I just need her to sign something for me. That's all. And your mama's right. It takes more courage to be nice than to be mean."

The kid bobbed his head. "I believe you. I know where she crashes sometimes, but you have to promise you won't tell on me. You got any cash?"

Jax was used to being asked for money. That's just the way it was when you were rich. But this kid asking made him chuckle instead of growl. Who could resist a kid looking out for himself?

"How much you looking for?" Jax asked, pulling his wallet out of his pocket.

The boy tilted his head, considering.

Jax knew the look. The kid wanted to get as much as he could but didn't want to ask for so much he came away with nothing. He was willing to pay for something useful, and he pulled out a hundred dollar bill.

"How about this?" he asked.

The boy's eyes almost bugged out of his head. He reached out his hand.

"No can do," Jax said, pulling the bill away. "Info first."

"Raven stays at her friend Elle's sometimes. I heard her talking to Mama about it. Elle has a hair shop on Z Avenue." His face fell. "I don't know how to get there, though."

"Lucky for you, I do," Jax murmured.

The boy held out his hand again and dropped it when Jax put the bill between his teeth and reached for his wallet.

"You change your mind, mister?" the kid asked, scuffing his toe on the faded linoleum.

Jax pulled out another hundred dollar bill. "No." He held up the two bills in each hand. "One for you, and one for your mama, okay?"

The boy grinned in excitement.

"Promise."

"Cross my heart and hope to die! Thanks, mister! Remember, don't tell on me!"

The boy ran away, the bills clutched in his fists.

Jax chuckled, but the fact he had probably just given that kid more money than he or his mama had seen in a long time made his smile fade.

As he turned to the door, a donation box bolted to the wall, secured with a large deadbolt lock, caught his eye.

Before he left the building, Jax shoved a check written out for fifty thousand dollars into the slot.

He thought nothing of it. He'd claim it as a charity donation on his taxes.

~

Z Avenue wasn't for the faint of heart.

Drug deals took place in plain sight. Hookers claimed corners and were a permanent fixture in that part of town. Stolen electronics were sold out of white industrial vans and the trunks of beat up cars. Gas station attendants were protected by bulletproof glass boxes. Bar fights were a regular occurrence because the bartenders couldn't be interrupted stealing from the registers.

Nobody dared venture into that part of town unless they belonged.

Jax, dressed in his suit and overcoat, being driven by a chauffeur in a spotless black Mercedes, didn't.

He could just imagine how the street would look in the summer at this time of evening. But now it was February, and the sun took what little warmth it brought to the day while it sank below the hazy chilled horizon. Not a soul lingered on the frozen sidewalk.

"Don't stay here," Jax told his driver before opening the car's door. "Give me twenty minutes, and then come back. It won't take me longer than that to know if I'll find what I need."

"Yes, Mr. Brooks," the driver said, meeting Jax's eyes in the rearview mirror.

Jax gritted his teeth against the cold air as he opened the door.

He wouldn't have bothered if there hadn't been any lights on in the grimy, rundown salon, but one light cut through the darkness of the shop. He bowed his head against the frigid air trying to find a way into his jacket and opened the heavy glass door decorated with a pair of scissors and the words *Jagged Edge*. The decals were peeling off the glass, the residue of the sticky backs outlining the missing letters.

A woman swept hair off the stained linoleum floor, and she glared at him. "We're closed."

Her platinum blonde hair was shaved on one side of her head, the other side hung past her ear, her bangs hiding her face.

Earrings ran up and down her exposed ear, and where the earrings stopped, a tattoo began, snaking down her neck, disappearing into a shabby tank top she wore under a stained white apron.

"Are you the owner?" Jax asked, not letting the pinch of her mouth or the anger in her eyes deter him from finding out what he needed to know.

"Who the fuck are you? You a cop?"

Jax stepped deeper into the salon. The woman ran a real business . . . or tried to. The smell of chemicals floated through the air; she'd recently given someone a permanent. And the fact that she was sweeping up hair indicated she'd had a customer or two not that long ago.

He had to give credit where credit was due. It would be next to impossible to try to run any kind of business on Z Avenue. How many times did she get robbed? By the look of her, she had a gun close by and knew how to use it.

"No, I'm not a cop. I'm looking for someone."

"Don't know, don't care," the woman clipped, bending to sweep the hair into a dustpan.

"I'm looking for a Raven Grey," he said and zeroed in on her expression.

The woman pursed her lips and blinked at the floor. "Don't know her."

Yes, you do.

Jax waited her out.

She emptied the dustpan and secured it to the broom's handle. After storing it in a closet in the back of the room, she met his eyes. "What do ya want her for? A quick fuck? You slummin'?"

Jax hated thinking about Raven that way. He'd been tempted, and he'd given in. Raven in a wedding dress made him feel things he hadn't felt before, and he succumbed to those desires before he could tell himself no.

But it hadn't been because he wanted to see what slumming was like. It'd been the look in her eyes after downing the contents of his flask. It had been the way she'd looked in all the satin and lace. It had been because he knew he could, and that little amount of power over her made him harder than he'd ever been in his life.

"I don't need to slum."

"Then I don't know what you need her for. If I knew her," she tacked on, realizing her mistake.

Jax leaned against a small desk the woman used to check in customers. He hadn't wandered too far into the little shop; he didn't want to spook her. Cops couldn't be bothered to come out this way, especially in the cold, but he didn't want to take the chance she would push a panic button. Maybe it wouldn't call the cops. Maybe she had a huge hulk of a husband upstairs above the salon pounding back beer and gobbling pizza who wouldn't give a shit about beating the fuck out of him.

"If you're her friend, perhaps she told you about something that happened about three years ago. Standing in for a bride?"

Anyone else would have missed it, but Jax caught the imperceptible widening of her eyes.

Raven spilled her guts.

The kid deserved another hundred.

He wouldn't have made it this far without the tip.

The woman pulled a pack of smokes out of the pocket of her apron and lit one up. She stared at him while she took a long drag. After she blew out a lungful of bluish-white smoke, she crossed her arms over her non-existent breasts. Tilting her chin, she said, "Maybe. What of it?"

"She signed the certificate with her real name. We've been married on paper for the last three years. I'm engaged and need to apply for another marriage license. I need to find Raven to divorce her."

The woman laughed, the sound coming out dry and hoarse like the smoker she was.

He cleared his throat, suddenly wishing for a glass of water.

Or three fingers of good scotch.

"Look at you. Your jacket cost more than what I make in a year."

He shoved his hands into the pockets of said jacket. A jacket he would need to send to the dry cleaners after standing in this woman's smoke.

"What does that have to do with anything?"

"She's not brave enough to take you for everything you've got. And even if she was, she'd never be able to afford a lawyer that could take on yours."

Jax hoped he'd slip out of this situation pain free, but that wasn't to be the case. Now he'd have to decide how much a divorce was worth to him.

He thought of the fury on Lucia's face if he told her he couldn't marry her on the date they decided. A divorce was worth a lot. More than he'd ever admit to this woman.

"Will you tell me where she is if I promise to take care of her?"

"Like you did last time?" she asked, then took another draw off her cigarette. "The two thousand you gave her is pocket change to a guy like you, and she didn't get a chance to use it, either." White smoke puffed out of her mouth.

"What do you mean, she didn't use it? What happened?"

"She's too trusting. She got ripped off one night at a shelter. They took every penny. It almost broke her. I never saw her so devastated. She had big plans for that cash."

Jax gritted his teeth. Raven getting beat up. Raven losing the money he'd given her. He fought against the feeling of responsibility that wiggled in the back of his heart. "You have my word that I'll look out for her. Better than last time."

A full ashtray sat on the corner of the desk, doubling as a paperweight, and, snorting, she snuffed out her cigarette.

She was close enough now Jax caught a whiff of a cheap perfume under the layers of cigarette smoke.

Rubbing her face, she met his stare.

He was taken aback by the fatigue, despair, and loneliness that filled her eyes.

"I don't believe you, but the fact is I'm worried about her, and right now you're the only one who can do anything about it. She hasn't stopped by in a while, and in the cold, that's not like her." She jerked her head toward the back of the salon. "Sometimes she sleeps in my storage room."

"She spent a night at Heavenly Hands a week ago," Jax offered. "It's how I found you. I paid off a little kid to tell me how to find you."

Her mouth tightened. "Well, that was a week ago. If you were searching the homeless shelters, where else has she been?"

Jax stared at the floor. "I don't know. She could have been at any of them. No one would tell me anything."

"Then they haven't seen her. Little kids aren't the only ones who will take money in exchange for information, no matter how uppity and indignant those bitches pretend to be. Loyalty to Raven or their other clients don't shut them up. They just didn't have anything to tell you. I've had to stay in one or two, and they're all scum suckers."

He rolled his shoulders. Her tone implied she lumped him in with the "scum suckers."

"Do you know where else she could go?"

The woman sank wearily into the chair that sat behind the desk and rested her head in her hands. "There're a bunch of abandoned apartment buildings along Pike. They were zoned for demolition a long time ago, but one of the buildings still has electricity and the temperature inside stays above freezing in the winter." She looked at him, her upper lip curling. "Raven doesn't stay there. It's dangerous for a woman to be alone in that building, and she knows she's welcome here. God only knows what kind of situation she's in right now."

"She's your friend."

The woman stood, her hands on her hips. "What do you know about friends?"

"Enough to know you care. Do you want to come with me?" Jax asked, unnerved by her display of emotion. No one felt like that about him, not outside his family. He tried to remember a time when he had felt like that toward another person. Love. Care. Concern.

Not since before the accident.

"I can't. I need to keep an eye on this place twenty-four/seven, or assholes will vandalize my shop quicker than shit."

Jax cocked his head. "If I give you money for helping me, you could relocate."

"Not everyone cares about money, Mr. Bigshot."

"That hasn't been my experience," he said smoothly, pulling out his checkbook. "Cash it, or not." He ripped the check out of the book and handed it to her.

Without taking her eyes off his, she tore it in two. "I don't need your money. I'm here because I want to be. Just let me know, somehow, if you find her. I want to know if she's okay."

A small pit at the bottom of his stomach began to grow.

"Because you don't think she is?"

"Because after everything you told me, I know she's not."

Three

L ooking for a homeless woman after dark in an abandoned apartment complex wasn't the best idea Jax ever had, but it wasn't the worst, either.

His driver was waiting at the curb when he'd come out of the *Jagged Edge*, and he hadn't batted an eyelash when Jax asked him to drive to Pike Street.

At first, he wondered how he'd find which building the woman was talking about, but when his driver pulled onto Pike, the light shining from various windows made it clear which building still had power.

"Stop up there." He pointed over the seat toward the building. It wasn't a high rise, and he thanked God, but it would require hours to search, especially if the people inside took an instant dislike to him and refused to help him.

His driver idled at the snow-covered curb, and Jax studied the gray crumbling complex before he spoke. "I'll need you to wait." Jax hated asking that of him, but he had little choice, and he hoped he wouldn't need as long as he thought. He had the divorce papers his attorney hastily drew up in his overcoat's inside pocket, and all he needed was a signature.

He didn't plan on giving Raven any more cash. It was her own damn fault she hadn't kept a better eye on the money he'd given her, and while he was touched the stylist at *Jagged Edge* cared about Raven, he did not. He certainly wasn't going to double back and let her know any news. He could pass on the message to Raven her friend was concerned, and that would be that.

"Do you need a weapon, Mr. Brooks?"

"No."

Jax was never far from his handgun, but since the accident he never carried it on his person. Being armed came with the security business, but he would never blithely carry a gun again.

"But—"

"No. If anything, it will give me a chance to practice my self defense. My instructor said I'm getting soft."

The driver flicked his eyes from Jax's in the rearview mirror back to the black street. The streetlights had been shot out and the building's dim glow did nothing to combat the complete dark of the winter night. "As you will, sir."

The front double glass doors were unlocked, and Jax walked into the lobby without incident. Broken mailboxes hung from the wall, and the carpet had been worn to less than threadbare many years ago.

The hairstylist was correct however, that it was at least above freezing, and while he wouldn't take off his coat, he could understand why this would feel like a safe haven for a person who had nowhere else to turn.

The lobby was empty, and Jax hit the button for the elevator, just to see if anything would happen. He wasn't surprised when nothing did, though he wouldn't have ridden in it anyway.

Even if he had a death wish, plummeting to his grave in a malfunctioning elevator was not the way he wanted to go, but that did mean he'd be searching a mid-rise building without a working elevator.

He wouldn't be able to do this all in one night. He should have went home and enlisted Erik's help and maybe a PI, but this was his last lead. With the way Raven was known all over the city, it wasn't too unrealistic to think she'd spend tomorrow somewhere else.

Jax had to search as long as he could tonight. If she slipped through his fingers, he'd be back at square one.

The hallway beyond the lobby on the first floor revealed little. Every apartment door was shut tight, and Jax heaved a sigh. Privacy must be hard to come by, and a chance to inhabit an empty apartment rent-free would be a once in a lifetime opportunity. But short of knocking on every single door, there wasn't much else he could do to find her.

He knocked on the wooden door of apartment 101.

Nothing happened, and Jax rubbed his forehead in resignation.

Anyone could be behind that door. Druggies on a high, blacked-out alcoholics, whores working over their johns. Or johns working over their whores.

He didn't pretend to be an expert at this kind of lifestyle, but working in security had shown him the underbelly of the city more often than he liked.

Moving on, he knocked on 102, 103, and on.

He didn't get any results until apartment 110, when a scrawny old man dressed in six layers of smelly clothes opened the door in a marijuana haze. He didn't look coherent enough to answer the simplest of questions, but Jax tried anyway.

"Do you know a Raven Grey?"

"Wha'?" The old man swayed and leaned against the doorjamb.

Jax should have brought Raven's picture. It might have been easier to flash her photo than to keep describing the thin woman with black hair and colored streaks.

"Raven Grey? She's a short woman with black hair?" Jax held his hand in front of his chest, approximating how tall Raven was compared to himself.

"Ne'er heard o' her," he slurred, then shut the door in Jax's face.

There were twenty apartments on each floor, and his knocking didn't earn him a single response at any of the apartments. He trudged up the stairs to the second. It was more of the same, no one opening their doors, or those who did refusing to help him.

Tired and defeated, three and a half hours later Jax found himself on the sixth floor. The hallway stank of urine and vomit mixed with the sweet smell of pot. Never mind dry cleaning his clothes after this. He'd throw them away. He didn't need the reminder of how low he sank to find a woman for her signature.

He struck pay dirt at apartment 620 when a woman opened the door and actually spoke with him. "I'm looking for Raven Grey."

Immediately, he knew the woman knew Raven, or at least had heard of her because a worried frown puckered her mouth and the lines between her forehead became more exaggerated.

She'd been pretty, once upon a time. Though streaked with gray, her blonde hair shone in the light of a lantern she used for light. The orange glow illuminated her clear skin. As tall as she was, the woman could have been a model, but stress and fatigue lined her face, aging her by many, many years.

Narrowing her eyes, she asked, "Why?"

"My name is Jaxon Brooks, and I met her a few years ago. I heard about her situation and want to help," he lied. His mother always told him he could catch more flies with honey and telling this woman the truth would only earn him another door slammed in his face.

She bit her lip and looked to the ceiling.

Jax followed suit expecting to see a large spider hanging above their heads, but the only thing above them was a ceiling full of cracks, the plaster coming off in chunks.

"The last I heard, Raven was on the tenth floor."

Trying to keep excitement out of his voice, he murmured, "Do you know which apartment?"

"1003." She ran a hand over her eyes. "I don't trust you, but I don't trust . . . Listen. If you go up there, be careful."

That was a given, but he tilted his head and asked, "Why?" He wanted all the information he could get before stepping into any kind of situation.

"She's not alone."

The woman retreated like a scared mouse, quickly closing the door.

Jax slid three one hundred dollar bills out of his wallet. He slipped them under the door, but he didn't wait to see if the woman would take them or thank him.

He almost wished he had his weapon. The comfort of the heavy piece in his hand. The knowledge he could take a life and the world would be a better place for it. Some people didn't deserve to live.

But that bullet could take the life of someone innocent. Someone who had a family who would mourn their loss for the rest of their days.

Trotting up to the tenth floor could have been a hell all its own if it wasn't Jax's number one priority to stay in shape. He tortured himself in his weight room every day as penance for all his sins.

It wasn't enough.

After running up four flights of stairs, his blood hummed and his muscles loosened.

He was ready for a fight.

Jax pushed his ear against the door of 1003. Voices murmured low inside, but none of them sounded female.

He trusted his gut. He didn't think the woman on the sixth floor lied to him. Raven made friends and evoked trust wherever she went, and the woman downstairs wanted Jax to help her.

Raven had trusted the wrong person, and a sick feeling twisted his stomach.

He never used to be the kind of person he was now. Now he

was just a cold, calculating, son of a bitch, and he had no intention of changing that.

For anyone.

Jax knocked on the door.

The murmuring stopped.

There were a few rustling sounds, perhaps they were hiding their stash, before the door creaked opened.

A bald, beady-eyed man peered at him through the crack. Black and blue bruises rested beneath his eyes, but they weren't caused by a fist. More than likely drugs, malnutrition, and lack of sleep made the bags under his eyes more pronounced, and his overall lifestyle gave his skin an unhealthy, waxy pallor. His lips were drained of color, and the lower half of his face blended into his neck.

The man stood shorter than Jax by at least a foot, but that didn't mean he wasn't armed and didn't know how to use his weapon.

Bringing a knife to a gunfight was one thing, having nothing against anything was something else entirely.

"What the fuck do you want?" Slimeball asked, revealing a mouth full of rotted teeth.

"I'm looking for Raven Grey," Jax said, fighting for calm. While his "catch more flies with honey" approach he used with the woman on the sixth floor worked, he didn't think it would go far with this guy. Only, he didn't want to start a fight if he didn't need to.

"Never heard of the bitch," Slimeball said, already shutting the door.

The fact that he called Raven a bitch, even when claiming he didn't know her, told Jax everything he needed to know, and he wedged his foot between the door and the doorjamb. Too bad the guy hadn't opened the door with the chain in place. Jax hadn't kicked down a door in a long time. And yeah, it looked just as cool in real life as it did on TV, as long as the person attempting it had the leg power to do it right the first time.

His foot sufficed in this instance, and he pushed his way inside, snagging his coat on an exposed nail in the doorjamb.

If that was the worst that happened tonight, he would consider himself lucky.

"I think you have," Jax said, scanning the room.

A bald lightbulb hung from the ceiling on an exposed wire over a card table. Two others looked his way but dismissed him, continuing to bag white powder.

"What the *fuck* do you think you're doing?" Slimeball roared.

"Cops ever come out here?" Jax asked absently, stepping into the kitchen. Pizza boxes littered the counter and a city trash receptacle that had been stolen off the street overflowed with garbage. The room was just warm enough that everything reeked, and Jax breathed shallowly through his mouth. He was curious if the faucet ran clean water, but even wearing his leather gloves, he didn't want to touch anything.

"That's none of your fucking business," Slimeball said, crowding Jax between his hefty body and the sink.

The woman on the sixth floor might have been scared of this guy, but Jax batted him away like an annoying fly.

He retraced his steps through the living room and searched down a short hallway. One open door revealed the vilest bathroom he'd ever smelled. A toilet that couldn't flush shouldn't be used as an outhouse. The stink was worse here than in the kitchen, and he gagged. He closed the door, hoping to trap the odor inside.

The hallway contained three more doors, and opening one revealed a storage closet with nothing inside it.

Another door opened to two bare mattresses laying on the floor, a hodgepodge of blankets and old pillows piled atop each one.

Just to be on the safe side, Jax checked the closet in the room, but the only thing in there, surprisingly, was what a closet was meant to store—clothing.

Slimeball waited in the hallway, but he wasn't empty-handed.

"You think I'm just going to let you look through my shit, you dumb fuck? I told you, I don't know no cunt named Raven, now get the fuck outta here."

Jax stilled. He'd been on the receiving end of a gun before. The best thing to do was act like Slimeball was in control. The timing couldn't be a coincidence, and Jax would bet his savings Raven was in the other bedroom.

He lifted his hands in surrender, but in one swift motion, he relieved Slimeball of his gun and pinned him against the wall, his hand around the asshole's throat. "I think I'll search where I want to search," he murmured, squeezing.

The overweight man struggled against Jax's hold, his feet dangling over the floor, kicking out at nothing.

Only when Slimeball's lips turned blue and his eyes turned bloodshot, did Jax drop the asshole to the floor, where he laid in a heap, wheezing.

Jax clicked on the gun's safety and pocketed it. The heavy weight of the metal inside his coat unsettled him, the feeling foreign and all too familiar at the same time, but he pushed the uneasiness aside as he turned the knob on the last door.

He was met with resistance.

The door was locked.

Tempted to kick it in as he wanted to earlier, he took a step back, then stopped. Instead, he grabbed Slimeball by the back of the neck and hauled him to his feet.

"Open this door."

With shaking hands, Slimeball pulled out a keyring out of his pants pocket and tried to shove a key into the lock.

Jax gritted his teeth. He'd been in the building going past four hours now. He was hungry and had to piss. He wanted a drink.

His driver probably felt the same, and a wave of remorse rolled through him. He should have made the man go home.

"I'll do it," Jax said, grabbing the keyring and shoving the druggie onto the floor, his head bouncing against the scarred and dirty wood.

He lost the key Slimeball tried to use, and he tried six different keys to open the door.

When he did, he wished he hadn't.

The room smelled like death, and he stepped back, as if the Reaper himself were in that very room waiting for him.

Fear slicked his throat. He wanted to be rid of Raven, but not this way.

The bulb remained black when Jax tried to turn on the room's overhead light, and he used his flashlight on his cell phone.

In the bright light, something scurried away, and Jax grimaced in disgust.

Rats.

Typical of a city apartment, the room was tiny, and there wasn't much in it except another bare mattress with a lump lying along the side, pushed against the wall.

"Raven?"

The lump twitched at the sound, and Jax knelt on the edge of the mattress. He pulled away an old blanket full of holes more than likely made by the rats that also used the room as a haven against the cold.

Raven's pale skin stretched against her skull, pasty, glistening with sweat.

She opened her eyes when he shone the light toward her, but her pupils didn't focus.

Drugged out. Typical.

He shook her shoulder. "Raven. Do you remember me?"

Her eyes rolled into the back of her head.

In frustration, he grabbed her chin, his thumb and fingers digging into her face. "Look at me, goddamn it." Her skin seared his fingertips.

"Fuck." She wasn't strung out on drugs.

She was sick.

Jax flung aside the dirty blanket that smelled of urine and sweat. Slimeball hadn't taken care of her, hadn't helped her. God knew how long she'd gone without food or water. He yanked up her shirt and pressed his palm against her side.

Her temperature was too high.

"Please," Raven whispered. "I didn't mean to be late. I'm sorry, I'm sorry, I'm sorry."

Delirious with fever, she babbled words Jax didn't understand.

What the hell was he supposed to do with her? Let her die? She wasn't in any shape to sign anything. She had no knowledge of her surroundings. Didn't know who he was.

Jax had only one choice.

He'd have to bring her home and nurse her back to health, or at least to the point he could make her sign the divorce decree before kicking her out on her ass.

Just like he did before.

Jax tried to lift her off the filthy mattress, hefting her into his arms, but he could only move her a few inches, a rattling and scraping coming from the wall. "What the hell?" he muttered. He laid her down again and grabbed his phone, sweeping it over her body.

"Jesus Christ."

Slimeball cuffed Raven to a radiator, and her wrist oozed blood. She'd tried like hell to slip the handcuff off her wrist.

Goddamn it.

Familiar with handcuffs, it took Jax only two seconds to find the right key off the keyring and unlock the thick silver bracelet. He held her hand for a moment and smoothed the hair from her face.

Lifting her into his arms, he held his breath. She stank of her own body fluids, blood, and grime.

He didn't even want to think about what Lucia would make of this.

Lucia.

How much would this cost him? Both financially and emotionally? He couldn't even imagine her reaction to Raven.

Maybe he could ask Erik to take her . . . no. Erik's taunt in Jax's office came back to him, and the jealousy that jabbed at him at the church seeing his brother and Raven together slithered down his spine.

Asking Erik to nurse Raven back to health would only set them up to fall in love.

He would force Raven to sign the minute she was of a mind to do so, and that would be that.

Raven wasn't anybody's business but his.

As he lifted her to his chest and stood, Raven curled herself into his embrace.

She weighed almost nothing, and Jax stepped easily into the hallway where Slimeball still laid on the floor, gasping, a sullen and hateful look in his beady eyes. "You can't fucking take her. She's mine."

Jax narrowed his eyes in return.

He hadn't thought about Raven that way while she was sick and it made him ill Slimeball was using her for his own pleasure while she laid unwilling, and perhaps, unknowing.

This time Jax did give into his own wants, and securing Raven to him, he kicked the druggie in the groin as hard as he could. The toe of his shoe connected with a satisfying *whap*, and the asshole assumed the fetal position with lightning speed.

He didn't stay to watch the sleazebag vomit in pain, but the sounds of retching that followed him down the hall and out the door was enough to bring a smile to his face.

"She wouldn't have lasted another day."

Jax stood in the hallway outside the bedroom he'd given to Raven in which to convalesce. Erik leaned against the wall, a foot anchored against the wooden paneling, a dour look covering his face. His arms were crossed against his chest, and Jax read the disapproval shining bright in his brother's eyes. The doctor who examined Raven snapped blue latex gloves off his hands.

"What?" Jax snapped.

"I said, she wouldn't have lasted another day. Her fever is a hundred and five degrees. She's dehydrated. Starved. She should be in a hospital." His mouth pulled into a displeased scowl. "If your father and I weren't golfing partners, I would insist on it. She needs twenty-four hour supervision."

"Stephen, you know I appreciate it—especially at this late hour—and hired a nurse," he said.

Monitoring Raven's temperature, the nurse was there, now, not dressed like any nurse he had in mind. She twisted her light brown hair in a bun, yes, but wearing yoga pants and a t-shirt, she appeared more of a college student than a nurse. The stethoscope hanging around her neck did little to make her look professional.

Erik had scoffed. "What do you want her to look like? A paper hat with a red cross perched on her head? A white dress, panty-hose, and old lady shoes? You don't live in a gothic romance novel, Jax, your haunted house only makes it look like you do."

Jax admitted that's exactly what he thought the nurse would look like. He wouldn't give Erik the pleasure of being right.

"You'll need to hire more than one," Stephen replied, bending over his black satchel and shoving the gloves inside a small white bag assigned for waste. "You don't understand how sick this girl is. She needs her temperature checked every two hours to make sure the antibiotics are working. She'll need the IV until she can begin taking liquids by mouth, and that won't be for several days —her throat looks horrendous. I've taken a swab, but I don't need the results to know she has strep. I've left instructions to keep her sedated. She's been through a very traumatic experience."

Jax ran his hands through his short-cropped hair, though not short enough for his taste. With all his searching for Raven, personal maintenance had fallen down his list of priorities. "She's been raped." That much was obvious when he'd taken her from Slimeball's possession.

"Not recently, if she has been. When I examined her, it appears she's had sexual intercourse, but nothing forceful such as rape." Stephen paused and regarded Jax with steely gray eyes framed with white bushy eyebrows that matched the cap of curly white hair on his head. Jax often thought Stephen kept a clean shave so as to never resemble Santa Claus. "Though, I'm not an OB/GYN, and someone in that field may see things I missed." Stephen picked up his bag. "But—"

Jax sucked in a breath. "She's given birth?"

Fear and something he might have called pain blossomed around his heart at the thought of Raven having his child. He pursed his lips. Of course, the regret was coming three years too late.

"No. Not that I can tell. Again, that's not my specialty, but from what I could ascertain, her pelvis has not cradled a child. She may have an STD, but I won't know until I get her test results. This woman, wherever you found her, whoever she is, she's lived a hard life."

"Thank you," Jax said, dismissing the doctor's examination results. He wouldn't let himself feel sorry for her. She chose to live the way she lived. Jax also ignored talk of an STD. Raven may have one, but he did not. He'd had himself checked after the incident—that's what he'd relegated him fucking Raven to, an "incident"—and he was always punctual with his yearly checkup. He would have known a long time ago if Raven had given him anything during their dalliance.

He turned toward the stairway to walk his father's friend out. There wouldn't have been anyone else he could call at four o'clock in the morning and taking Raven to a hospital wasn't an option. He needed to keep his eye on her so the minute she was coherent, she could sign the papers, and this way he could control her care.

He tried to tell himself that was the most important. He could hire the best.

If he took Raven to the hospital, she'd be tagged as a welfare case, and she'd be dumped onto the street at the first possible moment.

The lie didn't make him feel better.

"Wait, Jax," Stephen said urgently, and placed a hand on Jax's shoulder.

Erik straightened.

He'd forgotten his brother was standing in the hallway with them.

"There were rats?"

"What?" Jax asked, unprepared for the question.

"There were rats, where you found her?" Stephen whispered.

Jax nodded.

"Raven has several . . . wounds. I believed they were bites, and you just confirmed it. The antibiotics should fight against any infections the rodents carry. The nurses will keep the wounds clean, but if her temperature does not lower, if the wounds, after a few weeks, do not heal, she *will* need to be seen."

"Weeks?" Jax whispered. He hadn't signed on to take care of her for that long. A few days. A week. Maybe two at the most. But . . .

Stephen sighed. "Talk to your brother, Erik. Jax, if you weren't prepared to take care of this girl, why did you bring her here?"

Erik arched an eyebrow. "Raven has something Jax wants."

Jax shook his head at Erik.

Glaring, Erik revealed his teeth in what was supposed to pass for a grin but was really a disgusted sneer, and Jax tamped down the urge to punch him. While Erik had always been on his side, there were a few times, such as Raven, where they disagreed. Normally, they agreed to disagree and forgot about it, but Jax wasn't sure Erik would mind his own business this time.

At the front door, Stephen shrugged into his jacket. "What in the hell would that girl up there have you couldn't buy for yourself?"

"A divorce," Erik cut in.

Laughing at Stephen, whose mouth fell open in shock, Erik shut the door with a quiet click.

～

"Do you have to tell the whole goddamn city Raven and I are married?" Jax snapped, angrily trotting up the stairs.

"Who is he going to tell?" Erik asked, stomping up the stairs by his side.

"Our parents, for one thing."

"You didn't think you could keep this from Mom and Dad, did you?" Erik's face hardened. "I know the accident changed you, and I've been sympathetic and supportive all this time, but this is just too much. Did you hear what Stephen said? Rats. She's got goddamn pneumonia, strep throat, her temperature topped a hundred and five, and rats. Rats *chewed* on her. Forget for just a moment you saved her for her signature, and just think you *saved her*. She would have *died* handcuffed to a radiator, and all you can think about is what people will think once all this blows up in your face."

Jax blinked at his brother. He'd never heard Erik so impassioned. "Did you fall for her?" he asked, trying to swallow a mouthful of jealousy. There was nothing to be jealous about. He didn't want Raven. In fact, it would help him immensely if Erik did love her. Then he could dump Raven on his brother, and everyone would come out a winner. Once again, the idea curled like sour milk in his stomach.

Erik scoffed. "I know better than to try to take what's yours. I've been learning that lesson since we were kids."

"Where are you going?" Jax asked when Erik turned away. He wanted to ask if Erik would have a drink with him in the library. He didn't want to crawl into bed with Lucia, wasn't in the mood to be interrogated about things he couldn't control. Being alone was the only alternative, and he couldn't be his own company right now.

"I'm going to sit with Raven. She deserves to see a familiar face when she wakes."

"Stephen has her sedated. You heard him, it will be days before she wakes up."

"Then I'll wait."

Erik disappeared into Raven's room, and through the closed door, Jax heard his brother greet the nurse.

Jax stood in the dark hallway alone with nowhere to go.

Raven slowly came into consciousness, voices murmuring above her head, a smooth hand brushing her hair away from her face.

She didn't want to wake up, and she desperately searched for the darkness that kept her safe. But the pull of sleep didn't take her, and the voices became louder.

A man's voice.

But not Damien's.

Damien!

Raven sat up in bed, tried to force her eyes to focus. She searched the room for the guy who'd taken her in in exchange for work delivering drugs. He would kill her if she wasn't there to make the drops.

Something pulled at her wrist, and she clutched at her hand. Handcuffs. No, it was tape. She scrambled at it with broken fingernails. She had to get out of there.

Her skin burned, but not the way it had been. This pain radiated from her legs, and she thrashed under the smooth sheets.

Her vision zigged and zagged, like a TV unable to find reception.

Tears flowed down her cheeks.

"Hey, hey. Calm down, you're safe, love. Calm."

Raven braced herself to be pushed back onto the bed, for a hot, rancid mouth to cover hers, but soft, comforting hands only patted her back and cupped her cheek.

"Raven, look at me, love. Look at me."

She knew that voice. Somewhere, she'd heard that voice before.

Sweat ran down her back, and she tried to breathe.

"That's right, love, that's right. Breathe."

"Do you want me to—" a concerned female voice asked.

"No, it's okay," the man said, resting his hand on the nape of Raven's neck, "let her try to calm down first. She doesn't know where she is. Raven, can you look at me, love? You know me. We met a long time ago. I won't hurt you."

Raven tried to swallow, but her throat burned, and she gnashed her teeth against the pain. She stared at the plain white bedspread and tried to control her panic. No matter where she was, it would be better than where she'd been.

"The light, please," she whispered, unable to lift her head, her hair giving her a much needed curtain away from the blinding sunlight. She'd spent days and days in the dark, and the light streaming through the windows drove icepicks of searing pain into her skull, warring with the throbbing in her ears.

"I'm sorry, Raven, I didn't think." A pause, and then, "Will you close the blinds, please?"

Raven tried to relax when the room dimmed. The dark held secrets and pain. She was familiar with the dark, and the misery it brought with it was just as familiar and possibly, not entirely unwelcome.

Pain reminded her she was alive, that she could still feel.

Even if there were days she didn't want to.

"Lydia called and told me she's awake," a voice said.

A voice that made the blood in her veins turn to ice.

A voice she never thought she'd hear again in a million years.

"No!" she screamed, her voice ripping the inside of her throat to shreds.

Fast and furious, her heart beat like she'd taken a hit of the coke Damien sold.

She had to get away.

With new urgency, Raven tore at the tape at her wrist but her hair blinded her, and her hands trembled too badly. She couldn't swipe it out of her face.

"Raven, calm down, please, love," the other voice implored, but she recognized it now.

"What the fuck's wrong with her?"

Angel and devil.

Brothers.

"You're going to have to—" the angel said, but not to her. No, to someone she couldn't see through a cloud of tears and hair.

Someone comforting, someone who smelled of lilac.

The angel wrapped his arms around her, trapping her. Depleted of strength, she couldn't have moved another centimeter even if she wanted to. Instead, she sobbed in the angel's arms, and he smoothed her hair, murmuring things her fear wouldn't allow her to hear.

His voice was magic, and her heart calmed, a lightness filled her limbs. Raven wept into the angel's shirt.

"I won't let him hurt you," the angel promised.

But he lied. Raven knew he lied.

For no one could protect her from the devil.

No one could protect her from Jaxon Brooks.

The next time Raven opened her eyes, it was to the dark room, but dark because it was night, not because the woman who smelled of lilacs closed the blinds.

She laid still and mentally tested her body. She wiggled her toes, slightly bent her knees. She needed to shave, though she was rarely afforded the time or the water to do so. Once a week she tried to stop by Elle's salon, and there Elle would let her bathe and wash her hair. Raven moved her legs against the soft sheets, and something kept catching against the material. Bandages. She had bandages on her legs.

Raven continued the assessment, her mental eye roving from her hips to her breasts. Nothing. But that was a good thing. A woman who woke up sore but couldn't remember why wasn't in a good situation. She took a deep breath thankful Damien hadn't touched her.

She fluttered her fingers. A pain pinched her right hand, and licking her lips, she lifted her hand in front of her face. The tugging made her wince, but she blew out a sigh of relief. It was only an IV. Like in a hospital.

"How are you feeling, love?"

Now Raven could put a name to the voice. Erik Brooks. The man who walked her down the aisle. The memory was sharp: the church, Jax, and . . . after. When a husband and wife stole a few moments to themselves to enjoy each other before celebrating the rest of their lives with friends and family.

Cheeks burning, she sat up. The sheet fell into her lap, and she ran her hands down her breasts. Someone dressed her in a silky nightgown. A floral scent caught her nose, and she brushed her fingers through her hair. No knots. Smooth. Silky. Someone gave her a bath.

Clean wasn't a feeling familiar to her, and she lifted a lock of hair to her nose and took a deep breath.

"Raven?" Erik sat in a chair near the bed, and he leaned forward. "How are you feeling?" he repeated.

"My throat and ears hurt."

"You're very sick. Do you know where you are?"

"Am I at your house?" She prayed she was. She didn't want anything to do with Jaxon Brooks. To be in his house, under his care, would be almost as bad as being with Damien again.

"No. You remember me, don't you, love? I'm Erik Brooks. My brother Jaxon hired you to pose as his wife. That was some time ago. I wouldn't blame you if you didn't remember."

She laughed bitterly. "Hired? Is that what you call it?" Maybe Erik wasn't as kind as she made him out to be.

"I was trying to be . . . polite," Erik said.

Though it was dark, and she could barely see his face, she knew he was smiling. He hadn't forgotten what his brother had done to her. "Why am I here? How did you find me?"

"Jax looked for you for a long time. Days. But that's his story to tell, not mine."

"I don't want to be alone with him."

Erik sat on the edge of her bed. "You don't have to be. We want you to get well, and then we'll figure things out. But I'll be with you every step of the way."

She wanted to believe him, but they'd brought her here for a reason. Jax hadn't looked for her out of the kindness of his heart. He wanted something, though she couldn't imagine what. If he thought he'd fathered a child the afternoon he'd fucked her against the church window, and it only now occurred to him to look for his son or daughter, he would be mistaken. She'd been on the Depo shot for so long she didn't even have her period anymore. "There was someone else here. Last time . . ."

"Jax hired a nurse, or nurses, rather, to watch you around the clock. You have pneumonia and strep. The doctor who looked at you said you almost died. That's what the IV is for. Antibiotics. Vitamins and minerals. Fluids. You were in pretty bad shape, Raven. No matter how much you hate my brother, he saved you."

"Maybe I wanted to die," Raven whispered, but she didn't mean it. No matter how tough her life was, she'd never been tempted to kill herself. She couldn't do that to her parents. Though she hadn't seen them in many years, they at least knew she was alive, somewhere.

It was better than nothing.

Erik lifted her chin and made her look at him.

Her eyes adjusted to the lack of light, and again, she marveled at how different he was from Jax.

What had she thought when she'd been so panicked the first time she'd woken?

Angel and devil.

Never before had she been so accurate.

"Nothing is ever that bad," Erik chastised. "Jax has been through . . . well, again, that's not my story. But don't pretend to know my brother, Raven. Even with the way he treats you. We all have our demons, don't we, love?"

Blessedly, he released her, and she turned away.

Erik sighed. "I'm here because Nichole went on a break, and I said I would watch out for you. But you seem to be in a better place than the first time you woke."

She wasn't in a better place. Just because she knew more of what was going on didn't mean she was in a better place. It just meant she could look out for herself. Erik may say he'll never let her be alone with Jax, but Erik was Jax's brother, and family stuck together. She would never let herself believe Erik would choose her over Jax.

For now, she could take the comfort he was offering her.

"Will you stay with me?" she asked. She'd been alone for so long, emotionally hollowed out. Her heart and soul longed for intimacy. It was why she'd fallen for Jax's touch so quickly. A touch was a touch.

Even neglected children would rather have a spanking than nothing. She seemed to recall something like that in one of her short rehab stints during group therapy. But the therapist had been talking about them, too, not just little kids. When you're neglected, any touch, good or bad, was a chance to be *seen*.

"May I?" Erik asked, the mattress dipping as he leaned forward.

"What do you want to do?" Raven asked, moving away, though she was only a few inches from her own edge of the bed.

"I'd just like to kiss your forehead, if that's okay."

Kiss her forehead? The concept seemed so foreign to her she almost laughed.

"It's been so long for you, hasn't it, love? So long since you've been shown any kindness."

By a man. The words hung in the air even though Erik hadn't spoken them aloud. And that included his brother.

They both knew it.

"It's okay," Raven said, and she froze while Erik pressed his lips against her forehead. Chaste. The kind of kiss a brother would give his sister.

Tears welled in her eyes. She was usually good about the tears, allowing her anger to control her emotions. With anger she didn't have tears. She had fury. And hate.

"Your IV has sedative in it. Lie down now, and go back to sleep. It's one clock in the morning," Erik said, nudging her shoulder.

Falling back to sleep sounded heavenly, but she didn't want to be alone. "Stay," she begged again and tugged on the lapel of his jacket.

Raven tried not to think about what was next in store for her.

Erik could try to protect her, but what little she knew of Jax Brooks, the man always got what he wanted.

~

It was beginning.

Jax knew it was just a matter of time. Raven had been under his roof hardly forty-eight hours, and it was already starting. Not that he should be surprised.

Erik had always been more charismatic.

Jax shifted on his feet outside Raven's door. Nearing seven in the morning, he wanted to see how she was doing.

Quite well by the look of it.

She laid on her back, her black hair splayed across the bleached-white pillow. Erik laid next to her, one hand resting on her stomach, moving up and down with her breathing.

He didn't know what Erik saw in her that drew him so strongly to the pale, skeletal woman.

Hardly pretty, Raven was too skinny, but Jax pushed aside the fact it was probably because she didn't eat on a regular basis. Lucia was thin too, almost to the point of looking sick, like Raven.

But it was more appealing to him because she did it to be fashionable.

The way Raven lived disgusted him, but Erik, apparently, didn't mind it.

Jax tapped the tube of rolled papers against his thigh. He wanted them signed. Now.

He pushed the door open, and the young Black nurse who had just taken over for the day nodded at him. Stephen would call later to check on his patient, but Jax didn't plan to be the one the doctor spoke with. As far as he was concerned, Raven's time in his house was already approaching an end. If she needed more care, she could go to the free clinic. Or perhaps Erik would bring her to his apartment. He seemed to care about her welfare.

Jax did, too. Only up until she signed the papers. Then what Raven did or where she went was no matter to him.

"How is she?" he asked.

"The overnight nurse said Raven woke around one this morning," she whispered. "Mr. Brooks was here, and she said Raven's been sleeping since then. I texted Raven's vitals to Dr. Monroe just a few minutes ago. He said we could ease off the sedative, but to keep an eye on her temperature."

His brother spent the night with her. The information soured Jax's appetite. He'd been in the mood for a decent breakfast. Not anymore.

"Thank you," he said, dismissing her. This one was at least dressed in scrubs.

Jax nudged his brother's shoulder. "Hey. Wake the fuck up."

Erik rolled over and blinked at him. "What time is it?"

"It's seven. I'm going to the office, but I wanted to see if Raven was up to signing these." Jax forced himself to smooth out his tone.

Swiping at his eyes, Erik sprang off the bed. "She hasn't been here for a full two days, you heartless son of a bitch."

"Watch it," Jax warned. "You don't want Mom to hear you say that."

"Mom would be on my side, *will* be on my side, after she hears what you've done and how you're treating this girl," Erik whispered furiously.

"I'm doing what needs to be done," Jax said, wiping a speck of saliva off his cheek. "I don't understand what's gotten into you."

He didn't want to know the truth, and he cut off his brother before Erik could even open his mouth. "Just call me when she's awake."

"Leave the papers with me. She's scared of you, and she wants nothing to do with you."

Like hell he'd trust his brother. "No. I'll come back. She doesn't have to be alone with me. I'm sure you'll be by her side." The last was tossed over his shoulder in a splash of acid.

He couldn't control what Raven and Erik did, and he didn't care.

Rather, he tried to convince himself of that on the way to his office even though the memory of the way she tasted replaced the bitterness of coffee on his tongue.

Four

Later that afternoon, Raven woke alone.

Her appetite hadn't returned, and the pleasant woman who replaced the night nurse patted her shoulder and checked her temperature, unconcerned. "It will take some time for you to feel well."

"Do you know what's wrong with me?"

Erik said she was very sick, but she already knew that by the way her muscles ached and the way her ears thrummed in pain. By the way she wanted to cry every time she swallowed.

"You have pneumonia, miss, strep throat, and a double ear infection," the nurse said, noting her temperature on a chart. "The antibiotics will take care of it. Dr. Monroe prescribed enough to treat an elephant."

"How long will it take?" Raven rasped.

"You've only been here for a couple days, miss," the nurse replied. "You have to give it time. Your fever's coming down, though, so that's good. Dr. Monroe instructed us to decrease your sleep sedative, but perhaps you're still tired?"

"No!" Raven wanted to be awake as much as possible. While Erik was kind, she couldn't trust anyone.

The nurse rubbed her back. "Then I'll ask the doctor about

more pain meds, at least. Now let me clean your wounds, and maybe you'd like a cup of tea?"

"What happened to my legs?" Raven asked as the nurse pulled down the sheets.

"You don't remember?"

Raven froze; her heart stopped.

Jax stood in the doorway, his hands shoved into the pockets of his suit pants. His jaw was set hard enough to cut through stone, and the glint in his eye could have shot laser beams through her at a hundred paces.

"No. What happened?"

"Rats decided to turn you into a living buffet. That must have been painful. You don't remember?"

Raven flinched. Rats at Damien's didn't surprise her, not the way he lived in that filthy apartment, but no, she didn't remember. She must have been far too gone to notice. Thank God. Because Damien handcuffed her to the wall—she *did* remember that—and she wouldn't have been able to get away from them.

Rats had been eating her alive.

"I'm going to throw up," Raven whispered, bile rising in her throat, her stomach churning.

Dressing her wounds, the nurse paused, her eyes wide, but she took Raven seriously. A second later, she heaved painfully into a kidney shaped plastic dish while the nurse held her hair out of the way.

When she finished, tears streamed down her cheeks.

The nurse wiped her mouth using a pungent medical wipe and pushed her back against the pillow. "You should rest. I'll be done with your legs in a moment."

Raven closed her eyes against Jax's imposing figure. Mortified she threw up in front of him, she could feel his eyes boring into her with revulsion.

"I'll just leave you two alone," the nurse murmured, covering Raven's legs with the sheet and bedspread.

Raven's lips numbed with fear. She didn't want to be alone with Jax, and she envied the nurse's escape.

Erik promised she wouldn't have to be alone with his brother, but he said he had things he needed to do and would return posthaste. That was the word he used. Posthaste. At the time it made her smile, but nothing could make her smile now.

The quiet loomed between them, and she turned her head, hoping to shut him out, make him leave.

Too out of it to appreciate it before, Raven hadn't noticed the windows were actually doors that opened onto a balcony. The snow glittered in the watery sunlight, and the yard blended into the grayish-white of the winter sky.

The color mimicked Raven's own life. Cold. Gray. No color to be seen for miles. Empty and bleak.

"Why did you bring me here?" she asked when she could no longer tolerate his staring. She clutched the bedspread in her hands. The pressure tugged at her IV, and she loosened her grip.

"Saving you from the rats wasn't enough?" Jax asked, moving over the carpet without a sound.

"I'm sure it wasn't for me," she said, the cream and new bandages burning her legs. She hurt all over, and she would have been hard-pressed to tell anyone where she hurt more. "Do you need another fake wife?" she asked, taunting him.

In response, Jax threw a sheaf of papers onto her stomach. "You aren't fake. I told you to sign a false name on the marriage license. You did not. We've been married for the past three years. I would like to marry in the spring. For real. Imagine my surprise when I was told I could not do so."

Raven's hand trembled as she picked up the first sheet. The words blurred together. "What's this?"

"Those are divorce papers. I need you to sign them."

Her heart sank. Jax hadn't sought her out because he wanted to see what happened to her. He hadn't had an attack of conscience. He hadn't been secretly in love with her and finally succumbed to his feelings.

Of course not.

Every woman had fairy tales in her heart. Pixie dust glittering in her soul.

Why could Jaxon Brooks have everything he wanted? Because he had money? Because of his position in society? Because he was simply handsome, and everything fell into his lap the moment he crooked a finger?

No one told him no.

Even three years ago she had given him what he'd demanded.

This time she wouldn't buckle.

"No."

Jax knelt beside the bed.

He was so close she could smell the coffee on his breath, count the lines forming around his eyes.

Eyes full of hate.

He moved his hand with lightning speed, and he grasped a handful of her hair at the back of her head before she could even draw in a breath.

Pain shot through her scalp into her neck, and it fought with the flames in her throat and ears.

His breath fanned her face when he spoke. "What can I give you to make you sign?"

This was her last chance.

She'd tried, time after time, to do it on her own.

Failed.

Jax would be sure she made it out the other side. He'd have to, if she played her cards right.

Too bad she'd never been good at cards.

"A life. I want my life back."

~

Jax leaned against the doorjamb of the his-and-hers bathroom he shared with Lucia.

She refused to meet his eyes in the mirror as she applied

lipgloss to her plump lips she maintained with injections every six months. Though she was only twenty-nine to his thirty-eight, Lucia DuBois upheld a strict regimen of diet, exercise, and health and beauty treatments at the spa. Lip injections and Botox shots for the lines on her forehead only she could see were just the beginning. The list was long, and Jax had little patience for knowing exactly what Lucia did to herself. He only had the inkling he did because after Lucia moved in with him, she wasted no time sending him the bills.

"You know how it is to save face, Lucia," Jax said, willing her to look at him. "That's the way it is in our families."

"You can't make her sign?" she spat, her reflection glaring at him in the mirror over the vanity.

"How do you do that?" Jax sighed. "Force a pen into her hand? What could keep her from gouging a hole through the paper?" *Or my neck?*

He tried to appeal to her soft side, though it would be in vain —Lucia didn't have a soft side. "Think of the help we'll be giving her. You attend benefits and fundraising functions all the time. You can say you're doing a good thing."

"Then just give her some money and tell her to get out."

He'd tried that once, tossing two thousand dollars out the limo door, watching her scramble after the bills as they blew down the sidewalk. His skin crawled with discomfort. While he hadn't thought much of it, having gotten what he wanted, looking in hindsight at his actions made him grimace in revulsion. He was no better than Lucia.

But he wouldn't try to change. He was what he was.

"I just need enough time to dry her out, buy her some clothes, maybe help her find a place to live and a job. That's all. She'll be out by spring. It's February now. I just need March, April. Maybe some time in May. I know we were looking at a June wedding, but—"

"If you suggest we put off our wedding, I will never talk to you again." Lucia's green eyes shimmered with tears. "You promised me we'd marry in June. Your mother made us wait, and now you're saying we might not . . ." She pressed her lips together.

Jax looked away. He didn't know what was worse, her anger or her tears. He never knew which emotion was true, how honest her intentions were.

And what about him? He was thirty-eight years old and he wanted a family. He wanted children. He had a legacy in which to pass along to his first born.

Unfortunately, as Lucia's shoulders shook and she delicately wiped tears away as to not smudge her makeup, Jax couldn't picture her as a mother. Not the loving, kind, mother he'd grown up with. Grace Brooks hadn't baked cookies or set up blanket forts in the living room, but she hadn't shoved him into the arms of a full-time nanny the moment she popped him out, either. She'd made sure he and Erik had typical childhoods, and as small boys, they'd gotten into their fair share of trouble. Grace helped them with homework and for a few years was president of their private school's PTA.

Lucia would do none of those things. She acted like a child, expected to be given what she wanted the moment she decided it was to be hers.

"The timeframe may not be in my hands," he tried to explain. "The paperwork needs to be filed, our marriage license needs to be processed. If that happens in time, it happens. But if not, we can always have the ceremony and then marry in the judge's chambers later. No one would be the wiser," he said, hoping to appease her.

"It's not only the ceremony," she snapped, shoving the cap onto the tube of lipgloss. The tears were gone, and a hard look, devoid of any emotion, took up residence in her eyes. "I don't want that girl living in my house."

Jax resisted the urge to raise his eyebrows. His home wasn't quite hers yet, but she'd been living there for over a year, made decisions with the staff on his behalf. Had redecorated the moment she set foot inside, claiming the house was too stark for her taste. He'd let her. He'd let her do whatever she wanted if she'd stay.

"Just two months, possibly a bit more. She's sick now, pneumonia. She's staying in the east wing, far from our suite. I'll enroll her in classes. She's going to need rehab, therapy, probably. You won't even know she's here."

Lucia leaned into the mirror and viciously swiped mascara onto her eyelashes. Jax wondered how she didn't poke an eye out. "Fine. You do what you need to do, because I am well aware you will do whatever you want whether I agree with it or not."

"It's not that I don't value your input—" Jax started.

Lucia scoffed.

He rested his hands on her shoulders. "I value everything you do, Lucy, everything you are," he said, using his pet name for her. He met her eyes in the pristine mirror. Lucia abided no streaks. The cleaning woman made that mistake only once. "But she won't sign the papers if I don't help her." He buried his fingers in her hair, and she tipped her head back as she closed her eyes.

He pressed against her, trapping her between his hard-on and the edge of the vanity.

If he could say anything positive about her, it was that the sex between them bordered on explosive, when she deemed to give it to him. She used it, or the lack thereof, as a weapon. A lesson she learned, no doubt, at her mother's knee.

To punish him for allowing Raven under their roof, he wouldn't see, smell, or taste her pussy for months. But that wouldn't stop her from wanting it.

Or going elsewhere.

Lucia moaned and opened her eyelids into slits. "Then fucking do it. Or else I'll—"

Jax met her eyes and smirked. "Or else what? You'll leave me?" She turned in his arms, and he lifted her onto the counter.

Lucia dragged his head to hers and captured his mouth with lips that tasted of watermelon.

Jax ran his fingers up her thighs and under the hem of her dress.

She would let him fuck her one more time to remind him of what he'd be missing defying her wishes.

He knew what she'd be keeping from him in the following weeks.

And he'd take it while he could.

Raven's legs trembled, and she leaned against the cool glass of the balcony's French doors. The courtyard was full of snow, and trees dotted the property, evergreens with boughs heavy with fresh snowfall. Snowflakes floated from the white sky, the temperature above zero. If she'd been on the streets, she would have walked today, to get air. To fight the claustrophobia she often experienced in the winter when the dangerous temperatures gave her no choice but to seek shelter in places she didn't want to be.

Like Damien's.

She hadn't felt good prior to him finding her sitting on a bench on Z Avenue, and she felt downright horrible the night he had. She'd been hot, then cold, her muscles ached, and at that point she knew she was coming down with something.

Elle would have taken her in, but Raven didn't want to burden her. She had enough going on, and Raven didn't have any money to pay her for room or board. Elle paid her here and there for small chores around her salon, but sick, Raven would have been dead weight.

When Damien propositioned her, she latched onto the opportunity, as dangerous as it was.

She was lucky after she collapsed with fever on his spare mattress he hadn't killed her right then and there.

Had Jax not rescued her, she would have been indebted to Damien for a long time to pay him back for his "kindness." There was no way Damien would have let her go without expecting payback, and lots of it.

So, that's where she was. Raven wished she could contact Elle, let her know she was okay, but she didn't have Elle's burner phone number memorized. Axel would be worried about her too, when she didn't surface at any of their haunts.

Three weeks had passed since Jax brought her to his home. She hadn't seen anyone in that time besides the nurses Jax hired to take care of her and Dr. Monroe. He was a kind man, and he reminded her a little of Santa Claus.

Her cheeks burned when she remembered her conversation with him. He admitted to giving her a pelvic exam, and while he spoke to her of his findings, Raven hid her face in her pillow, unwilling to picture the kind old man with his fingers inside her, studying her private area. He told her she didn't have an STD, but she knew that. She and Axel were intimate sometimes, but she always made him wear a condom. She didn't have any interest in sleeping with anyone else, but she couldn't speak for Axel and where he crashed at night—and with whom.

Dr. Monroe questioned her bruises, but those came with the territory, and she shrugged off his concerns.

She pressed her cheek to the window.

Erik looked in on her, always fidgeting with an unlit cigarette. Sitting with her as a comforting presence while the nurse on duty knitted or crocheted, minding her own business until she would occasionally scoff in response to something Erik said.

Once he laid on the bed with her while they watched a movie. Jax poked his nose into the room and just walked away when he saw the two of them snuggled under her bedspread.

She wondered if Jax knew his brother was gay. That he didn't have any need to be angry because Erik would never look at her that way. If he didn't know, it was just a testament to how little Jax cared about the people in his life.

He only cared about himself and what he could get.

The nurse on duty, Toya, a Black woman with curves hidden

by baggy pink scrubs, looked up from her book. "Would you like a bath?"

Raven stared outside to the snow below. She felt rather like Beauty to Jax's Beast, high in the tower with no means of escape. Toya and the other nurses acted more as companions now. Her sore throat faded away, her ears back to normal, her lungs no longer feeling like she'd inhaled gallons of water.

Even the rat bites were almost gone.

She didn't know how long the nurses would be employed to keep her company, and she feared what she would do after Dr. Monroe deemed her well.

She needed to take her time at Jax's day to day, hour by hour, like she had on the streets. Though she had a roof over her head and food in her belly, they didn't make her feel any safer than she had fending for herself on Z Avenue or lying awake at night in a shelter, waiting for a woman to rifle through her things looking for anything she could fence on the street.

Raven learned to keep her most valuable possessions at Elle's, hidden in a box that used to contain permanent solution.

It had been a costly lesson the night the two thousand dollars Jax gave her was stolen out of her backpack. She cried for days over the lost opportunities.

"Yes, that would be nice," Raven said, fingering the pink nightgown she wore off and on during her stay. The clothing she'd been wearing when Jax found her vanished, and only for the nightgowns and panties that mysteriously materialized whenever she needed them, she had no clothes to her name.

Even if she wanted to run, she couldn't. She wouldn't last two minutes outside dressed like this.

Toya drew her a bubble bath, and steam and the scent of flowers permeated the room.

The nurse helped her sink into the bubbles and hot water. The tub resembled a deep Jacuzzi more than a regular bathtub, and she sank to the bottom, the mountain of bubbles hiding every inch of her skin.

"Call me if you need me," Toya said, before leaving the door open only a crack.

Raven didn't even have time to fantasize about what the rest of her day would bring before the door creaked open, and Jax stepped inside the cream and mint green bathroom.

Dressed in his usual navy suit—this time his tie was striped with silver and red—Jax leaned against the vanity, freezing her with his stare.

Grateful the bubbles hid most of her body, Raven gritted her teeth and tried to control her fear of the heartless man standing in front of her. Toya was just outside the door if Jax hadn't sent her away.

"Dr. Monroe said you're feeling better," Jax began, not seeming to care she was naked and bathing.

Not affected at all.

She didn't want him to be. She didn't want to be the one to thaw his frozen exterior. He was engaged—that would be his new bride's job.

"Yes," she agreed, bubbles caressing her chin. She wouldn't thank him for his concern—he wasn't here because of that.

"Then it's time we talk about the future. I need to know what your expectations are, and I'll have a contract drawn up with our arrangement. After I fulfill my obligation, I expect you to fulfill yours. You will not lead me on with any last minute negotiations. You said you wanted your life back. What does that mean, exactly?"

She couldn't concentrate with him staring at her. And while the bubbles hid her most important bits, she felt vulnerable. Naked. Physically, yes, obviously, but bare, her soul exposed for him to see.

"I don't know." Had she been warned of this meeting, she could have asked for a pen and paper and written a list. Prioritize. She knew what she needed to start her new life, but she had *too many* things she could ask for, like a college education, or money for one, and she didn't know how much Jax would let her have before he cut her off.

He shifted to his haunches near the tub, and Raven's heart pounded in dread.

He rested both hands on the lip of the porcelain. "What do you mean, 'you don't know?' Surely you had something in mind when you made the deal with me."

"I h-haven't had time to think." She hated the way her voice sounded. Like a blubbering idiot. That wasn't who she was. She would have been eaten alive, and not by rats, on the street, if she didn't have the courage and the guts to defend herself.

"Haven't had time?" Jax's eyes darkened, and his lips thinned. "Yes, I suppose you've been too busy cuddling up to my brother to think about anything else."

She wanted to sit up in protest, but she'd lose the protection of the bubbles covering her breasts. "I haven't been well." That was only partially true. She'd been sick, but she was feeling better day by day, and there wasn't any excuse she could give him.

And he knew it.

"Then let's start at the beginning and work from there," he murmured reaching out to her.

Raven cringed away. She didn't want him touching her, and blessedly, he withdrew his hand.

She wished he'd leave her alone and let her to soak in peace. It'd been so long since she had the opportunity to lie in a tub and do nothing but float and read a book. She used to take a lot of baths at home.

Before.

Instead, he sank to his knees and knelt in front of her.

His proximity took her even further off-guard. The unhappy pull of his mouth. The hard look in his hazel eyes. The tilt of his head that said he wouldn't tolerate any of her shit.

He was already pissed she had the audacity to say no to him.

Jax Brooks wouldn't make this easy.

She needed this chance. Whether he would make this palatable or not, she had to be strong enough to make it this time. Living on the street wasn't what she planned on doing with her life, and her parents made it clear if she wanted back into their house, even for coffee, she needed to visit sober, wearing decent clothes, and preferably holding a respectable job. They wouldn't tolerate her present state.

They had made it through, she could, too. That was their way of thinking. Only, she'd never been able to freeze herself off the way her parents could.

And like Jax apparently could, too.

Something happened to him, turned him into the way he was.

Erik wouldn't tell her what, only fed her enough to keep her from wanting to kill Jax in his sleep for being such an asshole.

"The beginning?" Raven shivered even though the water barely began to cool.

"The last time I saw you, you guzzled my whiskey like you hadn't had a drink in months. Are you an alcoholic? You don't seem to be. You've been with me for three weeks. You haven't had a drop of alcohol and you're not going through withdrawal."

"How do you know that?" she hissed, horrified he remembered that unsavory scene in the church.

"Because the minute I brought you home I marked all my liquor bottles. Tell me, do you have your drinking under control?"

She looked away, and the warm water lapped at her cheek. "I don't need it. I like it. It helps me . . ." She gave up. He would never understand.

"Escape."

Her gaze flew to his. There was a crack in his ice. Just a small one. A tiny fissure.

"How do you know?"

"This isn't about me. You don't need AA then, but you need counseling. You didn't get where you are by being mentally stable."

She tried not to be offended, all he said was the truth, but her cheeks flamed, hearing it said aloud.

Jax continued, "You can't go anywhere looking as you did. You need a haircut, makeup, lessons if you don't know how to apply it. Clothing. If you can look a part, it's that much easier to play. Do you understand what I'm saying?"

She did, strangely enough. Fake it 'til you make it. Even if she didn't feel put together on the inside, she would look it on the outside, and she would be halfway there. "I can't afford any of that."

Jax's mouth twisted. "Your signature will cost me plenty. It already has, though perhaps not financially. I'll pay for you staying here in different ways. But let's not kid ourselves, this situation is my fault. If I had come clean with Gwen leaving me, I wouldn't be in this hot mess with you."

"Who will help me with all of that? Certainly not you."

Jax scoffed. "No. And not Lucia, either."

She frowned. "Who's that?"

"Lucia is my fiancée. She's tolerating your existence under my . . . our . . . roof. She's made it quite clear she's not happy, and she would sooner spit on you than have a girls' day at Bloomingdale's. My mother will help you. Thanks to Erik, she knows all my dirty secrets, and I have to say, for some strange reason, she's looking forward to meeting you again."

Raven wanted to dunk her head. Meeting Mrs. Brooks was the last thing she wanted to do. While Jax's money would help her find her footing, his social circle would make her feel like mud under their Manolo Blahnik pumps. "Great."

Jax regarded her coolly, and his disapproval made Raven feel like a brat. His mother didn't have anything to do with this, and she should be grateful she was willing to help her.

"I'm sorry. It's kind of her to want to help me."

"That's better. You may be forcing my hand, but the least you could do is be cordial about it. Which brings us to the other things. You don't have an education."

"How do you know that?" The man knew everything about her, and she twitched with embarrassment. The bubbles in her bath were also starting to pop, and she hoped this conversation was almost over, or she'd be treating Jax to a show before too long.

"The internet is a wonderful tool. When you don't have access to a computer, the realization of the things you can find online can slip by you. I don't imagine you spend much time online."

The only place she could use a computer was the library, and library security rarely let her inside. She shook her head.

"I'll hire a tutor for you. Tutors, actually. One for GED classes. Another for manners and etiquette. Perhaps someone for speech. I'll want you ready to meet the Queen of England by the time you leave my house. If you pass the GED courses, we will see about university."

Raven's blood thrummed through her veins. College. More than she hoped he'd give her.

"Do you know what you would want to study?"

Before her life had changed, she wanted to be an English teacher. "I like English. A long time ago I wanted to teach it."

Jax nodded. "That's something. I'll see to it you have a diary. You can begin journaling. It will give your tutor an idea where you are in that subject, at least. Perhaps down the road you may want to write a memoir. Writing can be very therapeutic, I've been told. And if you were to publish, you would be helping others by sharing your story."

Speechless at the amount of insight and understanding Jax displayed toward her, she could only stare.

He stood, grimacing as his knees popped. "That's a start. I'll send up some clothing so my mother doesn't have to bring you to Bloomingdale's naked. It's much too cold for that, at any rate. Gwen left a few things behind, and since you fit into her wedding dress, I'll assume other things of hers will fit you as well."

"Okay." She didn't like the idea of wearing another woman's clothing, but wasn't that what she did? The clothes Jax probably burned after the doctor stripped them off her were castoffs she received during social service's "first snowfall" event. She'd needed the down jacket desperately and had slept outside the building to keep the first place in line.

"She'll come for you at ten sharp, Raven, and you'll meet her downstairs. You may go where you please, but you are not welcome in Lucia's and my wing. We must maintain some privacy, and I refuse to be responsible for what Lucia will do if she finds you where you are not permitted."

They didn't have to worry about her snooping around. As long as she had a book, she could turn a three foot space into her castle. "Do you have any books? The nurses have been sharing with me."

"I'll ask Mariah to give you a proper tour after the shopping trip with my mother. Yes, I have a library, and yes, you may borrow any book you like. But the books will be returned how they are borrowed, is that clear? Do not dog-ear to hold your place. Do not spill coffee on them. Do not eat Doritos and turn the pages."

She thought he was joking, and she almost smiled until he said, "I banned Erik from my library when he spilled scotch on a first print run edition of *The Sun Also Rises*. I learn from my mistakes. Do you, Raven?"

The bubbles receded to the point where she needed to ask Jax to leave, but he turned to go.

He didn't wait for her to answer, and she blew out a sigh of relief when the door clicked behind him.

She hadn't an answer for him, anyway. Did she learn from her mistakes?

No. Or her situation wouldn't have become so dire.

Living under Jax's roof, she would have to start.

~

She didn't sleep most of the night, anxiety twisting her gut. She didn't remember Jax's mother. Just a glimmer of a blonde woman dressed in a powder blue mother-of-the-groom cocktail dress peeking into the office while she signed the marriage certificate.

It was because of Grace Brooks she signed her real name.

Jax said something to her, but Raven had missed it entirely.

As the sun tried to make an appearance in the wintery sky, she crawled out of the bed she found herself in a little over three weeks ago.

While she showered, someone delivered Gwen's old clothes. Wrapped in a large, fluffy towel, she fingered the cream sweater, the nubby material catching on a ragged fingernail. She didn't know how old Jax was, but he appeared older than her own thirty years. He probably had his fair share of women living in his house, had several closets full of old clothes, not having the heart to get rid of them.

No. That wouldn't be why he kept things from previous lovers. The man didn't have a drop of sentimentality in him.

Whatever the reason, she was grateful. The black leggings were a bit long, and the bra gaped a little at the top of the cups, but the sweater fit perfectly.

She hoped the panties were brand new, or at least, worn very little if at all. That, at least, was one thing she insisted on. She bought underwear for herself. Or if she was given any, they were always still in the package. She wouldn't accept them otherwise. She may be homeless but she still had her pride, and panties were cheap enough to buy new, one by one as she needed them, at the dollar store.

When someone knocked on her door, Raven answered with gratitude. After she dressed, she didn't know what else to do. She was starving, but leaving her room to look for breakfast seemed wrong. She was an unwanted guest in Jax's house, and while she felt comfortable asking for something to read, food seemed different.

People took food for granted, but not her. Anything she could eat was a blessing, and she was grateful for every mouthful.

While she was sick, a maid or one of her nurses brought her a tray. Jax saw to it she ate well, but still, some meals there hadn't been enough food to fill her belly.

She never *ever* asked for seconds.

In Raven's world, there were no seconds.

"Mr. Jax left for the office, but he instructed me to offer you breakfast," a Latina woman said. She was short, like Raven, her skin an olive color Raven admired. Her hair was a glossy black, and her dark brown eyes were kind. "My name is Mariah."

Raven loosened her death grip on the doorknob. "Thank you. I'm hungry, but I wasn't sure if I should do anything."

Mariah's eyes darkened as she gestured for Raven to follow her down the hallway. "You keep to your room, miss," Mariah warned. "You don't want to run into Miss Lucia." She muttered something in Spanish that sounded none too complimentary to Raven.

If Mariah didn't like Lucia and Jax warned Raven not to get in the woman's way, then she definitely wouldn't leave her room unless it was necessary.

"You sit," Mariah instructed when they entered a dining room featuring a large dining table that could seat twelve.

Raven stared in dismay at the elegant, but cold, room. "Oh, I couldn't. I wouldn't—" Tears clogged her throat.

God, she wasn't cut out for this. She missed the comfort and warmth of the soup kitchen. The kind volunteers. The pancakes and spaghetti. The day-old bread the local bakery donated.

She was too far out of her league. She ran a hand over her face, embarrassed to cry over something so stupid as being asked to sit at a table.

Mariah placed an arm around Raven's shoulders. "You come into the kitchen with me. What Mr. Jax doesn't know won't hurt."

"Thank you."

She followed the cook into a bright and spacious kitchen. A TV bolted to one wall played a morning talk show, but too low for Raven to make out the words. The scent of coffee permeated the air and the bacon warmed on the stovetop. Her stomach rumbled.

Mariah jerked her head to a table half the size of the one in the dining room, this one painted white, the surface scarred.

Sinking into the seat, Raven blinked as a plate loaded with scrambled eggs, bacon, and toast appeared before her along with a mug of coffee and a sugar and cream service. "Oh, Mariah, you shouldn't—"

"It's my job. Now eat."

Mariah turned away to block out further objections, and Raven swallowed a lump of guilt along with a forkful of fluffy egg.

She was playing a game she couldn't possibly win, and she better quit while she was ahead. Maybe he'd give her something to tide her over until . . . well, she'd never do better without his help and resources. The stolen money proved that.

She needed to sign the papers and just go.

Before pushing her plate away, she made herself finish her food. This would be the last decent meal she'd eat in a while.

"Mariah, I—" Raven started.

A woman burst through the kitchen door. "Mariah, I looked for Raven in the—oh, for goodness' sake! What is she doing in here?" She stopped near the island counter, gloves clutched in one hand, her fist pushed onto a hip in amused agitation.

"She didn't want to be alone, ma'am," Mariah said, clearing Raven's plate.

"Jax wouldn't like it," the woman reprimanded, though a smile played with her mouth. "You know Jax likes things done the way he likes them done."

"Mr. Jax isn't here," Mariah returned, unconcerned she was speaking to Jax's mother.

Raven's heart slammed beneath her ribs, her breakfast rolled queasily in her stomach.

Grace Brooks.

She looked glamorous, polished in a way only a woman with money could look. She wore wide-legged black dress pants, the hems wisping over the tops of high-heeled black boots. Her blouse was hidden by a long forest green winter jacket. Grace's hazel eyes—Jax's were exact copies—crinkled with happiness, and her blonde hair was pinned into a stylish French twist revealing diamond studs twinkling in her ears, her earlobes pink from the cold.

"But guests don't—" Grace stopped, then pressed her lips together.

"This is the first day she hasn't eaten in her room, ma'am. I didn't think it would hurt," Mariah said, breaking the silence.

"It doesn't matter now, but she'll need to learn to be comfortable in a more formal environment. I suppose there's time enough for that." Grace blew out a breath. "Are you ready to go?" she asked Raven as Mariah started doing dishes in a large, white sink.

"Actually, Mrs. Brooks, I've changed my mind."

"You don't want to go shopping? Jax told me you needed clothes. I booked spa time."

Grace's scrutiny told her she needed it.

She tried to hold on to the anger so the tears burning her throat wouldn't reach her eyes. "I've decided I need to go . . . home."

Dammit.

Grace knew she didn't have one. Raven dried her palms on the smooth material of the leggings. "I just need my old clothes back," she said, though her chances of them being returned to her were slim to none.

Eyes softening with something Raven would have called understanding if she hadn't known better, Grace stepped farther into the warm kitchen, leaving behind a trail of melted snow Mariah would need to mop away.

She hadn't considered how much work she'd cause for everyone; how much time people would need to spend on her. She only wanted to make Jax pay for the callous way he'd treated her in the church, and after, watching her scramble after the fluttering dollars like a desperate whore.

She wanted to forget she ever met Jaxon Brooks, forget any of this ever happened.

Run back to Elle's.

Run back to Damien's.

To anywhere that felt familiar.

Grace leaned against the granite counter and thrummed her manicured nails against the surface. "Let's find you some proper clothes before you decide anything rash. If, by the end of the day, you still want to leave, I'll have Justin drive you wherever you want to go, and I'll tell Jax you gave me the slip. Deal?"

She wouldn't change her mind. "Deal."

Five

Raven sat in the back of a long black car with Grace while the driver stared straight ahead at the empty road that turned out to be Jax's mansion's driveway. Without trying to gawk, she took in the acres and acres of land his home sat on. She would need all day to make it to the city on foot.

By the time they reached the large shopping center, sweat prickled Raven's skin. Motion sickness and the faint scent of a perfume she couldn't name still clinging to the white and gray parka Jax set aside for her to wear churned her stomach.

"You're free to do as you like," Grace told the driver, twisting in her seat, a boot resting on the sidewalk outside Bloomingdale's. "We'll be a while."

"Yes, ma'am," he said, smiling faintly.

Raven wondered what the driver would do with his free day. It would be boring to be a driver, just sitting there, waiting on people's whims. But it wasn't any different, really, than being homeless. On the streets, Raven always had somewhere to wait. Waiting in line for a bed at the shelter, and then waiting for a shower if she was lucky. Waiting in line for clothes, or food, or some other handout. The only time she felt free was at the club with Axel if she already secured a place to sleep for the night, or when she popped her head into Elle's salon.

Justin opened the car door for her, and she sucked in the fresh wet air to calm her nerves. Snowflakes the size of cotton balls floated through the air.

Grace led her inside the shiny department store. "This way. Spa first. Jax gave me carte blanche."

Raven twisted her hands. It sounded so ominous; Grace could do whatever she liked to her, but this was what she wanted.

Five minutes later, she was pushed down into a stylist's chair, and a slim man with a stubby ponytail trailed his fingers through her snarls.

Elle usually did her hair. Raven liked the pitch black and the colored streaks her friend experimented with.

"Too dark," he declared. "It washes out her face." He spoke to Grace, knowing who was in charge.

Grace nodded, her coat draped over her arm, her purse hanging from the crook of her elbow. "I agree. Her skin is pallid, but that will change with regular meals."

The stylist looked at Grace out of the corner of his eye but didn't comment.

Raven knew what he was thinking. Who didn't have regular meals? Not anyone this stylist met.

"I like the black," she insisted.

The stylist shoved his hands onto his hips. "This is *not* your natural color."

She flushed.

"Dark brown." He glared at her. "Highlights around her face."

"Then a wax job, everywhere, but be careful, she has some scrapes that are still healing. Mani, pedi. Give her a massage. This poor girl has probably never had one. No alcohol. Perrier, coffee, or tea," Grace directed.

The stylist secured a plastic sheet around her. "She's in good hands. Don't worry about a thing."

Grace treated him to a dazzling smile. "I won't."

~

Grace didn't come back for nearly four hours.

Raven's hair was now the color it had been in high school. Dark, but not black, and that subtle difference made a significant one to her complexion.

The stylist also cut off many inches, giving her a sleek angular lob, but dismayed at the loss of length, she hadn't been in any position to complain. After the cut and dye, she sat under a hair dryer with conditioner in her hair.

Her muscles felt like jelly after an hour-long full-body massage, and the wax job burned her legs and bikini line. She hadn't been given a razor in the bathtub yesterday, and now she knew why. At first, she thought it was to keep her from inflicting self-harm, but other plans had been made for her, even then.

The woman who did her wax job waxed her eyebrows, too, though she left them full and beautifully arched.

The makeup artist highlighted her cheekbones, and lipliner made her lips just a bit fuller.

Her feet were smooth after a pedicure, and as the woman painted her toenails a demure pink, Raven thought back with regret to the mother/daughter days she spent with her mom.

While she was getting made over, Grace had been hard at work with a personal shopper choosing every piece of clothing Raven would need for any occasion.

Now, trying on clothes, her thin frame worked with her—fashionably thin. Not sickly thin.

Funny how that worked.

"For the tutors, for the classes, the parties," Grace announced, shoving her into a fitting area that couldn't accurately be called a stall. Damien's whole apartment could fit into the space that held a mini dais in front of a three-sided mirror.

"Why are you doing this?" Raven asked, standing in front of

the mirror dressed in tights and a sweater dress colored a deep purple.

She barely recognized herself.

Grace hadn't accurately guessed her size with some things, and she sent the personal shopper to replace a few clothing items leaving them alone.

There had to be another way for Jax to force her hand, rather than spend thousands of dollars on her. People divorced all the time, whether they wanted to or not.

He possessed all the power in the world. If he wanted a divorce without her cooperation, he could have one. Yet he chose to go along, and even asked his mother for help.

Grace stood from the plush loveseat she sat on while Raven tried on clothes, sipping on a frothy cappuccino. She set the huge porcelain cup onto the matching saucer and lowered herself onto the top step of the dais.

"Jax told me what happened."

Right before Raven's eyes, Grace changed into a completely different person. Her shoulders sagged, and all the sparkle left her demeanor. Suddenly, the overhead lights were not kind to the middle-aged woman, and her glow turned to sallowness in an instant.

"What did he say?" Raven asked, wanting to know the lies he told his mother.

"All of it," Grace said, squeezing the bridge of her nose as if to ward off a headache. "Gwen. The church. Looking for you and the time it took."

"Oh," she murmured, surprised. He told her the truth. "I wondered how Jax pulled off the wedding."

Grace looked up at her, and it unsettled her. The elegant woman should be looking down on her, not the other way around. For years people ridiculed her for being homeless, but no one bothered to ask her why. Not until Jax asked yesterday. People assumed she was lazy, or stupid, or bipolar, schizo. Mentally unstable. Jax hadn't *called* her that, exactly, not like it was something that defined her. He said it like she was afflicted with it or suffered from it. Like there was a reason she was the way she was.

Now his mother was looking up at her.

She didn't like it, and she sat on a step lower than Grace. Though it didn't make her that much shorter than the stylish lady who took her under her wing because her son requested it, Raven felt more like she was where she belonged.

"We knew you weren't Gwen. Me. Jax's father. Pastor Clark. Erik let us know. You resemble her, your height and coloring, and could be mistaken for her across a crowded room. It was quite easy, in fact, for Jax to do what he did. You wouldn't have fooled anyone at the reception, of course, but Jax took care of that."

She didn't know she shared similarities with Gwen, and it explained why Jax was so quick to blackmail her into doing what he wanted. "Why are you here now? Why go along with this? Jax has the money and power to force me to do anything he wants."

Grace ran her hands along the sides of her French twist, then fiddled with a diamond stud. "I feel I can be honest with you, Raven. Can I?"

"Of course." The better for her to know what was really in store for her if she stayed, and that was a big *if*. She was getting a small taste of what it will be like in Jax's world, and she didn't like it.

Sitting up straighter, Grace said, "When Jax explained what was going on, what lengths he'd gone to find you, there was something, Raven. Something in his eyes I haven't seen for a very, very long time. It gave me hope."

She wanted to scoff but held her tongue. There would never be anything between Jax and her besides revulsion and hate on his part and disdain and loathing on hers.

"There's nothing between Jax and me," she said as the personal shopper came back, her arms laden with garments.

"I would never spend the day alone with Lucia; I don't like

her. She's a greedy shrew. He's marrying the wrong woman this time," Grace said.

Raven smiled a little. She liked Grace, but she doubted Grace's opinion mattered to Jax.

"Let's find a late lunch," Grace suggested after Raven changed into new boots, skinny jeans, and a dark chestnut-colored turtleneck sweater.

"But what about—"

"We'll have everything delivered," Grace said, standing and picking up her purse. "A Brooks pays for convenience."

Raven stood in front of the mirror and studied the unfamiliar person standing on the dais. Her parents would let this woman into their home. This stylish woman, standing in leather boots and jeans that cost more than what Jax threw at her after dumping her on the sidewalk, would be welcome. She was the picture of sophistication and grace. But was she a convenience to the Brooks' family? Or an inconvenience?

Lifting her chin and gathering her courage, Raven decided to find out.

As promised, Mariah greeted her when Grace brought her back to Jax's house. It seemed silly to call it a house, because the size demanded a more proper description, but it sounded stupid to keep calling it a mansion.

She'd never been in a house of this size, and she got turned around more than once while Mariah gave her a tour.

Thick, heavy curtains blocked out most of the natural light, and as the tour went on, Raven felt like she was being led through a dark, stuffy museum.

Mariah showed her the library, and she waited patiently while Raven chose enough books to keep her occupied in her room for quite some time. Watching TV was not her usual hobby. Even before her parents kicked her out, reading had been her preferred form of entertainment. Sometimes, just to have somewhere to go, something to do, Raven would go see a movie at a little rundown theater near Z Avenue, but she wouldn't watch the TV in her room alone.

Mariah brought up a dinner tray a short time later, and Raven dug in, famished. Halfway through the meal she wondered if she wasn't invited to dinner downstairs or if Jax wasn't home. She didn't see Erik much anymore, but she couldn't expect him to visit all the time and she hoped Jax didn't tell him to stop spending time with her. Erik didn't seem the type to listen to what his brother said, though. Work must be keeping him busy, and Raven winced when she had to admit she didn't ask him what he did for a living.

She didn't know what Jax did, either. All she knew was he had money to burn, and she should be thankful for it.

Raven just turned out her light and burrowed into her bed when someone knocked lightly on her door. She slipped out of bed wearing the same nightgown she wore the night before. Grace chose numerous nightgowns and sleep sets for her at Bloomingdale's, but nothing would be delivered until later.

When she opened the door, she was surprised to find Jax on the other side, leaning against the wall, waiting for her. "Hi," she said, her heart pounding. The sight of him would never fail to intimidate her. His short blond hair held in place with product, the hard glint in his eyes. The stubble along his jaw. The impressive width of his shoulders tapering into narrow hips. Jax wore a tux, the bowtie untied and hanging around his neck. That answered her question—he hadn't been home for dinner.

"My mother said shopping went well."

"She okayed a lot of clothing," she said, blushing.

"I wouldn't have expected anything less," Jax said, pushing away from the wall. "Your lessons begin tomorrow at one. You'll meet your tutor in the library. Don't be late. He charges by the hour, and any minute you waste is a minute I have to pay for. Tomorrow night we're going to dinner."

"We?" she asked, confused. Surely he didn't want to be seen with her in public.

"Yes. You and me. You will have the clothing to dress for an evening out, and you need to start learning social graces. At least, I'm assuming that was part of your plan?" he asked.

She wanted an education, at least her GED. Finding classes to attend while she lived on the streets was next to impossible. There were several places that offered GED certificates, some of them free if she didn't have access to a voucher or scholarship, but looking how she usually did, well, places didn't always care to help her. But manners? Etiquette? Even if she could completely turn her life around, she'd never be able to afford to eat at the kind of place Jax would take her, so what did it matter if she knew how to behave in a restaurant of that caliber? Still, if he was willing to teach her which fork to use when, she should let him.

"Okay."

"You'll need a cocktail dress. I'm sure my mother bought you several and explained the difference between a cocktail dress and an evening gown. Dress appropriately and do your makeup. I'd bet a paycheck my mother bought you plenty of that, too. Actually, it probably *did* cost me a paycheck." He scowled. "I'll meet you downstairs at eight o'clock. I have dinner reservations for eight-thirty."

"Okay," she said again, but a pit formed in her stomach. She didn't have any clothing but for the new outfit she wore home. Gwen's clothing disappeared, and in the middle of shopping, she forgot all about the other woman's clothes. This didn't seem like a thing to mention to Jax, and she let him walk away.

"Oh, by the way," he said, flicking a glance at her over his shoulder, "I like your hair. It suits."

It was the kindest thing he'd said to her, and even after she fell back into bed, her mouth hung open in shock.

Jax waited in the foyer, pacing back and forth, occasionally looking at his watch. She wasn't late, he was early, just to get away from Lucia who was angry he was taking Raven to dinner.

"Let your brother do it," she demanded, and he bristled.

For the past week, he'd seen to it his brother had other things to do. Erik had worked at Titan since Jax opened the doors to his first paying customer, but lately his brother had grown soft. In retaliation, he assigned Erik a large project to oversee that frequently took him out of state. Erik accused him of not wanting him to spend time with Raven, and Lucia's comment grated on his nerves.

"He's not here. If you were around more, I could have told you I sent him to Seattle to head the Waterson cybersecurity project. I told them they would have to deal with Erik or no one. They took Erik."

Lounging in bed, Lucia sniffed.

"I would think you would look more favorably upon the company that keeps you in the lifestyle of which you'd like to stay accustomed," he said smoothly, choosing a tie in his armoire.

"I don't like you spending time with her."

Jax chose a tie and snaked it under his collar. He sat on the edge of their bed and ran a hand up Lucia's bare leg. Having a rare evening with no plans, she wore a satin robe and nothing else. "You don't have to worry about that." His hand trailed up her thigh, and musk radiated from between her legs.

She widened her knees, just a millimeter, and Jax grazed her heat, wetting his fingertips before she pushed him away, clamping her legs together.

He met her eyes and licked his fingers.

"You could have me if you kick her out," Lucia said, shoving a pillow between her legs, preventing him from touching her again.

Her arousal permeated the room, and her flavor . . . she knew what she was doing, cutting him off. He would do anything she asked, except throw Raven out onto the street.

The exchange made him hard, and he escaped their suite. If she wouldn't fuck him, there wasn't any reason to hang around. To punish him further for spending time with Raven, Lucia would be gone when he returned, and most likely, wouldn't be back until sunrise, her hair in a tangle and makeup worn off.

A noise behind him made him turn, and Raven stood before him in a burgundy off-the-shoulder cocktail dress. She'd left her hair down, but she'd added texture, the chunky locks framing a face she'd made up with a light hand.

Jax approved.

Nothing like how Lucia caked on her makeup, Raven added mascara to her eyelashes, a light sweep of blush, and lipstick. That was all.

But it was all she needed. Already regular sleep and decent meals were filling out the hollows of her face, and the purple bruises that had been so blatant under her eyes were fading.

She wore black pantyhose, her delicate calves accentuated by high heeled pumps. If she wasn't used to wearing heels, her feet would definitely be sore by the end of the night.

Betraying her nervousness, she held a small black clutch in her hands so tightly her knuckles turned white.

She looked perfect, and she frowned when he didn't say anything, simply stared. "This is all right, isn't it?"

He cleared his throat. "Yes, and you are on time. Thank you. Do you have a coat?"

"Grace said they would be hung downstairs. Wherever that means."

"She meant in the foyer, with the rest of the coats and jackets for Lucia and me. My parents and Erik also keep a few things here. My mother stopped by?" Jax opened the closet and selected a black cape with fur trim.

He draped it over her shoulders and secured the silver chain.

"She helped me put away all the clothes, going over again what was what," she said.

Justin waited for them, and Jax led her outside saying, "That must have been helpful."

After a long day at the office and the verbal sparring with Lucia, he wanted a drink and a good meal, and he took the stone stairs at a trot. When he reached the car, he realized Raven wasn't with him. He looked over his shoulder in irritation.

She stood on the top step, his house looming behind her in the dark, the stars bright pinpoints in the pitch black winter sky. Lights that flanked the house's red double doors illuminated her figure.

She stopped to carefully navigate the slippery steps in her heels.

Jax caught his breath, but it wasn't because a gust of wind chose that moment to hit him in the face.

He'd never been struck by a woman that way.

His heart had never stopped mid-beat.

He effectively shut off his emotions . . . or thought he had.

Gingerly, she stepped down the stairs, her gloved hand gripping the marble handrail covered with snow. "When I told her you ordered me to dinner, she helped me choose this dress."

That jerked him out of his stunned haze, and his mouth twisted. Pulling the car's door open he snapped, "You said you wanted to learn. If you didn't want to learn how to behave in public, you should have told me."

"I may have come from a shelter, but I'm not a dog," she retorted, sliding inside the car. "I know how to eat soup without letting it dribble down my chin. I don't know what kind of life you think I'm going to be living once I leave here, anyway."

"You may be accustomed to the local Olive Garden, but I won't lower my standards for you. I wanted to take you to dinner. We will go where I want to go."

He slammed her door shut and circled the trunk of the car.

Jax settled into his seat and said, "Go," to Justin who was used to his temper and did nothing but drive away from the house.

Jax settled into his seat and stared out the window.

Looking as she did, she wouldn't fit into an Olive Garden, either.

She shone too bright for the rundown chain.

When Justin parked in front of The Lighthouse, Jax said, "Let me help you."

"Help me do what?" Raven asked, but he was already climbing out of the car and rounding the back, the bitter wind fighting against his coat.

She clutched the handle of the door, prepared to push it open, and he pursed his lips in annoyance. The woman simply didn't listen.

He yanked the door open. "Let me help you out of the car."

"What for? Are my legs broken?"

"If the gentleman you are with doesn't help you from the car, get rid of him."

"The *gentlemen* I see don't even have cars," she said, gripping his gloved hand and stepping out of the sedan.

Jax kept his mouth shut. He didn't want to hear about her "gentlemen," such as they were.

Her shoe slipped on a patch of ice, and he steadied her, pulling her to his chest. A car stopped behind them, and the headlights made her eyes glow, like the scotch he favored. A puff of white breath escaped her lips.

"This is why you accept help. You would have been down on your ass in three seconds flat. Now hold onto my arm, and I'll assist you into the building." He pushed the car door shut and pounded on the side, letting Justin know he was free to drive away.

"I feel like a little kid. I've lived on the street for thirteen years, Jax. I can take care of myself."

Her scent tickled his nose, something light, something that smelled vaguely of cinnamon and apples, and Jax unstuck his tongue from the roof of his mouth. "There will be a day you won't be alone, Raven."

"A woman is always alone."

Jax didn't have a chance to respond. The hostess recognized him and immediately motioned for the coat check girl to relieve them of their heavy winter jackets. She didn't give Raven a moment to even fluff her hair before she stepped away to lead them to a table. When his assistant called to make the reservation, he'd instructed her to ask for a table in the back, somewhere in a corner, but the hostess, a curious glint in her eye when she looked at Raven, seated them in the center of the room.

He wouldn't argue. Not tonight. But any other evening, especially with Lucia, he would have asked for the owner, the chef who was indebted to him. Jax had invested in this restaurant many years ago, and his friend never forgot Jax's support. Tonight's date with Raven wasn't important enough to go over the hostess's head.

Raven was about to sit, and Jax growled under his breath, "Don't you dare." People stared.

He wasn't a stranger to the clientele, and his cheeks warmed. "Let me pull your chair out for you."

"I can't even sit without help?" Raven whispered, leaning in, her eyes darting every which way. "Are you going to cut my meat, too?"

Deliberately, he walked around the table and pulled out her chair, where she plopped in a cloud of burgundy skirt.

The moment Jax sat, a waiter brought them menus encased in thick leather binding.

Raven opened hers and ran her finger down the list of entrées. "Where are the prices? How do you know how much everything costs?"

"They bill my company," he murmured, perusing the menu.

"That doesn't answer my question. How do you know you can afford it?"

He closed his menu. "Raven," he said gently, "if you have that worry, you wouldn't eat here."

"What's the cheapest thing?" she insisted.

She looked down at her menu, and he missed looking into her eyes. He reached across the table and held her hand, and her gaze flew to his face, startled. "Order what you think you'll enjoy."

"Well, well, what do we have here?"

Under his breath, Jax groaned, and he casually let go of Raven's hand. Of course, Margo Brentwood, Lucia's best friend, would be here. At least he hadn't lied to Lucia about where he was going. The news would be in Lucia's ear in five seconds. Providing she wasn't . . . busy.

Jax stood and gave Raven the eye, warning her not to follow suit, but she set aside her menu. Muttering under his breath, he quickly stepped around Margo, rested his hand on Raven's bare shoulder, and held her in place. Men stood. Women did not. With her skin warming his fingertips and the ends of her hair skimming the back of his hand, small facts that made Margo arch an eyebrow, Jax said, "Margo, this is Raven, Raven, Margo. I'm helping Raven get settled in the city. She's . . . new to the area. Raven, Margo is a friend of Lucia's."

Raven only nodded.

"It's . . . kind of you to help," Margo drawled, discreetly studying Raven. "She's very . . ." Margo tilted her head. "Melancholy. I can see it in her eyes. You don't like the area, Raven?"

Raven stared, unflinching. "It's very cold."

Margo's smile turned smug. "That *is* a problem."

"Indeed."

Jax tried to hide his smile and failed. "Good evening, Margo."

After he took his seat, he motioned for the waiter. "I need a drink."

"What was she talking about?"

"That cold bit? She thought you were talking about me. She doesn't like me much."

"I was talking about her. She's not very nice."

"No, she's not, but she's receptive. She could see you're sad."

"It's a lot to get used to," she mumbled.

He ordered for them. Salad to start, then mushrooms stuffed with crab and cheese. Filet mignon, twice baked potatoes, and green beans with almond slivers, cheesecake for dessert. Appropriate wines for each plate, espresso with the cheesecake. Jax thought she would appreciate the simple meal.

Not wanting the topic to slip away, the moment the waiter walked away with their menus, he said, "My mother told me you almost changed your mind yesterday. What upset you to the point you would want out of our deal?"

"Grace told you that? Aren't I going to have any privacy?"

"Do you think I have any?" Jax asked, amused. Of course she wouldn't have any privacy. If anything, he would continue to watch her like a hawk until the minute she stepped out of his house for the last time.

"You can have whatever you want."

He lowered his eyes. If that's what she truly thought, she was mistaken. "No one can have whatever they want. Not even me. Especially me. Things have a way of happening that can ruin any chance at happiness."

She scoffed, and he wanted to kick her for being rude. Though kicking her wouldn't have been the best way to demonstrate manners.

"Like I feel sorry for you. Your mansion, your fancy job, whatever it is you do. A family who loves you. Like you have problems."

"Is that what you see when you look at me?"

Raven leaned closer, shoving her elbows onto the table.

He winced.

"What did you see when you first looked at me? Did you see a woman down on her luck, cleaning a church and trying to make ends meet? Did you see a woman, someone's daughter, someone's," her breath hitched, "sister, struggling to pay rent? Keep a roof over her head? What did you see when you looked at me?

You saw a druggie, didn't you? You saw a strung-out whore. And you used me like one, too. Go ahead and play victim. Whatever happened to you, go see a fancy shrink and leave the pain and suffering to the people who really know what that is."

The sommelier presented Jax with a white to accompany their salads and the mushrooms. He nodded stiffly in agreement after the first sip.

He stung. There was no doubt about it. Never in his life had his words and actions been flung back into his face.

At times, Erik tried to convince Jax to see reason. Other people had problems. Jax's accident wasn't the worst thing someone had gone through. But he was consumed by what he'd done, the family he'd destroyed through a simple act of carelessness, and he couldn't listen. Guilt ate at his insides like cancer, and the only way to keep his remains intact was to close himself off. Close himself off from love, from friendships. Only this woman sitting in front of him had, in the sixteen years since he'd pulled the trigger, made him feel anything but misery and vehement hate whenever he looked in the mirror.

He'd thawed, in that church, just for a moment, and ashamed he felt anything, even for a second, he'd made her pay.

"Then tell me, Raven. Why were you on the streets? What's your pain?"

She sat back when the waiter placed her plate of filet mignon in front of her. The salad and the mushrooms were taken away untouched and unnoticed.

The people in the dining room faded into nothing, and as Raven's eyes filled with tears, her beauty struck him. In the dim light, she looked like a painting. Her eyes shimmered with unshed hurt, her skin twinkled with candlelight, her hair sparkled. She could crook her finger at any man, and they would kneel before her and beg. For one brief second, he pictured Erik there, and though his mind rebelled at the idea, he thought he should let his brother have her.

She lifted a trembling hand to her lips and took a sip of the red the sommelier poured to accompany the beef. "I prefer red," she said, carefully setting the wineglass onto the white tablecloth.

He waited her out.

She sighed. "I lost my brother when I was younger. Not terribly young, but it hit me hard. We were close, and his death . . . was my fault. If I hadn't been . . . well, that doesn't matter, does it?" She met his eyes. "People can say all sorts of things, but that doesn't absolve you of responsibility."

Jax nodded. He knew that all too well.

"My parents couldn't deal with my behavior, and pushed to their limits, they kicked me out. It doesn't hit you all at once, you know? That you have nowhere to go. Until it starts to get dark and you realize you're not welcome at home and you can't go back."

"And the makeover, the classes?" Jax asked.

"My parents won't talk to me unless I'm 'normal.' That's what they say. 'Normal.' Like anyone can be normal after something like that happens, but I'm going to try. I miss them. They lost their son because of me. I think I don't deserve their love, but when I feel like that, I'm punishing them as well as myself. They don't blame me. They never have. I've taken that burden onto myself." She raised her hands to encompass the restaurant. "This is my 'normal.' Learning how to live like this. When Grace took me shopping yesterday, that's what I thought when I looked at myself for the first time. After the makeover. I thought, 'this is a woman my parents would let into their house.' After thirteen years, it was a surreal moment."

"Yet you told my mother you changed your mind."

"Asking you for classes, for new clothes . . . that's just money, and you can spare it."

Jax's mouth quirked. "Thanks."

She wiped her cheeks. "I mean, it wasn't the money you were spending on me. It was everything else. Mariah cooking for me, your mom taking me shopping. Even Erik when he stayed with me while I was sick. I'm using up everyone's time, and I don't deserve it. I didn't consider that part of things, that's all."

"So would you, right now, let me off the hook?" he asked, curious. "Sign the papers?"

"Yes."

He let her answer hang in the air, the murmur of patrons buzzing around them. She didn't want people to work for her, when that was one of many things he took for granted. He paid them, and he would have thought staying at his house would make her feel entitled.

Lucia certainly felt that way and had taken over from the first morning she woke in his bed.

But Raven would give up any chance of finding stability because she felt guilty Mariah cooks her meals.

"Where would you go?"

"Just drop me on Z Avenue, and I would find somewhere. I'm good at it." She tried to smile. "I won't freeze to death."

"Would you feel better if you worked?"

"Actually, yes. I need to feel like I contribute."

"That's admirable. A work ethic is valuable. Some people go through life expecting others to work on their behalf. Do you get along with Mariah? You should eat before it gets cold." He pointed at her plate with his fork.

She picked up her steak knife. "We get along, I think. I haven't spoken with her much, but she did warn me to stay away from Lucia."

Jax nodded, in appreciation for Mariah's advice, as well as for the piece of beef melting in his mouth. He swallowed and took a sip of wine. "Good. Why don't we ask her to teach you to cook? You'll be helping, but you'll also be learning a skill. We'll take it from there, okay?"

"Why are you doing this when I just said I would give you what you want?"

Jax didn't answer, only circled his finger in the air, encouraging her to finish her dinner.

Raven fell asleep in the car on the way home, and her head lolled against the seat until it rested on his shoulder.

Why was he giving her this chance?

Because as she was telling her story, he realized just because they looked different on the outside, they were the same on the inside.

The disgust he felt looking at himself in the mirror every morning was exactly how she thought about herself.

They weren't different at all.

They were exactly the same.

Six

R aven settled into a routine of sorts over the following weeks. Tutoring in the morning and afternoon followed by cooking lessons in the evening took up almost every minute of her day.

Her lack of education embarrassed her, and when the tutor gave her a laptop, she'd looked at it like it was an alien spaceship, afraid to touch it. Despite her lack of exposure to technology, her tutors introduced her to several subjects, and she soaked up the knowledge. It amazed her that after all this time she still remembered her times tables.

Homework assignments filled her evenings, and after eating a meal she helped Mariah prepare, she'd lock herself in her room and study late into the night.

She rarely saw Jax, and only once or twice a week did Erik visit, saying Jax was keeping him busy at work.

Raven knew the real reason, though. Jax didn't want him talking to her. It hurt, but Raven could understand the reasons why. There was no point in becoming close to any member of the Brooks family. Jax was ensuring she didn't feel as if she belonged in his house. Her stay was temporary.

No one knew that more than her.

Besides, even as the days passed and the numerous hallways in the large house no longer turned her around, the fact she felt more comfortable in the kitchen over anywhere else was telling.

Every once in a while she wondered where Lucia was, but only thanked her lucky stars she had never had the misfortune of meeting Jax's fiancée.

Her luck ran out one snowy evening after her tutor released her for the day. Carrying a heavy stack of textbooks, Raven took the stairs to her room, several pages marked with bright Post-It notes. She had quite a bit of homework to complete that evening, but she looked forward to it.

"I'll have to tell Jax we need an exterminator," Lucia sneered, coming up behind her. "We have a rat problem, I see."

Raven stopped mid-step. "Lucia, good evening."

God, but the woman was beautiful. She looked exactly the way Raven pictured a woman of Jax's ilk would look. Her blonde hair shone, waves upon waves floating around her shoulders. Her eyes were blue ice chips, accented by long, dark lashes. Her pink lips were pulled into an unhappy frown.

Lucia was dressed similarly to Raven: sweater, skinny jeans tucked into boots. But Lucia carried herself with an air of self-importance that Raven could never learn in a million years.

"You have some nerve," Lucia said, advancing on her.

Raven held her ground. She wouldn't be scared of this woman. "What do you mean?"

"Forcing Jax to help you. Do you know how many thousands of dollars he's spent on you?"

Narrowing her eyes, Raven said, "He blackmailed me first. He started this whole mess. I'm sure you know what payback means. There's no way a woman in your position has let an opportunity for revenge pass her by."

Lucia laughed. "You want more than payback. You want Jax." She stepped closer, fury sparking in her eyes.

Raven stepped back after all, trapped on the wide staircase between the handrail and Lucia's anger.

"But you can't have him," Lucia continued, her face close to hers. Unhappy lines framed the socialite's mouth. The woman never smiled. "Jax is mine."

Raven gripped her textbooks to her chest. Lucia looked ready to kill her.

"I don't want him," she said, trying to calm Jax's fiancée. She wished someone were around. Mariah. Grace popping in for a visit. Erik. Even Jax, though she knew which side he'd take.

But there wasn't a sound anywhere.

"I hate you," Lucia spat, bringing up her arm. "Get the *fuck* out of my house."

The impact of Lucia's hand connecting with the side of her face whipped her head to the side, and Lucia's nails raked across her cheek. She dropped her books and gripped the railing to keep herself from stumbling.

Meeting Lucia's eyes, she touched her stinging cheek, and her fingertips came away red.

Lucia stood on the stairs, victory, horror, then remorse taking over her features, one by one.

Raven knew it was all for show. There was no way a woman like Lucia, rich and spoiled, hadn't gone through life without slapping another person, without physically hurting someone and reveling in the pain she inflicted.

Unhappy people liked to share their misery.

But Raven would bet her new wardrobe the other women didn't fight back.

On the streets, Raven had to defend herself. She couldn't be pegged as weak, or she'd always be a target.

"You miserable cow," Raven whispered. "Don't you ever touch me again."

She only intended to make Lucia give her a little space, but in her anger she pushed too hard, and Lucia lost her footing on the stairs. The blonde tumbled down the remainder, her wrist snapping with a nauseating crunch when she broke her fall at the bottom.

Lucia let out a glass-shattering wail. "You little bitch," she screamed around her sobs.

Swallowing her heart and abandoning her textbooks on the staircase, Raven turned and ran. Jax would never let her stay after hurting his fiancée. He made it clear she played by his rules or she'd be out.

Desperately, her mind scrambled with ideas on where she could go, what she could do, and how quickly she could do it.

She had to leave before Jax kicked her out.

She rushed to her room, her heartbeat slamming in her ears. She only had a small amount of time before Lucia called Jax and he would come home.

The snapping of bone echoed in Raven's mind. She hadn't meant to hurt Lucia. Just push that horrid woman out of her face.

Frantically, she looked for things to bring with her. The weeks she'd spent in Jax's home hadn't buried the survival instincts she honed living shelter to shelter, and she was able to throw a few things into a backpack that would last her months on the street.

She wasted valuable seconds debating on whether to bring handfuls of the jewelry Grace purchased for her. Costume jewelry, all of it, but it would bring a fair price at a pawn shop.

In the end, she decided against it. Nothing in this room was hers.

She changed into boots more appropriate for walking, and she'd have no choice but to grab a winter jacket out of the foyer's closet on her way out.

Outside her room, she paused for a moment.

This was never going to be her life; she had no reason to say goodbye.

Lucia was blessedly gone when Raven ran downstairs, probably screaming on the phone to Jax right now.

She rifled through the foyer closet, her mouth dry, expecting someone to stop her at any moment. She grabbed the first jacket she saw, along with a hat and pair of gloves. March could be colder than any other time in the winter, even though spring was supposedly right around the corner.

Elle still had a few of her things, and her heart ached. She hadn't been in touch with her friend all this time. She hoped Elle hadn't written her off. Maybe someone told her Jax found her at Damien's. News like that wasn't kept secret for long.

She stepped outside, narrowing her eyes against the fading sun glinting against the pristine snow. She half expected Jax's car to be careening down the driveway, but only minutes passed since she pushed Lucia and she forced herself to breathe. It would take Jax at least half an hour to drive home.

Raven needed to use that time wisely. She shoved on her parka, hat and gloves, the cold already penetrating the thick sweater, her fear turning icy on her skin. She secured the backpack she took, stuffed with the things she hadn't felt guilty bringing with her.

Instead of using the driveway to reach the highway, she cut through Jax's acreage, hoping the fading sunlight and dense trees would hide her figure.

She groaned in dismay at the tracks she left behind, but there was no help for it. Besides, it would only tell them which way she went. Once she made it to the highway, she'd hitch a ride and disappear.

Jax wouldn't look for her.

He'd be glad she was gone.

Sweat ran down her back, but her thighs were numb with cold by the time she made it to the highway.

Her cheek stung, but she didn't touch it. Without a mirror, she didn't know how bad her scratches were, but she didn't care. She'd been hurt worse. Inside and out.

She began walking the opposite way than she wanted, toward a smaller town about ninety miles away, but she couldn't risk Jax happening upon her on his way home.

After forty-five minutes of walking through the cold on the shoulder of the highway, a car pulled along side her, the headlights cutting through the heavy dark of the country road.

The sun set long before. The veil didn't lessen Raven's nerves, but sliding into the car, pushing herself down so she could barely look out the window, did.

Anyone driving past the vehicle wouldn't be able to see her.

"Where to, chickie?" a teenaged girl asked, smacking a piece of gum between her teeth.

"Into the city's fine, anywhere. You shouldn't pick up strangers." Raven pulled off her gloves and held her hands to the heater vents to thaw her fingers.

Winter was a shitty time of year to have nowhere to go.

"You looked okay," the girl said, unconcerned. "You get in a fight?"

Raven remembered her cheek and used the mirror in the visor to look at her scratches. A passing car's headlights gave her the two seconds she needed to assess the damage. Three long and deep gouges oozed blood.

"Boyfriend," Raven lied.

"Been there, done that," the girl agreed, then turned on the radio.

Good. Raven didn't want to talk anymore, anyway.

When they sped by, Jax's house was lit brighter than a firecracker bursting at midnight.

He would be home by now, maybe even gone again, bringing Lucia to the hospital.

She wondered what Mariah would make for dinner, and if anyone would be around to eat it. She sighed. None of that involved her anymore.

~

The girl left her in an empty plaza parking lot, close, actually, to where Jax dumped her years ago. She offered to drop her wherever she wanted, feeling terrible it was so cold and dark outside, but Raven couldn't ask her to drive to Z Avenue. The area was too dangerous. She let the girl drive her too close for her liking as it was.

"Here," the girl said, twisting and grabbing her purse off the backseat. "You look like you're in a bad way." She pushed a fifty dollar bill into Raven's gloved hand, and she bit back a denial. She could stretch fifty dollars for a long time.

"Thank you."

"Be careful."

Raven limped down the empty sidewalk. The brand new footwear made blisters form on her toes and the backs of her heels, though she was warmer than she'd been in the past bouncing from one shelter to the next in the frigid winter months.

Rich people knew how to dress.

She walked for half an hour to reach Elle's salon, and she peered through the dirty and frosty window, searching for her friend, but the shop was empty. A lamp on the desk Elle used to write down appointments flickered, the bulb close to burning out, and it calmed Raven's heart.

At least her friend was there and nothing bad happened to her.

Raven went around back and banged on the door in the alley. One good thing about the winter months was that the temperature froze all the contents inside the dumpsters. People threw any and everything in them. Even bodies.

The door creaked open, and the point of a knife appeared, shining in the alley light that miraculously wasn't shot out.

"What do you want?" Elle snarled, hiding behind the door.

"Elle, it's me."

The door flew open. "Fuck. I've been so fucking worried about you." Holding the knife away, Elle enveloped her into a hug, and Raven drew in a comforting breath of cigarette smoke and hair dye.

"I missed you so much," Raven murmured.

"Come in out of the cold. Where have you been?"

Raven kicked her boots against the doorjamb and stepped into Elle's tiny salon. Hair dye, permanent solution, and other supplies filled the back room, along with the small cot Raven made her bed on more than one occasion.

Elle offered many times to let Raven room with her upstairs, but she never took advantage of Elle's generosity. She couldn't hold a job, therefore, unable to pay her share of the rent.

She didn't use her friends.

Only jerks who used her first and could afford to pay.

"Did Jax come here? Is that how he found me at Damien's?"

"You were with that sleazeball?" Elle's upper lip curled in disgust. "You know better than that." She flicked on a light and drew in a breath. "What the hell happened to you?"

"I need to go to the bathroom, then I'll tell you."

Raven sat on the toilet and fought back tears. She pressed a wad of toilet paper to her eyes. Now wasn't the time to cry.

After she calmed herself enough to step out of the bathroom, Elle started coffee and the soothing scent floated through the air.

Elle sank into one of the two padded salon chairs placed in front of the wide mirrors. They weren't cracked or scratched, and Elle saved a long time to afford them.

Clearing her scratchy throat, Raven sat in the other chair feeling a thousand years old. She explained her pneumonia and Jax finding her. "You told him where to look for me."

Elle lit a cigarette and blew smoke out of the corner of her mouth. "I was worried about you. The jerk said he'd tell me if he found you, but I never heard anything. Damien was fucking pissed. If he hears you're back, he said he's gonna get you good. I heard he couldn't walk for weeks without limping. Rich Guy kicked him in the balls. You should never have crashed at Damien's place. You better be careful."

"I know." Raven grimaced.

"Why didn't you come to me?" Elle asked. "I would have helped."

Shrugging, she said, "I didn't want to burden you. You're my friend, and I was sick."

Bitterly, Elle looked away. "But you'd run to Damien."

"I went *with* Damien. There's a big difference. Besides, it turned out all right."

"Not by the looks of it," Elle said, pointing her cigarette at Raven's cheek. "Catfight."

"Jax's fiancée was tired of me living in her house and let me know it. I got her back though." She tried to sound proud, but she could still hear Lucia's wrist snapping and her stomach churned.

That, and hunger.

How easy it was to get used to regular meals.

Elle nodded in satisfaction and blew more smoke. "Good. Don't need a rich bitch fucking with you. Got a plan?"

Raven nudged the peeling blue linoleum with the toe of her boot. "I'm good for now, I guess. I've had decent meals. No booze. I should go to social services while I don't look like something the cat dragged in. I stole a dress, for like, interviews and stuff."

"You're gonna try this all by yourself?"

Raven pursed her lips and fought back tears. Goddamn it, why did life have to be so hard? "I'd like . . . to . . . go home . . . one day."

"Z Avenue sure ain't it," Elle agreed.

"No. Maybe some people don't ever find a home."

Elle looked around her salon and met Raven's eyes. "I can't argue there. Come on, have a cup of coffee, then get some sleep. I have a full client list for the next couple of days. It'll be nice to have you around again to help."

Tired and irritated, Jax kicked the front door closed and dropped his briefcase onto the floor, not caring where it landed. He signed a new client, but even before the ink dried on the contract, they wanted results yesterday. It had taken many hours, and many lowballs of scotch, for them to understand results wouldn't happen overnight, but he'd have his team focused on the project first thing in the morning. It was the best he could do, even with the amount of money they were willing to pay.

There wasn't a sound throughout the house as he hung up his winter overcoat, and he found Lucia lying in bed, a cast on her wrist, watching TV.

"What happened to you?" he asked, undoing his tie. Just once he'd like to feel welcome in his own home, but the overwhelming sense of foreboding never went away. He told himself time and again it was how he felt inside, not what went on inside his house.

But that wasn't entirely true.

"I went out wearing new shoes, and I tripped and fell down the stairs," Lucia pouted, her eyes filling with tears.

He frowned and pulled off his suit jacket. "Why didn't you call me? Are you all right?"

She sniffed. "I didn't want to bother you. The clinic had an opening, and Justin drove me home again."

Assessing her, he said, "He should have said something. You don't need to do things like that alone."

"You were at work."

"I'm sorry I'm later than usual. I signed a high-maintenance client tonight. They'll need a lot of booze and manhours to keep them happy, but they're willing to pay for it, so that's all that matters."

Lucia patted her side of the bed. "Come here and tell me more about it."

Hanging his jacket in the walk-in closet, Jax narrowed his eyes. Something wasn't right. Lucia never voluntarily spent time with him. It wasn't a secret she was marrying him for social status and the perks of being Mrs. Brooks. Offering affection of any sort when they weren't in public wasn't the norm. It usually meant she wanted something. Something expensive. She probably had her eye on a new fur coat, or a trip to Paris. Something she needed his permission to have.

He stepped into the bedroom and undid his cuff links. After storing them in a drawer in his dresser, Jax perched on the side of the bed. If she was willing to meet him halfway, then he would try, as well. If he stood half a chance of having the kind of marriage his parents enjoyed, then he would need to put in the work. "Are you hurting?"

Lucia shook her head. "No. The doctor wrote me a prescription for pain pills."

Which you were happy to fill, he thought, but he didn't say anything. "Okay, well, it's late. Let me check on Raven first, then we should get some sleep." He wanted to ask how her tutoring went today, what she helped Mariah fix for dinner, but Lucia, pliant for the first time in a long time, enticed him to stay where he was.

Crawling into his lap, Lucia said, "I have something better we can do." She pressed her lips to his.

Jax, tired of the no sex mandate she'd imposed on them since Raven moved in, let her push him onto the bed.

It wasn't unusual for him to be up and out of the house before the sun even brightened the sky, and the next day was no exception. He spent the entire day working on the new client project, Erik hanging over his shoulder trying to help.

Even though he was beginning a project from hell, and it would require several days of grueling work to see any light through the sludge of the company's security issues, strong coffee and hot morning sex with Lucia put him in a decent mood. He missed talking to Raven the day before, and to Erik's surprise, he said he'd be leaving the office to be home in time for dinner.

Justin dropped him home at six o'clock, the sky pitch black

with winter night. While the stark setting fit his mood, he wished spring would come. Sometimes even he missed the sun.

After shedding his coat and dropping his briefcase in the foyer, he checked on Raven in the kitchen only to find Mariah alone, bustling around the warm, fragrant room that smelled of chili and cornbread.

"Where's Raven? She's supposed to be helping you."

Mariah eyed him while she stirred the contents of a large steaming pot. "I have not seen her, Mr. Jax. I took a tray up to her room for breakfast, but she was not there. I thought perhaps she had things to do in the city."

"Did the tutors come?" Jax swallowed and ran a finger between his neck and his shirt collar. He didn't like the sound of this.

"*Sí*. But I sent them away. Raven was not here," she repeated.

"Okay."

She wasn't a prisoner, and she was allowed to do what she liked. His mother may have ask her to go out for the day. Jax scowled. The tutors cost him a lot of money, and they should have been notified they needn't come today. Maybe he'd been working Raven too hard, and she asked Justin to drive her into the city for a shopping trip or to an art gallery. He could see Raven wanting to roam a museum for a time. Still, she hadn't complained about having too much homework, in fact, she seemed to enjoy learning, something else he admired about her.

"Thank you."

He called his mother as he made his way to his bedroom, but she told him she hadn't spent time with Raven today.

"Is she all right?" she asked, concern coloring her voice.

"I . . . don't know. I'll let you know when I find out anything."

He disconnected the call, and he pushed the door open to his bedroom. Lucia stood in the bathroom applying makeup, dressed in a black cocktail dress. "Where are you going?"

"Don't you mean, where are *we* going? We're having dinner

with the Tomlinsons tonight, don't you remember? Isn't that why you came home early?" In the mirror, she met his eyes.

Jax bit back a sigh. He couldn't admit he came home to check on Raven because he missed seeing her yesterday; Lucia would turn into a she-devil. She was displaying a side he hadn't seen since the early stages of their relationship, a fake side, but still, he appreciated her softer traits when she deemed it necessary to let them surface.

"Yes. Yes, it is."

Lucia offered him one of her rare smiles. "Liar."

Jax chuckled, enjoying the glimpse of a relationship he could have with Lucia . . . if she were a different person. The pain pills, or her want of something and changing her behavior to increase the likelihood of obtaining it, turned her into a woman he could only hope for.

"I'll change."

"Hurry. We're supposed to meet them in an hour."

Dressing in a fresh suit, he forgot about Raven.

After a pleasant evening of drinks, a good meal, stimulating conversation, and hot sex, he fell asleep with Lucia snuggled by his side.

"Have you seen Raven? Did she stay with you last night?" Jax asked Erik the next morning.

His mornings never differed. Up, maybe a quick breakfast in the dining room, and to the office by eight. Sometimes seven if he knew he had a large workload ahead of him that day. Like today.

He summoned his brother the moment his secretary told him Erik was in the building. Not only did he have questions about Raven, but they needed to go over the progress of the new project.

Erik sniffed at the cigarette he always carried but never lit. "No. Why would you ask me something like that? Are you telling me you'd approve?" He lifted an eyebrow.

The thought of Erik and Raven made his stomach clench, and he muttered, "No. I haven't seen her for a couple days, that's all."

Erik frowned and sank onto the loveseat near the window. "It wouldn't be like her to disappear."

"That's what I thought, but I have no idea where she could be. I checked her room this morning, and her bed hadn't been slept in."

It made him sick to think Raven had changed her mind after all, and she left without saying goodbye.

"This is good news for you, isn't it?" Erik asked. "You wanted her gone, and she did you the favor."

"You think I'm a real son of a bitch, don't you?" He ran a hand through his hair.

"Of course I do. You've done nothing for that girl that wasn't for your own gain. She's gone. Let her be."

"You're not curious where she is?" Jax found that hard to believe, not with the way Erik would hang around her before he put a stop to it.

"She's a grown woman. It's not like she was kidnapped and dragged out of your house. She left of her own volition, didn't she?"

"You're not helping."

"What's there to say?" Erik helped himself to a cup of coffee from the serving tray always present between seven and eleven before Jax made the transition to scotch or whiskey. "Maybe you weren't giving her what she wanted after all. Just be happy she's gone and file the papers."

"You're being a real asshole," Jax said, pouring a cup of coffee.

"Why would you say that? Are you looking for permission to go look for her? Are you asking for my approval to care about someone? My God, Jax, it's something Mom and I have been waiting for, for years. That maybe you would finally open your heart to someone. And if that someone was a real person, a real person who had a heart and thoughts and feelings, a goddamned *soul*, then good Lord, yes, go look for her."

"I don't have feelings for her." The denial was fast on his lips.

Erik sighed. "You're allowed to care about someone. You weren't meant to suffer your entire life for one small mistake."

"It wasn't small." Erik knew better than anyone it wasn't small. It was one of the biggest mistakes he would ever make in his life.

"Put it away. Put it away and go look for Raven if you're concerned about her . . . or if you miss her."

That was the crux of it. He missed her. He missed knowing she was in his house. Trusting Erik, he voiced his real fear. "What if she won't come back with me?"

He wasn't treated to any sympathy.

Erik glared. "Would you care? You still have Lucia. She was your choice. Perhaps something happened between them. Two women sharing the same man never ends well."

"They weren't sharing me." That was far from the truth.

Once again Erik raised an eyebrow and sipped his now tepid coffee. "Weren't they, now?"

He opened his mouth in automatic denial, then snapped it shut.

Two women sharing the same man never ended well. Lucia happy. Raven disappearing.

"You may be on to something. I'll dig deeper into it when I get home tonight. Someone has to know something."

"Don't wait too long. It's cold, and she has nowhere to go."

He nodded. If he found her once, he could find her again.

Jax poked his head into Raven's room on the off chance she'd returned, but her room lent a feeling of abandonment that sent a whisper of unease down his spine. Nothing was missing as far as he could see, though he hadn't any idea what his mother bought for her the day they'd gone shopping. Valuables remained in plain sight. Her laptop. Bags, purses. Jewelry. She left with the clothes on her back and precious little else.

He found Lucia in bed, eating chocolate, a Jerry Springer rerun blaring on the TV. Jax frowned in annoyance. "Don't you have something to do?"

He admired Raven's motivation. Even living on the streets took guts and a gumption Lucia didn't have.

"Like what?" Lucia asked, slipping another piece of chocolate into her mouth. "I can't plan our wedding. Everyone's been asking me questions, and I can't tell them anything. I had a fitting for my dress today, and I don't know if I'll get to wear it." Tears pooled in her eyes.

"Raven hasn't signed the papers," Jax reminded her, gently prodding.

"People get divorced all the time without the other party's cooperation. You know this." Lucia flung the box of chocolates toward the end of the bed. "You don't need her signature. I think it's an excuse to put off our wedding. You asked me to marry you the night we met. I thought it was so romantic. Love at first sight. Why are you delaying our marriage? Don't you love me?"

As much as you love me, kitten, Jax thought. "Where *is* Raven, Lucy? I haven't seen her lately and she's missed her tutoring sessions."

Lucia whipped her hair over her shoulder. "Who cares? She's gone. File for divorce so we can get married. I'm tired of waiting."

"I'd like to be sure she's okay before erasing her from my brain," he muttered, turning the TV off. The noise grated on his nerves.

"Why? I'm glad she's not here anymore. I hated her in my house." Lucia slipped off the bed and smoothed her hands along Jax's lapels. "I know it's early, but come to bed. Let's have Mariah bring up dinner trays, and we'll just . . ." She ran a fingertip along his jaw.

Offering more sex. He was more than a little suspicious.

He brushed his hand over her hair, twisting the strands

around his fingers. Jax cupped Lucia's cheek in his palm and leaned down as if he were going to kiss her.

Triumph flashed in her eyes for just a moment before she extinguished the spark, and it pushed Jax over the edge. He knew for sure, now, Erik was right. Something happened, and he was going to find out what.

He fisted his hand and yanked.

Lucia squealed in pain.

"Tell me what you know about Raven," he growled softly, not letting her hair loose even a millimeter.

"W-we f-f-fought," Lucia said, her lips trembling. "I hit her."

He swore. "And she pushed you, didn't she? She wouldn't have let you treat her like that. That's really how you broke your wrist."

It wasn't a question. Jax could see the whole thing clearly now. Lucia, alone with Raven, thinking she had the upper hand. Raven, having fended for herself for years, fighting back. "And after she realized she hurt you, she ran off, didn't she?"

Lucia couldn't answer through her tears.

"You bitch." He pushed her to the bed where she laid in a sobbing heap. "I don't want you here when I get back."

This brought Lucia's head up, and her eyes dried in an instant. "What do you mean?"

"I mean, get out. Pack your things and get the hell out of my house. You're nothing but an ice queen wrapped in a pretty package."

Lucia laughed, but it was full of bitterness and irony. "Ice queen? I'm nothing compared to you, Jaxon Brooks. You'll never have a heart. You'll always be alone. You call me cold? I'm practically a goddamned inferno compared to you."

With Lucia screaming expletives at his back, he ran out of the bedroom and snagged his overcoat as he rushed through the foyer.

He may be made of ice, but he was thawing, and it had something to do with a woman who had nowhere to go and had been back on the streets for the past two nights.

~

Jax took his own car into the city. He didn't know what to expect looking for Raven again, and he still stung with guilt that he made Justin wait in the car the whole time he looked for her in that rundown apartment building.

He would just have to hope the car's security system would deter anyone from trying to steal it.

Speeding along the highway, he checked his watch and swore. At this time of night, she could be anywhere. At any shelter, in any of the apartments in the building he'd searched before. He was back to square one, but at least he had the start of a thread he didn't have last time, and he drove straight to Raven's friend's salon. It made sense for Raven to run to someone she could trust, and he wasn't disappointed when the expression on her face told him almost everything he needed to know.

"She isn't here."

"But she was."

He knew that for a fact. The woman would make a terrible poker player.

"You didn't tell me you found her like you promised," she accused. "I spent weeks thinking she was dead."

He sank into a salon chair and watched her do busy work around the room so she didn't have to meet his eyes. "I was out of line. I should have let you know. Brought her by, let her send you a letter. Something. I'm sorry."

"Little good that does me," she said, lighting a cigarette, glaring at him through the smoke as she puffed.

"Look, I know why she ran off—"

"So do I, and I can tell you right now, if that woman's still in your house, Raven won't go back there."

"She's not. I kicked her out. Please, just tell me where she is."

The woman sighed. "She's at Club Nova. It's a dive a few blocks down. Said she missed her friends. I begged her not to go . . ."

"What?" The hesitancy in her voice made Jax jump to his feet. "What?"

The woman snubbed out her cigarette and ran a hand over her face. Suddenly, the wear and tear of her life and the darkness of the salon made her look a hundred years old.

"That guy you saved her from? Damien? He was pissed. Livid. Not to mention you wounded his pride kicking him in the balls. Didn't think anything of it, I'm sure. Not Raven ever coming back here, not her ever needing to hide from a dirtbag like that. I asked her not to go out, but you can't hide forever. She wanted to see her friends, and I couldn't stop her."

"She would have died if I hadn't brought her home and sought medical treatment for her." No, he'd never thought Raven would come into contact with that asshole again. No, he never thought he'd put Raven in harm's way by rescuing her. He didn't understand this kind of life. "Why didn't you go with her?"

"I can't leave. I never leave the salon. Only upstairs to bed. This is my whole life. In this room."

Jax stepped forward. Really *looked* at the woman he was speaking with. Tired. Sad. Miserable. Hopeless. "You speak of this place like you would a jail cell."

"We all have our prisons, even if there aren't any bars. What's yours?"

The first gulp of wine hit her like a boozy spell, knocking the tension right out of her. Who needed Jaxon Brooks anyway? Not her. She could make it on her own. She always had, and she always would.

Raven leaned back in her rickety chair in the corner of the dance club. Blue smoke clouded the air, a mix of cigarette smoke and pot. Cops didn't break up parties on Z Avenue unless someone died. Even then, the cops had to find out about it, and someone calling the cops on Z Avenue was about as likely as anyone in this underground warehouse winning the lottery.

She chugged the rest of her wine, and Axel filled her glass out of the bottle sitting among many in the center of the table.

"Missed you, girl," he said, pushing a little blue pill into her hand. "Valium."

Gratefully, Raven swallowed the pill with another mouthful of red wine. The flavor didn't compete with what she'd drank at The Lighthouse with Jax. She pushed the memory aside.

He hadn't come for her.

It was stupid to think he would, but in a small corner of her heart, she hoped, maybe. This was her third night on the street, and even though it seemed like Jax was maybe warming to her, apparently it better suited him she was gone.

That was fine though. It was good.

She'd fallen back into her life on Z Avenue easily enough, though she was spending more time with Elle than she liked. After tonight she needed to figure things out to get out of Elle's shop. She still *did* want to try to clean up, to maybe go home one day.

If she could funnel her self-preservation she depended on to live on the streets into some kind of plan to get *off* the streets, she'd be living in a decent apartment and going to a real job in no time. The only thing was, she still didn't have an education or decent clothes. She still wore the jeans and sweater she was wearing the night she pushed Lucia down the stairs. She shoved plenty of clean panties into her backpack, but beyond that, she wasn't any further than she was when Jax barged his way into her life at Damien's.

The Valium and the wine swamped her. Fuck Jax. She didn't need him. She'd been doing just fine on her own.

The music's bass slammed through Raven's bones. She was welcome at Club Nova, and Axel spotted her the minute she stepped inside. She missed her friend. Rumors spread while she was gone, he told her. Either she died and Damien hid her body, or a knight in shining armor came to her rescue.

Everyone was disappointed to hear neither was true. Well, no one wanted her dead, but a fairy tale broke up the drudgery of life on Z Avenue.

"Let's dance," Axel shouted at her.

Through her alcoholic haze, Raven struggled to pick up the beat. When she finally recognized Madonna's "Erotica," she grinned. He remembered it was one of her favorite songs.

They pushed their way onto the dance floor, and the crush shoved her against Axel's hard chest. He smiled at her, a soft, foggy cloud in his eyes. He'd been well on his way to fucked up when Raven stopped at the club, under the influence of whatever he carried that night and a few glasses of wine, and maybe a few shots of something else.

He gripped her ass and pulled her in close. It was that kind of song, and Raven didn't mind. In fact, she missed the closeness, and she plastered herself against him. It's what she'd come to the club for. The connection.

She wound her arms around his neck and pressed her lips against his neck.

There was no better feeling in the world than booze and a good friend.

Always feeling like she was walking on pins and needles in Jax's house, being back on Z Avenue was different. She belonged here. Was accepted here.

Axel covered her lips with his, wanting more, eager to pick up where they left off before she left Z Avenue.

Kind, and attentive when he wanted to be, there were worse men than Axel she could give herself to.

"If you wanted a good fuck, I could have obliged. All you had to do was ask."

Raven didn't hear the words so much as felt where they came from. In slow motion, she tore her lips away from Axel's mouth, her movements sluggish because of the booze and drugs.

Jax stood next to them, looking at her with so much contempt it she wanted to heave. Until she remembered why she left in the first place, and she stiffened her spine. He had no right to speak to her like that. He stood on the dance floor, cashmere and ice, as the drunk and disorderly bumped into him on all sides. He stood as firm as a tree in a gale, hardly moving, his eyes pinned on her.

Club Nova was dark accept for a few orange lights on the walls and the bar lights trying to glimmer their way through the basement's dense dark.

It was a wonder he found her at all.

"Who the hell are you?" Axel shouted.

Jax ignored him. "I want to talk to you."

Raven shook her head. There was nothing she had to say.

She buried her face in Axel's chest, and he wrapped his arms around her. "Bugger off," Axel said, his words vibrating under her cheek.

"Raven," Jax said, pulling on her arm.

The song melded into something wild, something hot, a lightning storm tangled with notes and chords, and suddenly, Raven wanted Jax's hands on her, not Axel's. She could blame the wine, blame the drugs, but the way she felt was Jax's doing.

Jax wasn't safe. He wasn't good to her, and he wasn't good for her.

He brought her to his world and abandoned her. She had to crawl out or get eaten alive.

This was her safe place. Club Nova. Surrounded by people just like her. Here, she wasn't the outcast.

Jax was.

"Leave me alone. I have nothing to say to you."

Sliding her tongue over her teeth, she hoped Jax understood what she said because the words hadn't felt right coming out of her mouth.

She needed more wine. She grabbed Axel's hand and led him

through the pack of bodies swaying, rocks on the unfinished floor crunching under her boots.

Club Nova was as basic as a club could be, a warehouse, underground, abandoned when the area was left to rot because better locations were built in more convenient parts of the city.

Left behind, like the living things on Z Avenue.

Raven tried to ignore Jax as he followed them to their table in the corner of the cavernous space. The music echoed off the cement walls, people's wailing lost in the pounding beat.

He took a seat beside her, pushing plastic cups out of his way with an angry swipe of his arm.

Sweat and must filled the heavy air, and Jax shrugged out of his coat.

Axel raised his eyebrows at her, and she shrugged. If Jax wanted to stay, he would stay. Nothing would deter him. But there was nothing for him to gain by hanging on. When it was time to leave, she'd crash with Axel, if he had somewhere to go, or at Elle's, and Jax would go home to his cushy life.

Her high was fading, and she poured more wine. She lifted the empty bottle to Axel.

He saluted her with a jaunty wave of his hand, grabbed the green glass by the neck, and pushed through the wall of people on the dance floor to the bar.

Raven downed the cup of red, the sweet, room temperature liquid soothing her parched throat.

"What are you doing?"

His lips moved, but she couldn't hear what he said.

She leaned closer and lost her balance, landing half in his lap. "What?"

Jax held her as he would an infant, looking into her eyes. "Why are you doing this?"

Using his rock-hard thigh for support, Raven pushed herself up. Close to his ear, she asked, "What else is there to do?"

"This."

Raven didn't understand what he meant until he pressed his lips to hers. He cradled her face in his hands, tilting her head.

Half in his lap, half on her own chair, Raven struggled for a moment, then his tongue slipped into her mouth, and she opened for him, forgetting her awkward position.

Kissing him now was the same as in the church. Rough, but tender, as if he were forcing himself to hold back.

She wished he wouldn't, but Jax would never lose control. He'd never lose himself in a moment. Rigid, every movement accounted for. Never a thought out of place. Everything he did had a reason, an explanation.

Except, he was here, on Z Avenue, in Club Nova, kissing her, and there wasn't an explanation to be found in her muddled brain. She sat up, the heat and smoke in the air turned her stomach. She needed the bathroom and some air. "I have to pee," she shouted, deliberately crass, and he grimaced.

She was so unrefined. So rude. The things he tried to teach her, she shed like a snake's skin the minute she stepped foot on Z Avenue.

Quicksand. The more she struggled, the deeper she sank until she couldn't breathe.

Grappling with the table to pull herself to her feet, she swayed, her vision slipping and sliding with the booze and Valium.

"What's wrong with you?" Jax demanded, gripping her chin, studying her face.

Raven wrenched away and weaved through the crowd to the bathroom in the rear of the building. *Lots of things*, she thought.

Lots of things.

Seven

Jax watched her go, darting around drunken dancers like a skilled quarterback, the touchdown line in sight.

Raven's friend bumped his way through the crowd, holding two bottles of wine over his head. Jax curled his lip in disgust and jealousy. He hated the way this guy had his hands all over Raven. Hated it more she enjoyed it. It was obvious they were more than friends.

She had a right to have someone. He wasn't in a position to tell her no. In fact, trying to persuade her to stay away from the guy would only push her into his arms.

That was how women worked. They were like children. Tell them they couldn't do something, and they laughed while they did it anyway.

Raven was like that.

No regard for his feelings.

Not that she should have any. He hadn't any regard for hers.

Seeing Raven ravished in some loser's arms, Jax knew there was a slim to none chance he could convince her to go home with him again and give their arrangement another chance.

Lucia's claw marks looked vicious, even in the poor lighting. They'd been half the reason he kissed her. He wanted to make up for what Lucia had done. Not that a measly kiss would make up for it. Not even his.

"Drink?" Raven's friend asked, and Jax tamped down the urge to knock the guy flat on his ass.

If he wanted a chance of convincing Raven to go home with him, he had to behave.

"Yeah." He held out his hand, his watch catching the light.

The guy raised his eyebrows but returned the strong grip.

"I'm Jax."

"Axel."

"Axel?" Jax shouted over the music. "Who names their kid that?"

Axel filled a red Solo cup to the brim and nodded at Jax to take it. "A woman high on crack," he said, grinning.

His steady gaze made Jax's mouth drop open. "You're not kidding."

"Nope."

"I'm sorry."

"Don't be. Chicks dig it."

The man had a friendly, easy-going way about him, brave too, staring Jax down, and he considered offering the guy a job. He could envision Axel getting along swimmingly with Erik. Swilling bourbon and not doing a goddamn thing but look pretty.

Jax gulped the wine Axel generously poured him, and as he rolled it around his mouth, found it wasn't that bad. "Raven, too?" He couldn't stop himself from asking.

"She's a good girl," Axel said. "She's kind, and people take advantage of that."

He dropped into a chair, and Jax caught a whiff of cologne and perspiration.

"Do you?"

Axel lifted a shoulder. "We take care of each other in a lot of different ways. What are you to her?" He smiled, but his eyes hardened. "I should throw you out on your billion dollar ass for how you treated my girl," he said, lighting a cigarette. "Your woman did a number on her." He tapped his cheek.

Jax didn't reply. It was his fault Lucia lashed out. He never should have expected Lucia and Raven to share the same house. Erik was right about that. He should have put Raven up in an apartment in the city.

But then he never would have been able to see her, and wasn't that what he wanted?

Axel's friendly demeanor dropped, and he snubbed out his cigarette after only a couple puffs. "What are you doing here?"

"I want Raven to come home with me. To try again."

Axel shook his head. "She doesn't belong with you." He jabbed a finger at the sticky tabletop. "She belongs here. This is her life."

Jax pictured Raven dressed in her cocktail dress, standing on the steps, his house towering behind her. "You're wrong," Jax said, pushing his cup away. "Raven's better than this."

Axel glared.

"And so are you."

Flinging out his arms, Axel said, "This is my castle, these are my subjects. I know where my home is. I know where I belong."

Jax gritted his teeth. He hated Axel just then, for knowing where he fit into the scheme of things. Ever since the accident, Jax struggled with finding his way, never quite feeling like he found any peace. And that's all he wanted, really, was to find some peace.

"Then where is your queen?"

"What?"

"Raven. She's been gone a while."

Axel scoffed. "You might not believe it, but she has a lot of friends here. She's probably just catching up with some of them."

Jax wanted out of this rat hole, and he stood, impatient. "I'm going to find her."

"Tell her there's more wine."

That would be the last thing he told her.

Moving along the wall to stay clear of the drunks and druggies, he made his way in the direction he watched Raven go. She may very well have a ton of friends in this godforsaken place, but he wanted to go home, go to bed. He'd been stupid leaving Lucia alone in his house, and he didn't doubt for one second she wouldn't use the opportunity to clean him out.

Nothing that couldn't be replaced, but he should have stayed while she packed.

He'd assess the damage in the morning.

Jax reached a narrow hallway, people sitting on the floor or leaning against the filthy wall. A couple made out in one of the doorways, the guy's hands down the woman's pants. She moaned against his mouth, and even the music didn't drown her out.

The darkness enveloped him.

The doorways weren't marked. There was nothing to indicate where Raven could have gone. He wandered the maze of back hallways, stepping around people who looked to be settling in for the night.

He turned a corner, and the sound of her voice whispered over his skin.

"Damien, it wasn't my fault," she wailed.

His hair stood up on end. Damien. That was the guy Raven's friend at the salon warned him about. The guy he'd kicked in the balls. The guy who let rats have Raven for a meal.

His body shook with rage, and he rushed toward the sound of her voice.

Another turn, then another.

How fucking deep did this warehouse go?

He didn't shake people either, who were using this place as a hideout from the cold, yet no one seemed to care Raven was in danger, minding their own business, not wanting to get sucked up into the trouble.

Jax had never been very good at minding his own business.

"You're going to pay me what you owe me."

Rounding yet another corner, Jax finally came upon them.

Damien held Raven against the damp and filthy wall, a knife

glinting in the hallway's flickering orange security light. He pushed the knife into the side of her neck, and the coppery scent of blood met his nose.

Damien grappled with Raven's pants.

It took only two seconds for Jax to realize Damien intended to rape her. If he had spoken to Axel for even five more minutes, he would have been too late.

"I thought I told you to never touch her again," Jax whispered. Despite the distance between them, the sound of his voice carried, and the sleazebag looked over to him, his eyes wide.

But it wasn't fear that made his eyes widen.

Jax swore under his breath. He didn't like the thought of fighting a guy strung out on drugs. Drugs made people unpredictable. Feeling like they didn't have anything to lose made them stupid—and dangerous.

"Just let her go, and you can run like the spineless creature you are."

"Fuck you," Damien said, pushing the knife deeper into Raven's neck.

She cried out, tears running down her face. "Just leave," she begged, meeting Jax's eyes. "Damien and I will work this out."

That was the last thing he'd do. He wouldn't leave her here to pay for what he'd done.

He pulled his phone out of his pocket. "I'm calling the cops. This place could use a good raid."

Damien laughed. "Cops don't come here, dickhead."

Jax stepped closer. "They will for me."

This deep underground he didn't have any signal, concrete walls barring him on all sides, but Damien didn't need to know that. He pushed on the browser app on his home screen and lifted the phone to his ear.

"Fuck!" Damien hollered. "Fucking bitch." He slammed Raven against the wall, her head smashing with a sick crack against the cement. He took off down the hallway, his heavy boots creating thumping footfalls that echoed to them even though he was long gone.

Raven sank to the floor, moaning, one hand on the back of her head, the other covering the cut on her neck.

"Are you all right?" Jax rushed to her and crouched. He didn't know what he could do for her or where he could touch her that wouldn't cause her pain.

She laughed ruefully. "I got off lucky, I think."

"He wanted to rape you."

"I got that, Sherlock," she said. "Help me stand up."

He grabbed her arm and steadied her. She rested against the wall for a moment, her breathing a heavy rasp that crawled across his skin and settled in his groin.

What a fucked up time to get hard.

He pushed the thought away and rubbed her shoulder. "How hurt are you? Do you need to go to the hospital? You're bleeding."

"I'll be fine. Come on, Axel's probably worried." She pushed her tangled hair out of her eyes. "You know, Damien's right. Cops don't come here."

Jax chuckled. "I don't have service down here, anyway. But I'm right, too. They would for me. I'm friends with the chief of police."

"Oh, God."

"Raven."

She looked at him out of the corner of her eye, sidestepping a woman sleeping in the fetal position, her back pressed against the wall. "What?"

"Please come home with me."

"I can't."

They stopped under another security light, this one stronger, the new bulb trapped in wire to prevent someone from breaking it.

"I know what Lucia did to you," he said, running his thumb over the scratches along her cheekbone. They scabbed over, but her skin still looked angry and red. He knew what Lucia's fingernails could do. He'd felt them along his back during sex often enough. "I'm sorry."

"Then you know what I did to her, but I'm not sorry for it and I won't go back to your house. If anything, the whole thing taught me I don't belong in your world. I'll figure something else out."

"I don't want you to do that. She's gone."

Raven shook her head. "Do you have the papers with you? You carry them around, right? I'll sign them, and you won't have to see me ever again. I know it's what you want."

Jax stared at the floor. In his haste to find her, in the moment he realized she was gone because of Lucia, the divorce hadn't crossed his mind.

He met her brown eyes, his heart slamming beneath his ribs.

They were married.

He was staring at his wife.

"Can we talk about it?" he asked, scared she'd press the issue. He didn't want to part ways, not now. He needed time to explore what he was suddenly feeling for this woman standing in front of him, blood still trickling down her neck, her skin pasty with pain. "Can you give us some time to talk about it?" He said a word that hadn't crossed his lips in a long time. "Please?"

She led him out of the maze of hallways, and he followed behind her, silent. She hadn't said yes or no, and he took his cue from her, keeping the rest of his words to himself.

The music grew louder, and they finally reached the dance floor. Even at this late hour, bodies still packed the space. If anything, the energy had grown more erratic, more desperate.

Jax could practically taste the tension.

Axel sat at their table, and he stumbled to his feet when he caught sight of Raven. "What happened?"

"Damien," Jax growled. "He had her pinned—" He broke off, unable to go further.

"Shit. Raven, I'm sorry."

"It's fine. He didn't hurt me. I'm leaving with Jax." She grabbed her jacket off the back of a chair occupied by a woman slumped onto the table, passed out.

Jax grabbed his jacket as well and blew out a breath of relief. Her acquiescence surprised him. He thought he would have to fight harder, make his case stronger.

Axel dogged them to the staircase that led to the warehouse's exit. "Are you sure this is what you want?"

"Jax, I'll meet you upstairs, okay?" she asked, slipping her hand into Axel's and squeezing his fingers.

He nodded tersely, hesitant to leave her alone with him. Who knew what Axel would say to change her mind? He couldn't police her, either, and reluctantly, he went half way up the stairs, just enough he knew he wouldn't be visible to them if they looked.

"Raven, don't do this," Axel pleaded.

Jax leaned against the grimy wall, his heartbeat rushing in his ears. He didn't know why this was so important, why all of a sudden he needed Raven with him. It wasn't that he was afraid to be alone, he'd been alone between relationships plenty of times.

But his house felt different with her in it. Lighter.

Raven gave him a sense of hope.

That maybe one day, he would be able to get past what he'd done.

"Axel . . . I need to. I can't explain it."

"I can give you whatever he can," Axel said, his voice floating up to Jax.

"Can you?" she asked. "Can you buy me decent clothes and food? An education? He's willing to give that to me, and I don't know why. I told him to leave me here, that I would sign those stupid papers, but he won't let me. I would be a fool not to take what he's offering."

"I can give you more than that," Axel said, and there was a rustling Jax couldn't identify. A silence that made goosebumps pucker his skin.

They were kissing.

"I love you," he whispered.

Jax almost missed it.

"Axel—"

"No, don't say it. I haven't said anything because, you're right. I can't give you what he can. But together we can give it a shot, huh? A better apartment, maybe. Not on Z Avenue. We could get jobs."

"I can't get a job without an education. Don't you remember? I don't even have my GED," Raven said, her voice low, breathless. "And where would we get money for an apartment? We don't have fifty dollars between us, and I can't sleep on Elle's cot forever. It's not her job to take care of me. It's not yours, either."

"But it's Jax's?" Axel said, bitterness saturating his words.

"I'm sorry. I'll come back for you."

"Yeah, right. Sure, you will. A few months in his palace, and you'll forget all about us."

"I could never forget about you."

Jax strained to hear. More rustling.

"Don't be mad at me," Raven said, her voice full of tears.

"Just be careful, sweetheart. I meant what I said."

"I know. I'm sorry."

Raven's ashen face appeared as she trudged up the steps to the exit, and Jax turned away, chagrined she caught him eavesdropping.

She didn't seem to mind. "I'm ready."

Jax slipped on his overcoat, the divorce papers he did indeed carry with him rubbing against his heart.

Grateful he won this round, he put his arm around Raven's fragile shoulders and led her out into the cold night.

~

Jax pushed her down onto the edge of the tub and swept her hair off her neck. "Let me clean this up for you before you go to bed."

"You don't have to. I can do it."

The ride home was quiet, neither speaking. Jax didn't know how to address what Axel told Raven before they left Club Nova. If she loved him in return, it wasn't Jax's place to interfere, didn't want to be the man who stepped between them.

Yet, his pulse had gone into overdrive when he buckled her into his car and drove away, no last minute decisions to turn around.

"I want to," he said, searching for a bandage and peroxide in the medicine cabinet. "In case you need stitches."

The bright light made him wince, but he needed to see what he was dealing with. Dr. Monroe would make another house call if need be, even at this time of morning.

"I don't think he hurt me that badly," she said.

"We won't know until we clean up some of the blood. This will hurt a bit, I think," he warned her as he lifted a cotton swab dripping with peroxide to her skin.

She shivered.

"I'm sorry I didn't get there faster," he said, smoothing the cotton ball over the blood that still oozed from the cut.

"I didn't thank you, and I should have. Damien . . . I don't like thinking about it, but yeah, he could have hurt me."

"He did," he corrected her, smoothing a new cotton ball along the cut, the liquid fizzing white.

"Not like that," she whispered, placing her hand on his arm.

Jax shook his head. "You wouldn't have let him do that to you. When it came down to it, you would have defended yourself. I have no doubt."

"I hope you're right."

Tilting her head with a finger under her chin, he said, "I know I am."

He threw the cotton ball away and reached for another. "I, ah, didn't know you were that close to Axel. You never said anything, the first time you stayed here, that you were leaving behind someone you . . . loved." He wanted a denial that didn't come.

"I've hardly left him behind. Z Avenue may feel a million miles away from here, but it's not. I can see him whenever I want, can't I?"

Jax stilled. While he'd seen no reason why Lucia and Raven couldn't live in the same house, he'd been mistaken and wouldn't go through that again, even if the roles were reversed. "I . . . hope you'll be busy with your tutoring sessions, and Mariah missed you."

As he fastened a large bandage over the cut, she asked, "How long, Jax? How long will this last?"

He shifted to his knees and knelt in front of her. "Let's play it by ear, okay?

She shook her head and his heart dipped. "I need some sort of time frame. I can't not know from day to day if it will be the last because you're tired of me being underfoot."

He grazed her hair, his hand trembling and fatigue weighing him down. "Summer then. Give me three months."

She frowned, and he realized his mistake. "I mean, I'll give you three months to get your life straightened out. That's all I can spare. If you can't do it in that amount of time, you're on your own."

That sounded more like him, gruff, unkind, unforgiving, and her face smoothed.

"Okay. Three months."

He left her wetting a washcloth with the intent of giving herself a sponge bath before crawling into bed.

Jax rested his forehead against the wall outside her room, nausea prickling his skin.

He had three months.

It didn't feel like enough.

～

Raven slid between the fresh sheets. Someone laundered her bedding while she was gone. She regretted her prickly legs and wished she'd taken a proper shower before crawling into bed. But the clock read after three in the morning and worry and stress weighed heavy on her mind and heart.

Somehow staying with Jax turned into spending time with him instead of cleaning herself up enough to go home. This *was* the best way to go about it—she couldn't deny he had unlimited resources to help her—but her time in Jax's house wasn't all about finding her way onto her parents' good side again.

That was bad.

He'd changed in the few weeks she'd been living in his house. Grown softer. His fingers whispered over her neck, cleaning the cut, and there was a kindness in his eyes that hadn't been there before. He seemed to sincerely regret what Lucia had done to her.

Raven pushed her head into the soft pillow.

She couldn't let herself think his transformation into a kinder man had anything to do with her.

Possibly she'd helped him see what a bitch Lucia was, but that was all. He probably already knew but didn't care. People married for all sorts of strange reasons, but her life would be easier now as he didn't seem to mind breaking his engagement with the evil woman.

Although, she was assuming. He may have made her move out, but they could still be engaged. It wasn't something that was any of her business; she was just relieved she didn't have to fear bumping into her again.

Axel's revelation surprised her. They'd always been close friends, friends with benefits when it suited them, but the idea of living with him, of trying to build a better life . . . all her excuses were real. It would be impossible trying to start living their lives on a better path with the few resources they had. Axel hadn't held a real job, ever, as far as she knew. He'd hate being trapped in a nine to five, a routine Jax seemed to enjoy. And Axel had just as much, or just as little, education as she had.

No, leaving with Jax was the right thing to do, and maybe, someday soon, she'd go back to Z Avenue and help him.

And Elle, too. Repay their kindness.

Raven rolled onto her side and willed herself to sleep.

The bandage pulled at her skin, but she was thankful that's all Damien did to her. If Jax hadn't come along . . . Damien would have gotten his payback.

Jax gave her three months to clean up, but that meant emotionally as well as physically, or she would never be able to move forward.

Her parents letting her into their house for coffee was only half of what she wanted. What she *needed* was to get her life back on track.

They'd ask why she lived her life on the streets for so long. Why she let herself go. And she'd need valid reasons so they would listen to what she had to say.

Her brother's death happened a long time ago, but that didn't take away her responsibility or the role she played.

Tomorrow she'd begin journaling, perhaps begin her memoir as Jax suggested. Work out her feelings on the page, and perhaps in the process she could help someone.

This journey couldn't be about him.

He wanted her to stay, and she was thankful for that, but she had to make this more about makeup and clothes.

Even her education.

This had to be about healing.

So she could stay off the streets for good.

"How's the Waterson project coming along?" Jax asked his brother the next morning.

Fog from a sleepless night filled his head. After he cleaned Raven's cut, he hurried to his own room where he'd thrown up in the toilet, heaving painfully even after he emptied his stomach while the scent of Raven's blood lingered in his nose.

Two months ago he would have said she'd gotten what she deserved, putting herself into that kind of situation. But Raven's pain sickened him, and what was worse, Damien had intended to hurt her even more.

He refused to think what that sleazebag would have done if he hadn't found her just in time. For the rest of the morning he laid in bed, tossing and turning, wishing he would have killed Damien instead of letting him run away.

He vowed it would be the last time the scum put his hands on her.

"You look like shit," Erik said, leaning against Jax's desk holding a steaming mug of coffee. "Late night with Lucia?"

Jax frowned, surprised the news hadn't traveled. Lucia couldn't keep her mouth shut. Hell, half the city should have known by now he kicked her out on her ass.

"No. Lucia told me she and Raven fought. You were right. Lucia hit her and scraped her cheek. Lucia's used to getting her own way, but she underestimated Raven. She fought back and pushed Lucia down the stairs. The dumb bitch broke her wrist."

Erik whistled. "A strong little girl, our Raven."

Jax wanted to punch him. Raven didn't belong to both of them. She didn't belong to either of them. He scowled, but Erik didn't look contrite. Only smug.

"At any rate," Jax continued through gritted teeth, "Raven got scared and ran. That's why she went missing. Lucia distracted me with dinner plans and sex, and I didn't look for her until last night." His cheeks heated. That he could be so easily manipulated rankled. He'd just been so . . . relieved Lucia had started to act like a real person. He should have known it was all a ruse.

Erik didn't look impressed, either, but said, "Well, I did say to let her be," then sipped his coffee.

"After Lucia told me what happened, I couldn't. I kicked her out of the house and went looking for Raven on Z Avenue. I found her in a bad way and brought her home."

That sounded good. Right. He brought her home.

Erik poured them more coffee out of the shining silver carafe. "You swapped women. I have to say, you moved up."

"I did no such thing. I gave her three months to clean up and get out."

"And then what will you do?"

Jax leaned back in his chair and sighed. What would he do, indeed. "Start all over again."

Sighing in return, Erik placed his mug on his brother's pristine blotter. "You could find someone to love," he suggested. "You equate finding a woman to marry the same as girding yourself for battle. It doesn't have to be that way."

"You don't understand."

"You're right, I don't. But it's not for lack of trying."

"I pray you never experience the things I've done."

"Accidents were meant to be forgiven. That's why they're accidents. Did you ever look to see who it was?"

"No. The department sealed the man's identity at Dad's request. You know that. Besides, I didn't want to know then, and I don't want to know now. It's better this way. The department shrink said I wouldn't have a face to fixate on. I tend to agree with her most days."

"Yes, I can understand the reasoning behind that, but it doesn't erase what happened. If you don't know, it's easier for you to hide from it."

"What would I do with the knowledge, anyway?" Jax asked, sweat trickling down his back. Like it always did when he thought about the accident.

About the life he'd taken.

"Find closure. Visit his grave. Do something to help yourself move on."

"*I took a life*," Jax growled. "There is nothing I can do to move on."

"It's been sixteen years," Erik murmured.

"When you take someone's life, you aren't meant to move on," he said. "Ever. The acrid smell of gunpowder, the slight resistance of the trigger, the blast that fills the air, even the sparkle of the stars that night. All those things permanently loop in my brain." He swiped a shaking hand over his forehead. "Now, let's go over the Waterson project. You may need to go out there for follow up. And I need you to help me with FlatIron Distribution. The CEO and board of directors are on my ass every five seconds. Their security breach freaked them out. We've plugged the holes but . . ."

Jax lost himself in work for the rest of the morning and tried to forget what Erik suggested. Find out the identity of the man he'd shot that fateful night?

He'd rather take his own life than do that.

It surprised Raven how quickly she fell back into her old routine. Tutoring in the morning, helping Mariah cook, studying in the evening until bedtime.

She asked Mariah to stop bringing meals to her room. Part of her problem before had been Mariah waiting on her. Raven didn't feel any better than the hired help, and she wouldn't let herself be treated otherwise. She began eating her breakfast with Mariah in the kitchen, preparing it herself and cleaning her own plate afterward.

Mariah reminded her she'd only been helping her stay out of Lucia's way, which was kind, Raven thought, shifting on a plush loveseat in Jax's library, but it had only delayed the inevitable.

Everyone acted a little bit differently now the icy blonde vacated the house.

Everyone but Jax.

He acted just the same as any other day, and she was hard pressed to guess if he cared Lucia was no longer warming his bed.

She sat hidden in the shadows of the spacious library, the loveseat positioned near a large stone fireplace. Mariah, a jack of all trades around the gigantic house, lit the fire in the evenings for Jax, on the off chance he would spend time here.

Their paths seldom crossed, and she sometimes wondered if he kept her busy so he wouldn't have to see her. She didn't lie to herself. She spent time in the library hoping to catch a glimpse of him now and again.

Her plan never worked particularly well.

That evening, after she settled into her favorite place with a book and a huge mug of café mocha Mariah taught her to make, his appearance gave her a sting of surprise.

It took her a moment to realize he didn't know she occupied the room.

Her heart broke for the man who sank behind the large desk and rested his head in his hands.

She sat still as stone, not attempting to even breathe; she didn't want to give away her hiding place.

A muffled sob drifted to her, and she set her book aside and almost went to him then, wanting to provide some small comfort.

He wouldn't welcome her intrusion. She'd grown to understand him enough to know that.

She sat, trapped, willing her heart to stop pounding, but it almost leapt out of her body when he said, "Are you enjoying the show?"

"I didn't want to disturb you," she said weakly.

"You'd rather spy on me," he accused, meeting her eyes across the room lit with only a small lamp she was reading by, and the fire, the bright flames casting shadows on the walls lined with other people's pain and heartache.

"That's not true." She pushed aside the throw covering her legs, and stood, taking a few steps toward him, her toes sinking into the plush carpet, before crossing her arms over her breasts. The nightgown adequately covered her, but with Jax's eyes on her, she felt naked, exposed. "I felt sorry for you."

Jax laughed, but it wasn't a happy sound and she winced as the sharp shards cut her as smoothly as Damien's knife.

He poured a glass of amber liquid and offered it to her, but she didn't want any. Not this time. With Jax's help, her reality was slowly changing into something better than she could find at the bottom of a bottle.

"Like I haven't heard that before. 'Poor Jax, closing himself off. Poor Jax, always working.' I know what my parents say, what Erik says. What people talk about at the social events I attend. I'm not deaf."

"Were you . . . is it about Lucia?" Raven didn't want to know, not really. She didn't want to hear that he was mourning a relationship with a woman who had a chunk of coal for a heart. He could do better, even if he didn't think so.

Jax knocked back his drink and poured another. "No. When I kicked her out of the house, I kicked her out of my life. No doubt that will bring repercussions, but what doesn't, dealing with a woman like that?"

"I'm sorry. You loved her. You didn't have to do that for me."

"Don't be sorry. I didn't love her, and I didn't do it for you." He ran a hand through his short hair. She wanted to skim her fingers over his scruff. Rarely did Jax let his five o'clock shadow go. But tonight, blond whiskers covered his jaw, giving him a disheveled appearance that looked good on him.

"I'm sorry," she said again, then winced. She wasn't educated, but for God's sake, she could do better than this in the conversational arena. "Did you work today?" she tried.

Jax narrowed his eyes. "I work every day."

She gulped. That didn't work. "What do you do for fun?"

Loosening his tie, he said, "I don't do fun." He pushed away from his desk. "I'm going upstairs. Enjoy your evening."

"Wait."

Jax raised an eyebrow.

"Would you want to do something with me tomorrow night?" Inwardly, Raven groaned. What was the point of that?

Spending time with Jax wouldn't do anything for either of them.

Yet, she could still feel the searing heat of his lips when he kissed her at Club Nova. He never brought up the kiss, and she hadn't either, but pretending it didn't happen didn't make it so. An evening, showing him some of what she did while on the streets, would be fun. Maybe.

Or maybe he'd think she was a complete idiot and renege on the three months he'd given her.

She had to do something. There was so much misery in his eyes.

"What did you have in mind? The symphony? The opera? A benefit?"

"I said something *fun*." She tamped down a pleased smile when a flicker of amusement moved across his face.

He nodded gravely. "I will leave myself in your capable hands."

"Be ready by seven."

"And not a minute later," he said, before easing open the library door and closing it behind him.

Raven stood in the room that was slowly growing cold as the fire weakened to embers. She may have been out of line. She may have made a huge mistake.

But she'd never forget the tear that glistened on his cheek when he thought no one was looking.

Eight

"You look like a cat burglar," Jax said as she came down the stairs.

"Do you always wear a suit?" she asked, adjusting the black beret resting on her hair. It wasn't her typical skulking-around-at-night-outfit, but Grace hadn't exactly been dressing her for that. She needed to make do with what she had in her wardrobe—black boots, black leggings, and a black sweater. Grace had chosen a black peacoat as part of Raven's outerwear selections, and she would grab it on the way out.

"You didn't tell me what we were doing, so I thought a suit would cover all the bases," he said, adjusting his tie.

"Don't you wear jeans and t-shirts?" Didn't he ever relax? She wanted to ask, but she didn't. She didn't want him to change his mind about tonight.

"No."

Raven stepped into the chilly air and groaned in dismay. Justin sat in the idling Mercedes, waiting to drive them wherever Jax ordered him to go. "I was hoping you would drive."

Adjusting his gloves, Jax narrowed his eyes at her, but stepped around the car's trunk and spoke briefly with the chauffeur.

The tires crackled against the packed snow as Justin drove away.

"Now what?" Jax asked.

The Mercedes' engine faded into the distance, and the air quieted.

Raven bit her lip. "What do you drive?" She paused. "You drive, don't you?"

"Yes, Raven. I can drive."

"Sorry," she muttered, kicking at the snow along the plowed driveway. The winter air chilled her to the bone. Though March was half over, spring wasn't in sight, and it could be weeks before the temperature finally rose and teased them with a hint of warmth.

Following Jax around the corner of his house, Raven's eyes widened. She'd never explored the back of his property, had never seen the several-stalled garage that seemed longer than Z Avenue.

"I have one of everything," he said, his breath coming out in a white puff. He opened the side door of the garage and flicked on the overhead lights.

Raven blinked against the sudden light and searched the row of cars. She couldn't guess the makes and models of most of them; they all looked too sleek and rich for her taste. "Don't you have something that would . . . blend in? We need to be low-key."

"What exactly are we doing? I could be working."

"All you do is work, and go to boring social events that make you miserable," Raven said, pointing to a bronze-colored Jeep. Brand new, the copper paint waxed to a gleam, it was the least ostentatious vehicle in the entire garage. "What do you do, anyway?"

Jax unlocked the Jeep with a key fob he selected off the wall. "I'm in security," he said, starting the engine and opening the garage door with the remote he pulled out of a storage compartment.

Raven fastened her seatbelt, breathing in the brand-new car scent. Classical music drifted out of the speakers, and she wondered if Jax enjoyed that kind of music, or if he only listened to it because he thought he ought to. "What does that mean?"

"What it implies," Jax said, pulling out of the garage into the dark. "Where are we going?"

"Head toward Z Avenue, but before you get there, turn left on Remington." She twisted in her seat to look at him. "No really, what does that mean?"

His profile seemed carved out of stone, no soft curves, only angles and edges.

She lived hard during her time on the streets, but she was fortunate her rough lifestyle hadn't marred her features. Elle's complexion was coarse and tough, but Raven had always attributed that to smoking, not to the kind of life she led. She didn't care to smoke, not like Axel and Elle, but she drank. Thankfully, not enough to cause irreversible damage to any part of her body.

In that regard she was proud of herself, too. Besides her slip up in Club Nova, Raven hadn't had a drink in a few weeks, thanks to Jax.

"It means I provide security. Cyber security for companies who have been hacked online and want to prevent it from happening again, or for companies who haven't been, and want to keep it that way. Bodyguards, bouncers for events. When high profile guests visit the city, like the President, they hire my company for extra detail."

An oncoming car's headlights lit up his features.

"Do you do that?" He looked like he would be capable of guarding the President. Stoic. Focused. Like nothing could ruffle him.

Jax shook his head. "I work behind a desk. I don't want to carry a weapon."

"I don't blame you," Raven murmured, hearing the gunshot that haunted her dreams. It seemed surreal that something so small could end a life. Could cause so much damage. And for so long. She'd been dealing with the destruction caused by a bullet for sixteen years. "Axel's good with computers, when he wants to be."

"I have a feeling Axel's good at anything . . . when he wants to be."

Raven studied Jax's face, trying to determine if he was teasing her, but he looked serious enough, focused on the highway and the shining patches of black ice.

"Like a boyfriend. Or a husband."

"I . . . we're friends. I haven't thought of him that way."

"He's thought of you that way," Jax said, and she stared out the window, wishing he would let it go. She wasn't ready for a relationship, not the kind of relationship Axel offered her. While getting back on her feet was a good thing, she had a long way to go before she could think about being with someone, and it would take a very special man to convince her to start a family, have children.

Her brother, Levi . . . his death . . . how could her parents wake in the morning, shower, dress, live their lives, day after day? Live in the shadow of their dead child's absence?

She'd never be able to survive something like that.

"Raven?" Jax asked.

"Why are you pushing this? It's not something you can do when you're on the streets. Even if I were so in love with him I wanted to marry him, what good would it do? Neither of us have jobs. There are days he's no better than Damien, dealing drugs. His are just higher-end." Raven pursed her lips. She hadn't meant it like that. "He's happy where he's at. It's why I didn't stay with him. He could promise me anything, but he wouldn't keep them, *couldn't* keep them and I would have turned down a chance, maybe my only chance, to finally make my life better." She drew in a shaky breath.

Jax rested his hand on her thigh, and his palm's heat radiated through his leather glove. "I'm sorry. I . . . was wondering if a relationship with him would be something you wanted after . . ."

"After my time's up, you mean," Raven said, staring at the cold, abandoned streets.

"You'll have a life, after you leave my house," Jax said, his voice husky and deep.

She thought she felt his hand shake, but it was only wishful thinking on her part. They were married, husband and wife. But it was stupid to think he'd want to keep her. This outing was just supposed to be about lifting the weight he always carried on his shoulders. Tease a smile out of him, if even for a moment. Not try to trick him into feeling things for her he'd never feel.

"Turn here," she said, instead of acknowledging him, "and go down three blocks. If there's space, park in the lot on the corner. You don't need to pay. No one monitors this section of the street, and I've heard the card swiper's rigged to copy your credit card number."

He parked in one of two open spaces, cramming the Jeep between two plain white service vans.

"This is a good spot." Jax's vehicle looked too new to be in this part of the city. "And we're right on time. The movie starts at eight."

"Movie?" Jax asked, opening his door and letting in a gust of Arctic air.

"You'll see."

The lock to the theatre's back door was always broken, and Raven took the chance it hadn't been repaired during her time with Jax. She pulled off a glove, and with her skin stinging, pushed her fingers between the door and the jamb, searching for the catch.

A streetlight flickered; a car drove past the alley.

Behind her, Jax stomped his feet, and Raven hoped it was because his toes were numbing from the cold, not that he was irritated with her.

"We could just pay."

She tried to lighten the mood and giggled. "Where's the fun in that?" Her fingers found the latch and she pulled, the door clicking open. "But we'll pay for popcorn," she whispered, gesturing him inside. "There's no good way to steal any without getting caught."

"That makes me feel better," Jax said sarcastically, and she elbowed him. "What movie are we sneaking in to see, anyway?"

"*Casablanca*. Have you seen it?" Raven knew the building like the back of her hand, and it took only but a few moments to find the correct theatre. She trotted up the shallow stairs and took a seat in the middle of the aisle at the very top of the stadium seating.

Jax sat next to her and pulled off his coat. "No. I'm not one for movies."

Raven met his eyes, an ad for a cell phone company flickering over his face.

"What do you do, then?" she asked, her voice barely loud enough to be heard over the commercial.

"Try not to go crazy." He raised a hand like he was going to touch her cheek, and she waited, anticipating the smooth brush of his fingers, but instead he said, "Here," and pushed a twenty-dollar bill into her hand.

"What's this for?" she asked, folding her fingers around the crisp bill, disappointed he didn't go further.

"Popcorn?"

"Oh, right."

Sitting next to Jax in the dark was more intimate than she expected it to be. Especially when Jax loosened up a little and started to nibble at the popcorn, their fingers bumping into each other's when they'd dip into the tub at the same time.

"Sorry," she'd mutter.

Still, he didn't seem to mind, at least, he didn't stop eating popcorn because he didn't want to touch her anymore.

Toward the end of the movie, they ran out, and Raven set the cardboard container on the floor. She rested her arms on the armrest and leaned back in her chair, propping her feet on the empty seat in front of her.

Jax shifted, and Raven hoped it wasn't to lean away because she was hogging his armrest. But when he casually put his arm around her shoulders, she smiled, and she breathed in the heady scent of his cologne until the movie ended.

When the lights came on she asked, "What did you think?"

"That was . . . nice," he said, and Raven laughed at the surprise in his voice.

"Life's more than just work," she said, gathering her jacket where it slipped onto the sticky floor.

"It hasn't been for me."

"You should fix that."

"Now where?"

"We finish off the night with pie and coffee."

A twenty-four hour diner sat directly across the street, and an older waitress who wore too much makeup, her hair plastered to her head with hairspray hollered, "Raven! Aren't you a sight for sore eyes!"

"Hey, Dorothy, how have you been?" she asked, shaking her head when Dorothy waved a menu in front of them.

"Same old, same old." Dorothy jerked her head to the left. "Sit where you want. I'll bring the coffee. What else?"

"A plate of my favorite, of course."

"You got it, girly."

Raven led Jax to a red booth, the vinyl cracked. She slid in across from him and pulled off her gloves.

"Do you come here often?" Jax asked, doing the same.

"If we have money." Raven wrinkled her nose. "We'll buy pie, and Dorothy keeps the coffee coming. She's kept our asses from freezing off more than once."

"We?"

"Axel sometimes. A friend once in a while. Never Elle, because she doesn't leave her shop, but I'd usually bring her back a piece of pie. Dorothy's sweet and she'd slip me a piece before we left."

Jax turned a salt shaker, half empty, old food crusting the tarnished silver top. "You miss your friends."

"They've been part of my life for years. We've helped each other through some rough times," Raven said, leaning back as Dorothy approached their table.

"Let me know what else you need," the waitress said, tucking the circular tray under her arm after serving them coffee and pie and slowly ambling away.

Jax took a sip of the steaming coffee. "Hey, this is good."

Raven laughed. "Try the pie." She pushed the plain white plate nearer to him. The apple pie slice was almost as big as a half pie, and a huge blob of vanilla ice cream melted on top. "Don't tell Mariah how good it is, you'll hurt her feelings."

She pushed her hair aside. Her hair was growing out, but she didn't want to bother anyone for a trim. And she didn't want to ask Elle. Raven wanted to keep her hair looking more grown up, and Elle liked to . . . experiment.

"Your neck looks like it's healing."

"It is." She cleared her throat and poked at her coffee cup. "Thank you, again, for stopping Damien from, you know." Her cheeks warmed.

"You're welcome, again. I'm sorry Lucia made you run, but I'm glad you stuck up for yourself."

She blinked in surprise. "You are?"

"It was my fault you were put in that situation. I should have rented an apartment for you in the city. My mistake."

Raven's heart sank. Stupid girl. Why did she keep hoping maybe he'd want to spend time with her?

She swallowed her disappointment with a bite of pie.

"I should be the one who's sorry. You really want to get married, huh?"

"I am," he said, forking up a bite of pie, and she forced a laugh.

"I keep forgetting about that."

"Me, too. To answer your question, I would like to share my life with someone. But I'm not . . ."

She waited.

Jax sighed. "I'm not normal. Finding someone to put up with me seems an impossible feat at times, and I'm willing to take what I can get."

Raven covered his hand with hers. "Maybe you just need to loosen up a little."

Jax pulled his hand away. "I'm afraid that's not possible. I hold myself in check for a reason, Raven."

"But—"

"It's late, and I have work in the morning." He laid a twenty-dollar bill on the gold-flecked Formica table. "Are you ready?"

"I guess so."

After a quiet ride through the snowy night, they parted ways at the top of the dark stairs. He'd put as much distance between their rooms as possible. Even with Lucia gone, it didn't seem like a situation he'd be changing anytime soon.

Shoulders slumped, she started trudging to her room.

"Raven."

She stopped. The way he said her name gave her goosebumps.

"This weekend it's my turn. Saturday night, six o'clock. Black tie."

Raven's shoulders slumped even more. Black tie meant an uncomfortable dress. High heels.

"What are we doing?"

Jax bared his teeth. "Something fun."

Raven highly doubted that.

~

Jax knotted his bow tie.

The forlorn expression on Raven's face when he told her about tonight mirrored his feelings.

He didn't want to go, either, but he had no choice in the matter. He hadn't been seen in public since he'd thrown Lucia out of his house, and he needed to prove he wasn't hiding.

His mother had been doing her fair share of defending him,

and while he thanked her for it, he also regretted putting her in that situation in the first place.

She warned him Lucia would also be attending the March Madness Ball, but that didn't bother him. He'd bumped into Gwen here and there, and they'd silently agreed to ignore each other.

Gwen might even be there, he mused, trotting down the stairs to the library where he planned to help himself to a drink while he waited for Raven.

He needed to be careful. He'd become a laughingstock if he notched too many more ex-fiancées on his bedpost.

Thinking Gwen or Lucia could have, or would have, supported him through life's ups and downs was downright lunacy.

Jax needed someone strong, who could weather his storms, who would bend instead of break.

Lucia was tough, but not in the way he needed her to be.

"Why are you making us do this?" Raven complained, standing in the doorway. "I'd much rather watch a movie and eat pie."

So would I, Jax thought, his mouth dry as he drank in the sight of her.

Gold dripped down her body, pooling at her feet. Gold dust decorated her cleavage, and her amber eyes were accented by gold eyeshadow.

She blushed. "Your mother sent me instructions. I hope I carried them out to your liking."

Jax cleared this throat. "You'll do."

He hated himself for dimming the light in her eyes. But while Raven was tough, maybe even brave enough to put up with him, she did not belong with him. Her feelings were too real.

He needed a Gwen or a Lucia who would know how to play the game.

To the end this time, goddamn it.

"Are you ready?"

She nodded.

"Justin is waiting for us outside."

Jax draped a fur over Raven's shoulders, and she moved ahead of him, her dress dragging behind her on the floor.

She stopped, her hand on the door handle and looked at him, her hair shading one side of her face. It hurt to look at her, and he wanted more than anything in the world to carry her upstairs. To shield her from the world.

This night wasn't only to save face. It was to continue the studies Raven asked for. How a gentleman should treat a woman.

He quirked his lips. He hadn't exactly been a stellar example in that department.

"What is this for, now?" Raven asked, wiggling in the limo's seat. "You rich people try too hard to have fun."

"This is the March Madness Ball. It's a fundraiser for at-risk youth basketball. Schools need new courts, gymnasiums, uniforms. Money for tourney fees."

Raven stared out the window, the blackness relieved only by pinpricks of lights from the houses farther away. "That seems like an odd charity to take up."

"Like you said, we try hard to find excuses to have fun . . . and spend money."

The dance was held downtown at the ritziest hotel in the city. Located on the top floor, the ballroom showcased the bright lights of the cityscape through floor to ceiling windows.

Jax passed their jackets to the attendant, and with his hand on her back, he guided Raven into the enormous room.

Chatter ceased when the guests realized who arrived, and he tried to appear unruffled, though he tightened his grasp on the nape of Raven's neck hard enough to make her gasp.

"Sorry," he muttered.

"Jax, Raven, you made it!" Grace Brooks cried, giving both of them fierce hugs. "Raven, you look gorgeous! Whatever happened to your neck? Come, let's find some champagne and you can tell me . . ."

Raven threw him a panicked look over her shoulder, but all Jax could do was lift his hands in surrender.

"I see you decided to swim with the sharks," Erik said, handing Jax a lowball glass of scotch.

He needed it. He hadn't wanted to start Raven off too early, or they would have had champagne in the limo.

"I'm usually one of the sharks," Jax commented wryly.

"Not after kicking Lucia out on her pretty little ass," Erik said cheerfully. "Now you're chum."

"I'm surprised you're here. Mom ask you to come?"

"I haven't seen Raven in a while, so I thought I'd stop by. I knew you'd bring her whether she wanted to go or not. You never do this kind of thing alone."

Jax scowled. "I'm returning the favor."

"What do you mean?" Erik asked, tugging on his bowtie.

"The other night Raven took me to the movies and then to a little dive for coffee and pie."

"That doesn't sound like you," Erik commented. "What possessed you to say yes?"

"She caught me in a private moment, and I agreed to make her go away."

His brother could read him too well, much to Jax's chagrin. "Bullshit. You said yes because you wanted to spend time with her, and you enjoyed yourself."

Jax searched through the crowd for her. He trusted his mother, but he wanted to see for himself Raven was holding her own.

She spoke to a man near the bar, a smile lighting her face.

The man, whom Jax couldn't identify from where he stood, placed his hand on the bare skin of her back.

Deep in his throat, Jax let out a possessive growl.

Erik whipped his gaze from Raven to Jax and back again, and he whistled. "Holy shit. You're falling for her."

∼

Raven didn't care what anyone thought of her. She *really* didn't. It wasn't as if she needed the approval of any of the people here tonight.

It didn't matter rumors circulated around her, denser than the sweet aroma of the dessert buffet along the far wall of the room. She felt more for Jax who *did* want to fit in, whose world was encased in these four walls.

Raven could go back to Z Avenue and be accepted for who she was. Be welcome, not in spite of who she was, but because of it. She was willing to bet Jax didn't have one real friend in this room besides Erik.

She beamed at the man who had the audacity to touch her after offering her a hundred dollars for a blowjob in the cleaning closet down the hall. She brushed him off easily enough, joking he couldn't afford her real prices.

He had the grace to blush and changed the subject.

She couldn't wait to tell Jax. On the other hand, she didn't want to cause trouble. And honestly, she wasn't quite sure if he'd come to her defense. It hadn't been that long ago Jax shared this man's assessment of her.

"You're causing quite a splash, my dear," Grace said, interrupting another proposition.

"I'm sorry," she murmured. She forgot this was Grace's territory as well as Jax's.

"Don't be," Grace said, waving her hand and gliding across the floor toward the dessert buffet. "This is the most fun I've had in years. These things can be so stuffy. Not that I'm taking pleasure in the rumors about you," she backpedaled quickly, "but you are a bright dollop of color."

"No offense taken, Mrs. Brooks," she said, accepting a plate decorated with dark pink swirls and the smallest sliver of cheesecake placed in the center. "I know I don't belong here."

"You belong here better than you think." Grace nudged her until they stood in the shadows. "There's not one woman here who knows what it's like to live. Their days are full of spa appointments and luncheons. Fundraisers like this and vacations to the Bahamas."

Raven tried a bite of cheesecake and the whipped sugar and cream cheese concoction melted on her tongue. "Didn't you grow up with all this?" She didn't mean to be rude, but Grace acted much like these women.

Grace laughed, a low throaty rasp. "Good God, no. While I do enjoy my husband's wealth, I grew up poor. I did the books for my father's mechanic shop. My mother left us when I was a baby . . . motherhood didn't agree with her, I guess. My father never got over her." She nibbled on crumb of the chocolate cake she held on a silver dessert plate. "He turned to drinking and was rarely sober. A gifted mechanic," she said wistfully, her eyes scanning the crowd, but seeing a different picture. "He could have done so much, yet he barely fixed enough cars to put food on the table. I should have worked somewhere else, but I wanted to look after him too, you know?"

Raven nodded. She did know. It's why even though her parents didn't want to speak to her, she still kept an eye on them. It helped to know they were all right.

"One day a car broke down a block from our little shop, and in walked a man who lit up the whole city. Jax's father. The minute I saw him . . . well, you know what they say. He paid for my dad to dry out, but it was too late. Three weeks after he walked me down the aisle, he died of liver failure."

"I'm so sorry," Raven murmured, touching Grace's arm.

"Thank you. The main point is, my dear, men don't want women like this. They think they do, all shiny and bright, but it's an illusion. Like gold paint. It chips off, and you're left with what's underneath. Do you like my son, Raven? Besides what he's doing for you?"

She didn't want to get the woman's hopes up. It didn't matter how she felt about Jax. The way it disappointed her when he closed himself off, or the way he held her at arms' length. It didn't matter that her heart picked up speed when he looked at her, or how happy it made her when he'd put his arm around her in the theatre. Jax's father may not have cared where Grace came from, but Jax did.

"He's very cold."

She flinched away, waiting for Grace's retaliation in response to the insult, but Grace only nodded. "Yes, he is. He used to be a cop. Did he tell you that?"

Raven took another bite of cheesecake. Listening to Grace's story, she forgot she was holding it. "I didn't know what he did presently until just a few nights ago."

"He's not one to be forthcoming with details," Grace murmured sadly. "He shot someone in the line of duty. He never recovered."

"That's terrible," she whispered. No wonder Jax was so reserved. Books and movies made it seem like nothing, a man pulling a trigger and walking away. But it wasn't so simple as that. Watching the blood drain out of someone as life flickered out of their eyes. Only someone evil could walk away unaffected.

She called Jax the devil, but it wasn't true.

"None of these women will ever be what Jax needs, yet he'll keep looking. He's cut himself off from real emotion, and has for sixteen years. He's drawn to you, Raven, even at this moment. Can you feel his eyes on you?"

She hadn't, she'd been too caught up in Grace's words, but now she felt Jax's steely gaze boring into her and she looked into the crowd where Jax stood off to the side clutching a glass and staring at her.

"If you tread carefully, you could cut through his veneer, if you wanted to."

Did she want to, she asked herself, self-consciously smoothing her hair. He hadn't taken his eyes off her.

He'd hurt her, while she tried, but she was no stranger to pain.

"Yes," she said, taking a step toward him, "yes, I do."

❧

"Lucy, you're looking lovely tonight," Jax said, offering the blonde a flute of champagne.

"Jax, I'm surprised you're here."

He breathed in her perfume. Poison. Apt. But it also made him lonely. While it hadn't been long since he'd thrown Lucia out of his house, he missed a body warming his bed.

If she would let him—though hell had more chance of freezing over—he'd drag her into a back room right now and ram his cock into her, over and over, searching for some kind of human contact, no matter how slight.

Human contact without risk.

That's what he needed.

An escort, perhaps.

A woman who would take her feelings with her. Along with the cash he paid her.

"Maybe I wanted to apologize," he said smoothly, appraising her frozen blue eyes, her perfect blonde hair.

Lucia smiled, and Jax waited for her face to crack in two, her skin stretched so tightly across her cheekbones, courtesy of a recent facelift.

"You never say you're sorry," she whispered, stepping closer to him. She leaned her body into his, and Jax forced himself to keep his arm at his side. He wanted to draw her in, feel her heartbeat.

Lucia was alive, and Jax was tired of being alone.

"I'll pay you back," she murmured, her lips feathering against his earlobe, sending shivers down his back. "I'll pay you back for making me look like a fool. Gwen isn't much for revenge, but I am, and I have plenty for both of us."

She kissed his cheek. "Enjoy your evening."

～

Frozen in place, Raven watched the whole scene, her mouth dry, the sweet flavor of cheesecake turning to dust on her tongue.

Had they made plans to see each other after the ball?

Would Lucia move back into Jax's house?

"You look like you're about to throw up," Erik commented, passing her a mug of coffee.

Gratefully, Raven accepted the warm porcelain and breathed in the earthy scent. "How did you know?"

"That you want to throw up, or that you needed a cup of coffee?" he asked, a smile tugging at his lips, a mug of coffee in his own hand, his usual unlit cigarette tucked behind an ear.

Raven laughed, trying to brush aside the sting of Lucia kissing Jax. "Both. What time is it?"

"Not late enough," Erik said, pushing his arm out to pull his sleeve away from his watch. "Not even nine. We're in it for a few more hours, at least."

Hidden speakers floated music to them, something dreamy, frothy, and couples began to drift to the dance floor.

"Would you like to dance?" Erik asked.

"I don't know how," Raven said, equal parts hopeful and terrified. She didn't want to look like a fool. Her reputation had already done enough damage.

"It's easy," Erik said, placing both of their mugs onto the narrow lip of a decorative column. "Like this."

He pulled Raven into his arms, one arm around her waist, the other hand holding hers. "Taller women wrap their arms around a gent's neck," he said, "but rest your hand on my shoulder. That'll work."

"Now what?" Raven asked. It felt odd being in Erik's arms when two seconds ago she'd been jealous of Lucia's proximity to Jax.

"Stand here. Move on your feet back and forth. That's it."

"Oh. But there're more complicated dances."

Erik's hazel eyes, so much like Jax's, twinkled. "Sure there are, but I don't know how to do them. This is the best I can do, love."

He tightened his hold on her waist.

"It's good enough for me," she said patting his shoulder. "Aren't you here with someone?"

"Well," Erik muttered, looking away.

"I know. It's okay."

"You would, wouldn't you?" Erik asked, tilting his head. "You see people."

"It's easy when no one sees you in return."

"They're missing out on a wonderful woman," Erik murmured into her hair.

"Thank you."

"I have someone, but we aren't close. I mean, I'm too busy for a relationship."

"Why?" Raven asked. "Everyone deserves someone."

Erik shook his head and looked over her shoulder, his gaze drifting over the dancing couples. "I've spent most of my life protecting Jax in some way or other."

She shuffled her feet, the hem of her dress catching on a heel. "Grace told me he used to be a cop and he shot someone in the line of duty."

They danced behind the column, deeper into the shadows, a forgotten and dying potted plant collecting dust in the corner near an emergency exit.

"It wasn't exactly like that. Mom pushes aside unpleasantness, and it can distort the facts. It was more of a . . . well, Jax panicked. What he saw wasn't what he thought, and it was just one big messy accident. I've been protecting him, mainly from himself. I'm older than he is by a couple of years, and I keep an eye on him. For Mom and Dad."

"It was an accident," she murmured, more to herself than to Erik. Yet, even when there was an accident, there was always someone to blame.

"Yes. And he's paid in guilt all these years. I . . . stick around to make sure he's okay."

"You deserve your own life," she said.

"I wish I could see him settled. If a woman could take over . . ."

She shook her head. "No, Erik. If Jax is going to make a relationship work, he has to forgive himself. He has to accept what he did, he has to accept it was an accident. But maybe you don't need to worry. I saw him talking to Lucia earlier. Maybe they'll get back together."

"She's not good enough for him."

Reaching up on her tip-toes, Raven kissed his cheek. "You're a good brother."

He smiled at her, and was about to say something, but a voice, explosive with anger, stopped him. "Just what the *fuck* is going on here?"

Jax couldn't explain his rage finding Raven in Erik's arms. He often thought Erik would be a better match for her, anyway. But after his exchange with Lucia, loneliness, grief, and maybe a little bit of fear roiled in his heart, and seeing Erik and Raven together intensified those feelings a hundred-fold.

"It's not what you think," Raven said, her eyes wide. "What's wrong with you?"

"Jax—" Erik tried, but Jax cut him off with a glare and pulled Raven's arm. "We're leaving."

"But—"

He stopped, not caring he was making a spectacle of himself. It wasn't the first time. "Do you want to stay?" he snarled.

Raven lifted her chin, fire blazing in her eyes. "No. But I thought you might. I saw you cozying up to Lucia earlier. Didn't you get back together?"

The mention of Lucia's name made electricity zip through his veins, and his brain crackled with fury. "We are going home."

"It isn't my home," Raven snapped.

Jax ignored her. He had no choice because he was afraid if he gave in to his feelings, he'd hurt her.

He needed someone to share his pain.

"It's not yours, either."

Jax brushed off her words. As they waited for the coat attendant to retrieve their jackets, he surveyed the ballroom.

Erik stood off to the side, his hands clenched into fists.

His mother stood alone, tears in her eyes.

Lucia huddled with Gwen, a smug smile on her face. Gwen's expression held little emotion, only looked over his shoulder with sympathy at Raven who smoldered behind him.

He hoped she would explode when they were outside. He hoped she would tear into him, give him an excuse to let loose.

As if Justin could read his mind, his driver was waiting with the limo when he and Raven stepped outside.

She stomped to the car through the snow and brushing him off to open her own door, flung herself into the backseat.

Her indifference at letting him help her into the car the way she was supposed to topped off his anger, and he seethed in his seat, thrumming with tension.

"That was unnecessary," Raven spat when they cleared the hotel's circular drive. "And you're supposed to be teaching me how to behave in public? What kind of aftermath do you think Erik and your parents have to deal with now?"

Simmering with temper, Jax bristled at Raven's defense of his family, and his rage boiled all over again.

He rose the divider between them and Justin.

Raven scoffed in disgust.

Jax sat in silence for one moment, then he struck.

He fisted her hair in his hand, the silky strands tight around his fingers. Jerking her head, he made her meet his eyes.

His heart stirred in a way it never had before. Not when he'd been engaged to Gwen, and certainly not when he'd been engaged to Lucia. No. Raven's eyes possessed something he'd never seen looking at his ex-fiancées.

Compassion.

When Lucia stared at him, it had been with hate, resentment, and jealousy. She wanted what he had, but marrying him was too much of a price to pay, though she'd been willing to do it.

Raven never looked at him with anything but concern and empathy.

He loosened his hand in her hair, but she didn't pull away.

Roughly, he took her mouth with his, satisfaction running through him when she whimpered.

He shoved his tongue between her teeth, invading her space, tasting the sweet of a dessert and the smoky flavor of the coffee she'd been drinking with Erik.

Raven leaned against her door, and Jax followed, crowding her until there wasn't any space between them.

This was what he needed, this was what he craved.

Touch.

When she wrapped her arms around his neck, he nearly came undone. He ran a hand up her leg, his mouth moving from her lips down her neck, skirting the bandage, to her shoulder.

She moaned and widened her legs. "Jax."

His fingertips brushed her panties, and she whimpered again, but this time the sound was full of desire, not pain.

"Touch me, please."

"In a few minutes, darling. We're almost home."

The words Raven threw at his back on their way out of the ballroom echoed through his mind.

He'd never given his living situation much thought. He'd bought the house when he began thinking about marriage, hoping a woman would be enamored with the floors, the rooms, the staff.

A woman wouldn't marry him just for himself, Jax knew he was unlovable, and he'd hoped the woman he chose to be his wife would be content with the consolation prize.

The mansion was just a building containing several rooms he had no use for, a place he called home because besides the house where he'd grown up, he never felt at home anywhere.

His house came into view as Justin rounded a curve in the highway. Lights blazed, but they offered no warmth. Stark. Cold. Mariah did her best, but it wasn't enough. He'd sell it. Before he found another woman to marry. She wouldn't want to live in the shadow of two ex-fiancées and an ex-wife.

A fresh start in a fresh relationship.

Thinking of Raven as his ex-wife chilled him, and he took her mouth again to chase away the feeling of dread the thought of her leaving gave him.

Of course she'd leave.

He wanted her to leave.

He played with the hem of her panties, her skin's heat warming his hand.

Justin let them out in front of the stone steps and he kept a tight grip on Raven's arm. He didn't want her slipping on the icy ground, but he didn't want her changing her mind, either.

He'd never force a woman. He never needed to. Money was a brilliant motivator to entice women to spread their legs.

But Raven was different.

She'd survived without money.

She'd survived without him.

And she could do it again.

He walked her to his room, the tension sizzling between them.

Or at least, *he* buzzed with it.

She didn't seem to think twice, more caught up with the hallways of the wing she hadn't been allowed to enter.

For a moment he wondered at bringing her to his room—how she would feel being taken in the same bed Gwen and Lucia had warmed before her—but she was his wife. That trumped everything.

He opened his bedroom door and nudged her inside.

Raven looked around the huge suite and he tried to see it through her eyes.

The king-sized four-poster bed.

The sunken sitting room.

The fireplace.

There weren't any pictures. There weren't any knickknacks or souvenirs. Everything functional. Everything in its place.

This very well could have been a hotel room, and the sterility of it shamed him, and spurred his anger all over again.

He jerked Raven's fur off her shoulders and tossed it onto a chair. He did the same with his own jacket.

She stood in the middle of his bedroom and watched him take off his cuff links and undo his tie.

Strip off his jacket and unbutton his shirt.

He took his time, enjoying the anticipation.

Anticipation was all he had.

He'd be quick—in and out, so to speak—and in less than half an hour she'd be back in her own room.

Afterward, he could get drunk and sleep; the release would finally calm him.

He needed something, someone, to take the edge off.

It gave him a small hint of satisfaction to take what his brother wanted. Even though Erik had always been there for him since the shooting, he resented his brother his peace of mind, and he'd done what he could to try to keep that resentment hidden. He didn't deserve it. Then Erik had to set his sights on Raven, and it pissed him off.

Jax clenched his jaw, his teeth gnashing, and reached for her, but she flinched away, stepping back.

"You'll be nice."

He blinked in confusion. "What?"

"You'll be nice. You fucked me once in anger. I won't let you do it again. You'll be gentle, or I won't let you. Do you understand me?"

In fury, he screwed her in the church, angry Gwen walked out on him. He was furious he'd found Raven attractive while at the same time repulsed by her looks and lifestyle.

He'd been full of rage nothing ever went his way.

Nothing had changed. He was in the same place now as he'd been three years ago in that church.

The shooting was still there, always, under his skin, never

letting him go. That was something else that would never change, would never go away. It would always be a part of him.

His eyes hardened, and he pursed his lips.

Like hell she'd tell him what to do.

He advanced, and she stepped back, stepped back until her body was pressed against the wall near his closet.

She stared at the floor, and when he reached for a gold strap of her dress, she lifted her head, tears wetting her cheeks.

"Please," she whispered.

She pressed a kiss to his chest, her lips searing his skin, right above his heart.

And Jax did something he'd never done before. He let a woman lead.

Nine

Raven took advantage of the extra inches the high heels gave her height and peppered kisses over his chest while he stood there, heaving, his breath escaping his lips in shuddery gasps.

It took a lot of control for him to rein in his anger, to pause instead of attacking her in rage and lust.

He'd already used her and thrown her away. Tonight he'd have her on her terms or not at all.

She was glad he made the correct choice because she *would* have walked out. He wouldn't treat her the way he treated the other women in his life. He may not think her better than that, but she did.

If she wanted to be treated like trash, she could find Damien.

She was sure he'd gladly enjoy another chance to teach her a lesson.

"Raven," Jax rasped.

She pressed a kiss to his neck under his pulse that skittered out of control. "Slow," she murmured, pushing off his shirt, and it fluttered to the floor. "Do you think we can turn the lights out?"

Jax lifted a small remote off his armoire. The overhead light darkened, and a fire flared to life in the fireplace. "How's this?"

Raven smiled. "Perfect." She paused. "Is kissing okay?" she asked.

"Why wouldn't it be?"

He kissed her in the car, but he'd done it to punish her for being with Erik.

"Not the way you kissed me in the limo," she said. "Like this." She nudged him onto the bed, and she stepped between his knees.

She kicked off her heels, no longer needing the extra inches.

Soon they would be heart to heart.

She framed his face with her trembling hands. The fire reflected in his eyes, exposing the emotions he couldn't keep banked.

Pain and heartbreak.

Guilt.

Maybe even a bit of hate.

For whom?

Himself, surely, for ending a life too soon.

Lucia, for not being who he needed her to be.

Maybe even for her, for the same reason.

Jax was looking for someone to rescue him from what he'd done, but no one could.

She covered his lips with hers, light at first, to let him acclimate. Had he never been kissed like this? Like he mattered.

Like someone . . . loved him?

She slipped her tongue into his mouth as she ran her fingers through his hair.

He encircled her waist with his hands, and she stiffened, waiting for him to hurt her somehow, but all he did was tighten his fingers, and she relaxed.

She increased the pressure of the kiss, and he fell backward onto the bed. She followed, startled, falling onto his chest, laughing.

Jax rolled her onto her back and looked into her eyes. "You're beautiful. Do you know that?"

She felt beautiful when he looked at her that way.

"Can I undress you?"

Raven nodded, impressed he bothered to seek her permission.

"I've never asked before," Jax admitted, "I've always assumed it's what they wanted."

"It probably was," Raven said, goosebumps appearing on her arm where his fingers pushed down the strap. "But it's romantic, don't you think? To ask?"

"I've never given it any thought," Jax whispered against her skin.

She sucked in a breath to say something, but she paused. *To hell with it.* "It could be part of your problem. Gwen and Lucia, *all* women, they . . . we . . . need to be treated as more than a quick and dirty lay."

Jax lifted his lips off her shoulder. "The women I've been with knew the score, Raven. Sex isn't love."

She knew what he meant underneath his words. He may be doing what she asked, but love wasn't part of it this time, either.

Placing a hand to his cheek, rough with stubble, she said, "It's something to keep in mind. For next time."

His eyes darkened, but he didn't refute her words.

She stood and let him slid the dress from her body where it laid in a golden puddle at her feet. She wore a bra and garter set Grace chose, in the same color as the dress. Raven wondered if Grace had insisted on purchasing lingerie because she hoped Raven would end up where she was now. In Jax's bed.

"There's something to be said for taking your time," Jax said as he unclipped a garter snap. He rolled the stocking down her leg, then did the other side.

"Undo your bra?" he said, making it sound like a question instead of a demand.

Raven turned around. "You do it."

He released the hooks. She held the material to her breasts and looked at him over her shoulder.

"Tease."

She turned around, clutching the gold lace to her chest.

"That's what one of the men said tonight. He thought I was a hooker who . . . wouldn't service him."

Jax frowned. "Who? I'll pound some manners into that son of a bitch."

"It's what you thought," she reminded him.

"You're better than that now," Jax muttered, red staining his cheeks.

"Why?" Raven demanded. "Because my bra's La Perla and my dress is Tom Ford? I'm the same person in here." She slapped the flat of her hand against her chest. "Clothes don't change a person."

She gripped Jax's chin and made him look at her. "You're still the same person, Jax. The same person you were before you accidentally shot someone. A good man."

He shoved her away and stood from the bed in one fluid motion. "Who the hell told you? It's no one's business."

"Your mother," she said.

At the minibar in the corner of the room, he poured himself a drink. "It's none of her goddamned business. And it's none of yours. Get out of here."

"No."

"What did you say to me?"

"I said no. It's time to stop hiding from what you did. Own it. Then maybe you can get past it."

Jax drained his glass, then poured another. He tipped it to her, offering, and had it been any other time, she would have smiled at the manners so engrained in him he couldn't even fight without being polite.

She shook her head.

He drained that glass too, his Adam's apple bobbing as he swallowed, his skin cast gold in the fireplace's flames.

"What the hell do you think I've been trying to do all these years? I *have* owned it. I make myself pay for it *every goddamned day*. I get no rest. I get no relief. I can find no salvation. I took a life. And when I did, he took mine."

"It doesn't have to be that way."

"It doesn't?" he asked, pouring a third drink. He brought it with him to the bed. "Isn't that what you did? You say you lost your brother, but you didn't keep living life like nothing happened. No, you stopped living. So how is that different, Raven? How is that different?"

She lost her fight and sank onto the mattress. It wasn't different. The minute her brother's body hit the ground, she lost her life along with his.

The guilt she felt because he'd been in the park to find her and bring her home was the same Jax felt for pulling the trigger.

Jax knelt in front of her. "It's the same, Raven."

She lifted her head. "Then let's help each other."

~

It was different, and difficult, for Jax to be gentle. It'd been so long since he made love with a woman he cared about.

He unbuckled his belt, then unbuttoned his slacks and slid down the zipper.

The fight stirred his blood, and the thought of sinking into Raven's pliant body made him rock hard.

Naked, he pulled the bra away from Raven's breasts.

His breath caught.

He told her she was beautiful, but that was inaccurate. Her skin sparkled in the flames. She looked like a goddess.

"Lie back," he murmured, and she complied.

He smoothed her panties down her legs and dropped them onto the floor next to her dress.

Grabbing her legs behind her knees, he positioned her at the edge of the mattress. He wanted her so badly he could taste it. Quivering with anticipation, Jax ran his hand along his cock and prepared to push into her heat.

Raven rose to her elbows and glared. "What are you doing?"

"I think it's clear," Jax said, annoyed at the delay.

"Not like this, you're not. The first time you hammered me against a window. You can do better than this."

"But—"

"You just told me I'm not a hooker, so don't treat me like one."

Jax kept the growl to the back of his throat and turned down the bed.

Obstinate.

Stubborn.

Entirely correct.

Raven scrambled between the sheets, and he sat, thankful time had passed since Lucia occupied his bed. At least Mariah had laundered his sheets.

"I'm sorry," he said, embarrassed. He should have led her to a guest room. He had six.

She scoffed, rearranging the pillows, dumping two onto the floor. "What? You think I don't know you've had women in your bed? I haven't been a nun, either. You know Axel and I have a history. It's fine. Besides, you didn't love them."

I don't love you, either, he wanted to say, but the words jammed in his chest, like he'd taken too big a bite of a peanut butter and jelly sandwich and he couldn't swallow it down.

He slid into the cool sheets beside her and laid on his side, his head propped in his hand. His other trailed down her stomach, past the trimmed frame of her hair, toward her delicate, deliciously warm skin.

"Will you kiss me?" she asked.

The question turned into a moan as he slid one of his fingers into her.

As he played, he kissed her lips, her neck, her breasts, and she did the same for him, the friction of his whiskers against her sensitive skin turning her lips scarlet.

He'd never known such romantic foreplay, and by the time she was panting, begging, he too, felt like he could explode at any moment.

"Now, Jax, please," she choked, and he complied, pushing into her, so gently, so easily, as she was ready for him.

He needed all his self-control not to blow the moment he was fully encased inside her.

He cuddled into her, his breath on her neck, his lips at her ear. "Is this what you wanted? Is this what you like?"

She met his eyes. "Isn't this better?" she whispered, her thumb tracing his bottom lip. "Do you feel it?"

Burying his face in the warmth of her neck, he knew exactly what she was talking about. How her legs cradled his hips, how her fingers twisted in his hair. How her breath tickled his ear, how her mumbled words of encouragement and pleasure cocooned him in a haze of safety and passion.

If he'd had his way, he would have fucked her, sent her to her room, and showered by now. Sat in front of the fire, alone, for the rest of the night, with only a glass of scotch for company.

When he came, it was almost painful, the quaking so strong he cried into a pillow so she wouldn't hear.

He shuddered, and Raven wiggled her hand between their sweat-slicked bodies. As he released the last of himself inside her, she made herself come, her muscles convulsing around him.

He collapsed on top of her, breathless.

"I'm sorry," he huffed, straining with the effort not to crush her. "I'm not used to, well . . . I should have made you come first."

"I can take care of myself," Raven said, laughing as she nipped at his neck. "But maybe next time?"

Next time. "Yes, I can do that."

He dozed next to her, their limbs entwined, and at three in the morning, he woke to use the bathroom. Gently, he rolled out of bed, but despite his efforts not to jostle her, when he came out, Raven laid awake, lying on her side, hugging a pillow.

"I'm sorry. I didn't mean to wake you. Are you thirsty? There's bottled water in the bar."

"No, I'm okay, thanks."

Jax slipped between the sheets and kissed her forehead. The

fire still burned, the flames flickering across her face, and the sad look in her eyes made him worry. "Are you okay? Are you sore?"

"No, I'm not sore. Not yet, anyway." Raven sat up and covered her breasts with a sheet. "Jax, there's nothing going on between Erik and me."

"It isn't any of my business," he said, angry she brought up his brother while they were lying in bed after just making—having sex.

"Yes, it is. It is if we're sleeping together. And that's not all of it, either. Will you look at me?"

God, she looked like a siren, bee-stung lips and mussed hair.

"Jax, Erik is gay. There will never be anything between us but friendship."

Jax clutched the comforter in his hand. "Erik's what?"

"Gay. Erik likes men?"

"Raven, I don't know—"

"He told me at the ball. He said it wasn't a secret, so I'm not outing him by telling you. He's even seeing someone . . . when he's not keeping track of you."

"I've never asked him to do that," Jax said defensively. While he hadn't asked, he'd needed Erik by his side all these years.

"But he has. It's not the point, anyway. Why didn't you know?"

He wanted a drink, but he didn't want to get out of bed and risk Raven taking it as a cue to leave. He wanted to spend the rest of the night with her. He wanted to wake up with her, nuzzle her breasts, have her open for him as the sun came up.

Groaning, he backed against the headboard. Why hadn't he known about his brother's sexual preference? He could say because he didn't care. He would love Erik if he were attracted to rabbits. No, it was because . . . "Ever since the accident, I've been wrapped up in my own life. My own grief. I never gave a thought to anyone else. Including the women I tried to marry."

"You owe him an apology."

Jax flicked a piece of hair behind her ear. How much she cared about other people charmed him.

"I'll talk to him tomorrow. You're right. I should have known."

Raven bit her lip and tucked herself into his side.

It unsettled him how she fit like she belonged, like she'd been doing it for years. Like they often woke in the middle of the night to talk.

"What else, Raven?" he asked, a sense of foreboding slithering down his back.

"I'd like to see Elle, if that's okay?"

His heart calmed. "Of course it is. You're not a prisoner here." He forced cheer into his voice. "In fact, it's the other way around —you're forcing yourself on to me, remember?"

Which brought about its own set of problems. Problems he definitely wouldn't think about right now. "Would you like a car? Do you have your driver's license?"

Raven shook her head, her hair brushing his chest.

"Then I'll have Justin drive you."

Raven skimmed a hand down his stomach. "I can catch the bus, I just need a ride into the city. I don't want Justin to wait for me on Z Avenue. It's not safe."

He understood. He'd had to tamp down his own guilt asking Justin to wait in front of that dilapidated building the night he looked for Raven. "But you need a way back, sweetheart."

She sat up, looked at him with pools of smoky whiskey. "Can I come back, Jax?"

Oh, God, Raven.

"Yes, sweetheart. You can always come back."

That was when he fell. The next morning, after he analyzed and tore to pieces every second of that night, that's when he knew.

That was when he fell in love with Raven Grey.

～

On Sunday morning, Jax did something he hadn't done for many, many years. He visited his brother.

Erik lived in the city, a loft apartment along the river.

Justin let him out on the sidewalk, and Jax looked up the side of the gray stone building, the height dizzying.

He had other motives for visiting Erik. Raven also left his house that morning to spend the day on Z Avenue, and he didn't want to be at home without her.

They'd woken that morning how he wanted. Watching as sleep let her go, her eyes blinking, at first confused, but then a smile on her lips as she remembered where she was. How she'd turned to him and lifted her head for a kiss.

Jax had never felt more content, and he'd kept her in bed for as long as he could.

He couldn't hide her, she wouldn't let him regardless, and she'd been out of the house by ten. After Justin returned from dropping her off at the nearest bus stop, Jax asked him to drive him to Erik's.

He tried not to worry overmuch about Raven spending the day on Z Avenue. She'd spent thirteen years of her life there, and she knew how to survive.

Opening the door of Erik's building, he admitted it wasn't Raven he was worried about. It was Axel. He bristled when she brought up Axel's name, the night before, in his bed no less, but he'd been called many things since the shooting, and hypocrite was not one of them. He'd held his tongue.

Raven kissed him so sweetly this morning before she left. He could only hope she meant the feelings behind the kiss and the look in her eyes when she said goodbye.

The elevator creaked as it carried him to the twentieth floor, and it took so long for the doors to glide open Jax was afraid he'd spend the day trapped in the box rather than apologizing.

He shifted the container of bagels to one hand and knocked on his brother's door with the other.

Erik answered, opening it just a crack, and peered out, an

unlit cigarette dangling between his lips. He quit smoking years ago but never gave up having a smoke around.

The affectation made the women crazy, the sexiness of it without the stink and bad breath, and it was a light blinking on in Jax's brain why Erik never noticed.

"Jax! Is everything all right?" Erik slid the chain off the lock and opened the door. "Is it Mom or Dad?"

Chagrined, Jax realized he should have called first. "Is my visit that out of character?"

"In a word, yes. What's this?"

"Bagels. Your favorite, I think, from that deli on Cornell."

"Thanks."

"Are you going to let me in?"

"Sorry, sorry."

Jax stepped into Erik's loft. Nothing much had changed, but the stark difference between Erik's apartment and his own house was more evident than night and day. Erik's walls were filled with pictures of their family and old friends. A coffee table full of magazines and books sat in front of a couch that looked comfortable, lived-in. Before they made love, he would have pictured Raven there, reading a book, sipping on a coffee, a throw covering her legs to ward off the chill, and it would have made him angry.

Raven did that in *his* house, in his library.

He had to control his jealousy. She hadn't acted the jealous tart last night, though she would have had the right.

"Where's your suit?"

"I'm wearing a suit," Jax said, following Erik into his kitchen.

He'd always liked Erik's kitchen, and maybe, if—when—he sold his house, he'd buy a house with a kitchen more family-orientated.

The white with blue accents was cheerful, and the earthy scent of coffee emanated warmth. But not heat—warmth of a good life, a happy life.

"No, your jacket's missing."

Raven's teasing made Jax leave off the jacket that morning.

Still dressed in slacks and a dress shirt, he felt on a lazy Sunday it would suffice.

No tie, though.

And he hadn't shaved.

He must look like a completely different person.

Well, he felt different.

"I'm not going to work today."

"Oh?" Erik said, pouring coffee.

"Raven and I have plans later."

Jax sat on a stool at the breakfast nook, pushing a vase of flowers out of his way.

Flowers.

Now there was something that hadn't been in his house for a long time.

Erik plated bagels, set out flavored cream cheese, and he slid a mug of coffee to Jax.

"Thanks. You're still not going to tell me where you buy your coffee?"

Erik laughed. "No. It's the one thing I have over you. I'll never tell."

Jax sobered. "We've never been in a contest."

"No, we never have. We didn't need a contest, Jax. You've always been the winner. Did you come to apologize to me about last night?" Erik leaned against the counter, his expression blank.

"Actually, yes," Jax said, and was happy to see the surprise that flitted across Erik's face. He rarely apologized. It meant he was in the wrong somehow, and he never admitted he was wrong. "I . . . had no claim on Raven, and I was out of line."

Erik wasn't stupid, and he tilted his head at the choice of words Jax used. "You had no claim on her last night. But now you're saying you do?"

Jax sipped his coffee to wet his mouth. "We . . . I . . . we made love last night. I mean, we *made love*. It wasn't anything like what I've been doing with my ex-fiancées. She wouldn't let me. I intended to. I didn't want her to mean anything to me. But she . . . she went to Z Avenue to see some friends today."

"Ah," Erik said, nodding. "She'll come back. You two have an agreement. She's an honorable woman, and she'll fulfill her end of the bargain. You don't have to worry. You'll get your divorce."

Jax stared.

"Right," Erik said quickly. "You don't want it now."

"No. No, I want to stay married . . . if she'll have me. She said it was just an accident. She didn't blame me, didn't point fingers. If she can accept what I did, if she can sleep in the bed where I've only fucked other women and not given a damn about any of them, if she can forgive me how I treated her when we met . . . It's a lot to ask of her."

Erik poured more coffee into his mug. "That's nothing. All those things . . . that's nothing. You're forgetting the most important part."

"That I love her."

Erik nodded. "I'm happy for you. You're a very lucky man. I know men say that to each other all the time, but Raven, she's special. She's the kind of strength you need. She'll make you a good wife."

"Yeah. I think so, too." He paused and rubbed tiredly at his face. "I'm sorry about not knowing."

"Not knowing what? Oh." He paused. "Raven told you."

"She did. Last night, we fought about how I treated you at the ball. I've been so self-absorbed, I had no idea. Well, maybe I did, but I didn't care about anything except you watching my back."

"You're my brother and something horrific happened. I won't pretend to know what it's like to have gone through that. Killing someone, accidentally, you hear about it, you know? Parents stepping away from a bathtub and their babies drowning, or hunters shooting their friends because they look like deer." Erik rolled his eyes. "Drunk drivers killing people because they wouldn't order an Uber. It's all over, but that doesn't mean I know how it feels. I wanted to be there for you."

"You've been there for me too much." Erik opened his mouth to disagree, but he cut him off. "No. I'm not blaming you for giving me your time. I appreciate it, and I needed it, more than you'll ever know. But it's time for me to stand on my own. You have a life to live, a man to date, I've been told, and you have a right to do that. You've never liked working at Titan, you've done it to keep an eye on me. So, not only did I come to apologize, but . . . you're fired."

Erik gaped.

"You'll receive a fine severance package, of course," Jax said, slipping off his stool to pour more coffee.

"I don't know what to say."

"Say you'll take your man on vacation. Say you'll find a job you like going to. Say you won't be a stranger." A curious burn started in Jax's throat at that.

"But Jax, Raven—"

"She could never take your place, not as a brother and not as a friend. I won't turn her into my keeper, either. We need to spend time together, get to know each other, if I want a relationship with her. But as we do that, I need to learn to stand on my own. I need to face the accident head on."

"How will you do that?"

"I'm finally going to find out just whom I shot that night and make amends any way I can."

It was a bit presumptuous to throw away sixteen years of hiding because he spent one night with Raven. In fact, he had no idea what she felt for him, and he could only hope as she continued her education while she lived with him, her feelings for him would grow.

And when he asked her if they could stay married, she would say yes.

It was a long shot. She wasn't trying to change just for herself.

Raven had family she would want to spend time with. She would need to get to know them all over again, as people, and as parents. Kind of like him and Erik. When they spent time together now, it would be as friends.

Jax looked forward to that.

He hadn't planned to fire Erik, the words just slipped out, but the shocked and stunned look on his brother's face made it worth it.

He'd need to fill the position, and he knew just the person.

Of course, that would be a risk and commitment in and of itself, but he wouldn't make a decision like that purely to make Raven happy—that was just a bonus.

Jax asked Justin to drive to a jewelry store he favored when he needed to buy a gift. He'd never bought an engagement ring before. Gwen and Lucia picked out their own. But he would for Raven. Something small, tasteful.

Elegant and classy.

Like she was.

Jax had them bring out the tray of rings from the back.

Anything store-front wasn't good enough for Raven, and he knew it the moment he saw it.

Set in rose gold, a small heart-shaped diamond sparkled. Discreet, but possessing some weight, it was perfect.

It didn't take long for him to walk out of the store with the black velvet box nestled deep into his pants pocket.

Part of healing after what he'd done was learning to be alone, learning to be comfortable in his own skin, and Jax forced himself to go home despite the chance Raven having not returned from Z Avenue.

He wished he thought to purchase her a phone, but she seldom left his house, and when she did, it was with him. The inability to contact her made him pace the library, and Mariah poked her head into the room, concern wrinkling her forehead.

Jax waved her away.

He wouldn't stoop so low as to call Justin. She would have told him what time she wanted him to pick her up at the bus stop.

He'd always been the one in control, and he would learn to give it up. Once in a while, at least.

To pass the time, he logged into his work email. He'd have more to do until he replaced Erik. Knowing his brother—and Jax liked to think that even though the last sixteen years had been centered on him, he did—Erik would still come in to work for the next little while.

The sky was growing dark when Jax looked up from his computer and he frowned at the time. He thought for certain Raven would be back by now, and just when he was going to cave in and call Justin after all, she shuffled into the room, her cheeks pink.

This feeling of uncertainty was new for him, and he willed his heart to stop pounding. But God, she looked beautiful, her hair spilling out of her winter hat, her eyes twinkling, her skin clear and bright, a smile on her lips.

"You had a good day?" he asked, not rising from his chair.

Rushing to her, crushing her against him, reeked of desperation.

"I did," she said, pulling off her gloves and flopping into a chair in front of his desk. "I saw everyone. They wanted to know when I'd be back."

"What did you say?"

Raven laughed. "There was nothing I could say. Back where? Back on the streets? Back to Club Nova? Back to a homeless shelter? I said you gave me three months to figure things out, and I plan to. I plan to use those three months, not waste a minute. I can't go back there. I want a different life, and I won't waste the time you've given me, or the money you've spent on me. Nothing you give me will ever be taken for granted. Nothing."

Jax could have taken her words as a goodbye, but he didn't.

Instead, he took them as a promise.

"Let's go out," he said, shutting his laptop. He wanted to celebrate.

Raven narrowed her eyes. "Your idea of fun and my idea of fun differ greatly," she said, and he laughed.

"Yes, but I think you'll enjoy this."

~

Jax hadn't been ice skating since he was a child. Doing something that wasn't sitting at a stuffy dinner party or making excruciating small talk at a charity ball was a new departure for him, and it made him realize just how much he cut himself off from the world.

"Where are we going?" she asked for the third time.

He hadn't told her his plans, only requested she dress warmly as the March evening still had the ability to freeze from the outside in.

The city's lights glittered in the frozen air, and for once in his life, Jax appreciated the beauty of the city he called home.

"What did you do today, then?" he asked a question of his own. He wanted the information as much as he wanted to distract her.

"You're not going to tell me."

"Nope."

Raven lifted a hand to his cheek, the glove warmed by her body heat. "You look happy."

Jax swerved around a slow-moving vehicle. "I am."

"I'm glad."

He pressed a kiss to the back of her hand. "Your day?" he prompted. He wasn't asking to check up on her. Okay, fine, he was. Technically, it wasn't his business what she did. She had every right to have laid in a sweaty heap of sweat and sex with Axel. Jax only prayed to God she hadn't.

He may have confessed his feelings about Raven to Erik, but he was a long way off from saying anything to her. They were on shaky ground at best, and he had no idea how she felt about him. She could be interested only in her education and viewed spending time with him as part of a necessary evil to obtain her objective.

But after last night, he didn't think so.

Patience had never been his strong suit, but he'd need to take it slow. They hadn't exactly met in a conventional manner.

His courtships with Gwen and Lucia had been rushed affairs. He hadn't wanted them to discover what kind of a man he really was.

They had anyway.

No, he looked forward to dating Raven, getting to know her as a person and not just a woman he'd marry for the sake of being married.

Raven bit her lip. "I'm worried about Elle."

"What's wrong?"

"She's tired of her life there."

"Well, it isn't any wonder . . . Raven." He almost called her sweetheart. "She never leaves her shop. She's a prisoner in her own salon. No one could be happy living the way she does. Why doesn't she ever leave?"

"Her husband was beaten to death protecting her store," Raven said, tucking her hands between her knees. "She went out for the evening. A couple of men saw her go and thought they could rob her register or pillage the back room for stuff to sell. Her husband tried to fend them off. It was a long time ago."

"Were you on the streets then?" Jax asked, his hands trembling on the steering wheel.

"Yeah, but I hadn't met her yet. Someone targeting the salon again is a very real possibility. Her shop's one of the few legitimate businesses on Z Avenue."

Jax slowed his Jeep. The traffic thickened as they entered the city.

"What do you think you could do for her? I thought making amends with your parents was important to you."

Raven sighed. "It is. It's what I've been trying to do since before we met at the church, but I can't leave my friends behind. I've lived on the streets for too long to just walk away. Elle helped me when there was no one else around. I owe her. I'll be able to get my GED soon. My tutors say I'm on the right track. If I could do that, if I could figure out a job . . . Elle's a good hairstylist. She could open a real business if she could move. Z Avenue is one step away from hell."

They idled at a stoplight. Worry strained her face, her eyes shadowed with fear.

"What about your parents?"

Raven twisted in her seat, looked at him directly. "I want to talk to them, hope they let me move back home, if I can prove to them I'm stable enough. Then I could save money. I want to go to college, but Elle won't last that long. I need to help her first."

Jax opened his mouth to say he'd pay her way through school, but Raven shook her head.

A car honked. The light turned green.

"I know you said you'd help me, and I appreciate it. But you gave me three months, not four years. I don't intend to take up any more of your time than that. You've already been very generous."

Jax swallowed painfully. No talk of maybe hanging around. No talk of even staying friends. He couldn't blame her. He hadn't given her any indication he wanted to stay in contact with her. "When you leave you'll . . ."

"Talk to my parents, but I need to help Elle as soon as I'm able. She's my family, too."

Jax didn't bring up the future while they skated. They both wobbled on the ice, falling into each other, and Jax was relieved to see some of the sadness on her face fade.

It worried him she felt so attached to her old life on Z Avenue.

It worried him she'd choose her parents over him.

He just needed to make her see she didn't have to choose, that she had a big enough heart for everyone.

And so did he.

~

He drove home, stiff, sore, cold, but laughing, the taste of hot chocolate lingering in his mouth.

She sat with his hand tucked in her lap. "Thank you for tonight. It was a good day."

"Thank *you* for coming with me. I enjoy spending time with you, Raven." He wanted to tell her more, but stopped. She already had so much on her mind.

"I like it, too. I spilled about my day," she said, "but you spoke to Erik this morning, didn't you?"

Jax turned into his driveway and parked his Jeep in the garage. He shut the engine off, and for a moment, they sat in silence.

"Yes, and you were right about everything," he said. They only had a minute or two before the interior of the truck cooled to the point they would be uncomfortable and need to go inside.

"You didn't fight, did you?"

"No. Erik and I never fight, but I did fire him."

Raven sucked in a breath. "Jax, that wasn't—"

"I know, but he hated working for me. I did him a favor, and he wasn't offended. Stunned. Concerned I'd lost my mind, but generally happy I seemed to be moving forward. He won't be watching over me anymore. Well, maybe a little. I guess by now looking out for me is as natural as breathing, but I want him to start living. He's too old to play babysitter. Come on, let's go in."

Holding her hand, he walked her to the side-door of the house. He tried to think of a subtle way to ask, but there was none. "Will you spend the night with me?"

She stood on a step, making herself eye-level with him.

He loved looking at her. The scratch on her cheek was barely perceptible in the hazy moonlight, her delicate breath turning white in the frigid temperatures.

"Yes. You can kiss the bruises I'm sure I have all over my butt because someone didn't catch me the two thousand times I fell," she said, laughing.

"I'll make it up to you," he promised, scooping her up into his arms, breathing her in as he carried her up the stairs.

They made love in front of his fireplace. He memorized every inch of her skin, every flicker of desire in her eyes.

He didn't need to be told to be gentle. He didn't need to be told to go slowly. He loved her, and while he didn't say it, he tried like hell to show her.

Ten

It was more important than ever she get on the right track. Visiting Elle on Z Avenue reminded her that more was at stake than just her relationship with her parents.

Jax had access to some of the city's best therapists, and while she'd been seeing one regularly, one Jax paid handsomely to make house calls three times a week, Raven didn't put as much energy into the sessions as she did when her tutors came to call.

The next day, she met Dr. Wheland having an adjusted attitude and a new determination. She wandered the library as he organized his notes on the coffee table in front of the loveseat he liked to sit on during their sessions.

"Is there anything specific you'd like to talk about today?" he asked, opening his notebook.

He always began the conversation the same way, allowing her the floor. Most times she brushed him off, and he'd skim his notes, going over what they'd talked of previously.

For the amount of time she'd spent with Dr. Wheland, they hadn't covered much ground.

Not that she didn't want the help. She appreciated these visits and was grateful for the money Jax spent for the best, but Levi's death was a painful topic and she hadn't been brave enough to talk about it.

She was still that scared fifteen-year-old girl.

The look in Elle's eyes, the pain and utter hopelessness she'd displayed, made Raven see that it was time to admit her role in her brother's death.

"I'm ready to talk about Levi."

Dr. Wheland sipped his coffee and carefully set the mug on a coaster before replying. "Can you tell me why?"

Raven perched on the leather chair near Dr. Wheland's loveseat. "I visited Z Avenue a few days ago. I saw Elle." Bouncing her leg in agitation, she said, "She's not doing so well."

"I'm sorry to hear that. But what does that have to do with opening up to me?"

Raven liked Dr. Wheland. His brown hair threaded with gray, and his dress shirts and sweater vests reminded her a little of her father. The easy way he had about him that said, "Come, sit. Let's chat."

"I realized I need to get going with this. Start moving. Elle needs my help. Jax only gave me three months to figure this stuff out. I need to take advantage while he's paying." She tried to smile, turning it into a joke.

"Raven, you can see me anytime, talk to me anytime. No payment required. But let's get back to Elle. What's happening there? What makes you worry about her so much now?"

Raven bit back a groan of frustration. She had to be patient with his line of questioning.

"She's tired of life on Z Avenue, Dr. Wheland. She needs my help, but I don't have anything to give her now. I need to talk about Levi, then maybe I have a better chance of talking to my parents, sooner, rather than later."

Dr. Wheland propped an ankle on his knee, revealing argyle socks and the brown loafers he always wore. "Raven, I don't think this is about Elle. I don't think it's about Levi. Isn't this about Jax?"

Raven's cheeks flared with heat. "What do you mean?"

Flipping through his notes Dr. Wheland said, "When we talk, we always talk about Jax. How he treated you before, how he's only helping you for your signature now. How he's given you three months to get back on your feet." He tapped his pen on his notebook.

She smoothed the skirt of her black dress. "Yes."

"Take me back, Raven. When did your feelings for him change? When we first started speaking, you hated him. The power he had over you. The control."

She stared at the carpet, her black pumps mussing the freshly vacuumed fibers. She *had* hated him. No. That wasn't true.

She'd feared him.

"Then later you ran away after Lucia attacked you. Were you . . . surprised he came for you?"

"Yes." She was shocked when he'd shown up at Club Nova. She tingled when she thought of him kissing her after she fell into his lap. The gentle way he'd cleaned the cut on her neck still brought tears to her eyes.

"Let's do a little word association, shall we?"

The exercise caught Raven off guard, but she agreed. Dr. Wheland loved to change tacks to keep her thoughts and answers honest. It used to put her on edge, these games, but more than once he'd pried out a kernel of truth or a feeling she wouldn't have known had even existed.

She made herself relax and repeated to herself what he always told her. There were no wrong answers.

"Let's begin," he said. "Z Avenue."

"Friends."

"Your parents."

"Guilt."

"Mariah."

"Food."

"Books."

"Learning."

"This library."

"Comfort."

"March."

"Snow."

"College."

"Money."

"Jaxon Brooks."

"Leaving."

The word popped out of her mouth and silence hung in the air.

Dr. Wheland made a few scribbles.

"You associate Jax with leaving. Are you afraid he's going to leave you, Raven?"

She was surprised to find tears dripping down her cheeks. She wiped them away with a tissue she pulled out of the box sitting on the coffee table.

Before she could reply, he said, "Talk to me about that night."

Raven took a deep breath, closed her eyes, and tilted her face to the ceiling. "I was at a friend's house. I was fifteen and allowed to come and go as I pleased as long as I didn't stay out past curfew, but I was running late. We were working on a project for the end of the school year and lost track of time. I knew I was going to be in trouble, and I took a shortcut through the park."

"The one along Cherry Blossom Boulevard."

"Yes. My mother said never go through there at night, but I did. Just this once. It took off close to ten minutes."

Raven balled the hem of her dress in her hands. The night seemed so real. The chirp of crickets, her backpack heavy with books against her back. The cool breeze in her face. The stars twinkling overhead.

"I saw him across the park. Levi. He'd taken the same shortcut. Mom and Dad told him to go find me. He never would have been there if I hadn't been late."

"Then what happened?"

"I heard two cops. They were all, 'Stop! Show us your hands!'

One even drew his gun. Like my brother looked like a criminal," she said bitterly. "He stopped. He'd only been walking through the park, minding his own business. He had no reason to run."

"What were you doing at that point?"

"I was a ways away. I'm not good with distances, so I couldn't tell you how far, but I stepped behind a tree when I heard them yell. One had an edge to his voice I didn't like. After they got out of Levi's face, I planned on doubling back. I didn't want Levi to go all the way to my friend's house for nothing."

"Reasonable."

Dr. Wheland's voice didn't make her react. She was too pulled under, caught in the moment of that evening.

"I could tell by Levi's body language he was relaxed, easygoing. We were brought up in a middle-class family in a decent part of town. We were taught in school to find an officer if we needed help. There was no reason for us to fear cops, you know? He took a step forward, reached into his pocket." She met Dr. Wheland's eyes. "During the investigation, they came to the conclusion he was reaching for a pack of cigarettes in the inside pocket of his jean jacket."

"How could you see Levi?"

"He stood in the square, under an overhead light. The cops stood just out of the circle—I could see two figures, but that was all. It was past midnight, and their blue uniforms made them blend into the darkness."

Agitated, she stood, her fingers clasped together, her knuckles white. Sweat pooled under her arms and dripped down her sides.

"A shot blasted. I'd never heard a gun fired before. After that, it was like slow motion. Levi fell. There was a clatter. The cop dropped his gun. He was a good shot. The autopsy said Levi was dead before he reached the ground. I don't remember screaming, but by the time I made it home, my throat . . . I could barely speak."

Dr. Wheland stood and placed a hand on her shoulder. She

tried to focus, tried to concentrate on the heat of his hand on her skin.

He led her to her chair and pushed her down until she sat. She was grateful for the support under her shaking legs. Her heart slammed, and her blood rushed in her ears with the memory of it. She hadn't told the story to anyone for many years.

"Thank you for telling me."

Drained, she sagged against the cushion. She wished she could go upstairs and lie down, but being it a typical weekday, she'd have tutoring, and a cooking lesson with Mariah.

"Am I better now?" she tried to joke.

Dr. Wheland smiled. "Therapy doesn't work that way." He sat in his place on the loveseat, bracing his elbows on his knees, his hands folded as if he were about to pray. "But guilt does. Denying yourself a home, you've made yourself pay for Levi's death. Living on the streets is hard—it's your penance—but I don't think this is anything you haven't thought of before."

"No."

"Do you think after the three months are over, and you leave to start your new life with your family, Jax will come for you?"

The change of direction in the conversation confused her for a moment, the meaning of his question fighting through the fog of mental fatigue.

Jax had been so gentle with her the night they'd made love in front of the fire. Afterward, he'd wrapped her in a throw and they sat, drinking wine and talking until neither could keep their eyes open.

After that night, if someone would have asked her if she thought Jaxon Brooks loved her, she would have said yes, but she'd woken early the next morning, the dark winter sky only thinking about succumbing to the sun, having to go to the bathroom. After relieving herself, she stood at the window to see if a blizzard the weather channel predicted came through. The storm hadn't—the moon shone on the same amount of snow in Jax's yard as the day before. As she turned, her hand still holding the curtains aside, she caught sight of papers on his desk.

They weren't special. Not colored. Not decorated in any way.

But they looked official. They looked familiar.

Raven held them to the window, reading by moonlight.

Romantic, some would say. If it were a love letter.

But the papers weren't declarations of love. Quite the opposite.

They were the divorce papers.

Signed by him.

Waiting for her.

She would have signed them right then and there and disappeared like a thief in the night, but she couldn't forget her time at Jax's would be her only chance to better herself.

They had a bargain.

She couldn't squander it.

Too much depended on getting her life together.

Her parents.

Elle.

Even Levi's memory. He wouldn't want her to keep living on the streets.

"Raven?" Dr. Wheland prompted.

"No. I think . . . he may regret how he treated me. I think . . . he might see me as a friend, or even a lover. But," she drew in a breath, "he doesn't see me as a wife. I appreciate the help he's given me, even if I had to bribe him for it, but when the three months are over, he'll let me go. He'll want me to go."

"Sometimes people move into our lives for just the briefest moment, and then they move on. But there's always a reason for them to come, and there's always a reason for them to go."

She nodded. "Yes. Jax will fulfill his promise, and I'll walk away with a new start. In return, I like to hope I've been showing him that even though he made a mistake, he's still worthy of love."

"As are you."

"As am I." Raven stood and wiped her damp palms on her dress.

She forced a smile and held out a hand.

"Thank you, Dr. Wheland. I'll see you soon."

Jax looked for Raven in his suite first, which was stupid of him, he admitted, when he came upon his empty room.

Though they'd grown closer as the days went by, there seemed to be a wall Raven would not let him breech. They still made love, and whenever he asked, she still slept in his bed. They invited Erik to dinner, and they met the man Erik was dating. It had been a satisfying evening all around, and Jax had fallen asleep with Raven in his arms, a glimpse of how his future could be if Raven were his wife flitting behind his eyelids as he willed himself to sleep.

But no matter how happy he seemed to make her, no matter how hard she laughed, there was something he couldn't move past, and her ring stayed in his pocket.

Jax pushed her door open and leaned against the jamb, watching her sleep. Mariah said Raven had practically collapsed in exhaustion at the stove while stirring gravy, and the cook shoved Raven upstairs to nap.

He supposed he should let her get some actual sleep at night, but lying with her body so warm next to his—it'd be like a starving man turning down a steak dinner if he didn't take what she offered.

It was different . . . having sex with someone he loved.

Tonight, he wanted to take a walk, the temperatures warming for the first time that winter, and he turned away, disappointed.

"Hey, you're home."

"Hey yourself, sleepyhead," he said, stepping into her darkened room. "Are you feeling okay?"

Raven smiled and held out a hand. "Yes. I . . . I had another good session with Dr. Wheland this morning. I guess it wiped me out more than I thought. And my tutors are saying I'm close to taking the GED exam. They gave me a practice test and the answer key to get me started."

Jax sat on the edge of her bed, pleasure and pain mixing in his heart. He was happy that she was moving forward, that she was finally grabbing hold of the life she wanted and deserved. But when she finished her studies, when she felt she had a firmer grasp on her mental health, she would leave. She could talk to a counselor anywhere, she could get a full-time job and rent an apartment with Elle, go to school part-time in the evenings. People did it every day. It would be a struggle, but Raven could handle it. This woman lying on her bed, holding his hand, grit and determination in her eyes, she could do it. Jax had no doubt.

"That's excellent news," he forced himself to say. "Have you been out today?"

Raven shook her head, her hair scratching against the pillow.

"It's warmer than it has been in weeks. Would you like to take a walk?"

"That sounds wonderful. Meet you downstairs?"

Jax kissed the tip of her nose. "I'll give you ten minutes."

He wanted to ask about her session but thought it better to wait. They would have plenty of time to talk while he showed her the land he purchased with the house.

Less than ten minutes later, she bounded down the stairs. "I'm ready."

"Are you hungry?" he asked, concerned. She looked happy, but a current ran between them, setting his nerves on edge.

"Maybe after?"

"Yes, of course."

Beyond his garage laid acres and acres of wooded area, and they walked side by side, the deep snow crunching under their boots. Stars twinkled in a rich black sky, and a brilliant moon lit their way. The slight breeze felt almost . . . warm against his cheeks.

He scrambled for something to say, then relaxed. Raven didn't need idle chatter. Taking a deep breath of country air, Jax enjoyed the comfortable silence.

In a few moments they'd enter the, well, it wasn't exactly a forest, but the trees were thick, and his property contained a creek that didn't freeze over in the winter, no matter how low the temperatures dropped.

"What made you want to be a cop?" Raven asked as they walked toward the tree line.

Jax forced a laugh. "I can't leave you alone with my mother anymore." He rarely talked about his time on the force, and though he was reluctant to start now, whenever Raven asked him for something, he would do anything within his power to give it to her.

She rubbed the side of her body against his. "Are you afraid she's going to reveal some horrible secret?"

"Between my mother and Erik, you've already heard my worst. But I don't need her showing you any of my baby photos."

Raven playfully wrinkled her nose at him.

"I think I was in love with the idea of being a detective, you know? I wanted to work my way up, be a plain clothes detective, catching killers. After a hard day's work, sit in a bar and drink whiskey sours while I tell my lady woes to a sympathetic bartender."

"Wow, someone was reading too many mystery novels."

"You're not kidding," Jax said, stepping over a large branch partially covered with snow. He held her hand and helped her over it. "And they left out what a pain in the ass it is to wear blue."

"I guess it's like the medical field. Some people are cut out for it, and some people aren't."

"Are you still thinking of teaching English?" he asked, taking the opportunity to steer Raven away from his days as a uniform. He wouldn't be able to avoid telling her the details of the shooting. Just like, at some point, he'd like to hear the full story of how Raven's brother died. He didn't even know his name.

They came to the creek where two deer were having a drink.

Meager provisions over the winter had made them thin, and startled, they ran off into the woods.

Raven heaved a sigh. She brushed snow off a rock and sat, stretching her legs, her boots buried in the drifts. She looked adorable in her black hat and black jacket, bright red mittens protecting her hands.

"Maybe. Not really. I need to earn a good wage, and teaching, especially starting out, won't give me that. What can I do that I would be good at that pays well? Elle went to beauty school and started making money right away, but I have no interest in cosmetology. I don't want to be a dental hygienist poking around in people's mouths all day, but I don't have time for four or five years of school."

"Because of Elle?" he asked, stepping to the creek's bank, crunching debris under his boots.

"A little. I mean, my parents may be willing to let me live with them, but I don't want to depend on them for a place to stay. The goal was to visit them with my looks improved, yes, but also a roof over my head, a good job, and future plans in place. My GED will be a good start. It will prove I'm serious, but it won't be enough."

Jax's mouth dried, and his skin prickled. Now or never. It would be now or never.

All she could do was say no. All she could do was break his heart, and that wouldn't be any worse than what he'd experienced before.

He'd lived through it.

Summoning his courage, he could use that whiskey sour now, he turned to her. "Raven."

"What I need is my own place, somewhere I can afford. Then Elle, I doubt she'd be able to sell her shop on Z Avenue, but at least she'd—"

"Raven."

"—have options."

"Raven," he said, standing in front of her.

She looked up at him. "I'm sorry. What?"

He swallowed. "Stay with me."

"I am staying with you. You gave me three months, and that's fine. My tutors assure me I'm doing great and—"

"I mean, stay with me. Forever." He dropped to his knees in the snow. "Raven, I . . . Because of the accident I've felt like I didn't have the right to move on. I took someone's life, and I didn't let myself find happiness. I worked seventy- to eighty-hour weeks, and I forced myself into relationships that made me miserable. I've done enough jail time, so to speak, for something that . . . I can't say it wasn't my fault, because it was, but like Erik says, accidents are just that. Accidents. The way I treated you, in the church, I mean, and the way I acted when I brought you back after looking for you at Damien's. I wasn't . . . kind. So, I have no right to say any of this, but, I love you. The first night we slept together, when you showed me what making love to someone could be like, that night I knew."

The snow made his knees numb, but he didn't care. The sparkle in Raven's dark eyes captured him, the tremble of her lips urged him on.

"Marry me, Raven Grey. Be my wife, and I'll help you pick up the pieces. We'll get your education sorted out, we'll help Elle. I was thinking Axel may make a good replacement for Erik, if he wants to give it a try."

Raven covered her mouth with her hand.

"You've shown me what love is, Raven. Let me give you a home."

"But, but, we're already married," she stuttered. It was all she could think of to say.

"Then let's stay that way." Jax pulled a black box out of his pocket and opened the lid.

Even in the moonlight that wavered through the evergreens, the rose gold sparkled and the diamond twinkled.

"You still have the divorce papers." She waited for the anger to come. She'd been snooping through his things. But he only blew out a deep breath, a sigh that sounded full of regret.

"I kept them in case you wanted out of our marriage. Whenever you spoke of your parents, it never sounded like you'd still want me in your life. But it doesn't have to be that way. I'll give you all the space you need. I just . . . when the three months are up, you don't have to leave. I'm asking that you don't."

His hazel eyes were full of hope, and a hesitant smile twitched on his lips.

He was serious.

His proposal was everything she thought she wanted, everything she thought she'd never hear.

Jaxon Brooks telling her he loved her. Loved her, despite her past, despite her time on the streets.

One day she'd tell him everything she'd told Dr. Wheland about the night her brother was shot, and her role in it.

Jax knew what it meant to make a mistake.

Knew what it was like to live with the guilt.

They'd both been alone, but now they didn't have to be.

She flung herself into his arms, pushed aside a glimmer of doubt that was so quick through her heart she wasn't even sure if that's what it was.

She didn't need his house to feel like she'd come home, the house other women lived in before her, answering the same question she was about to answer.

Raven found her home the second he wrapped his arms around her.

"Yes," she whispered in his ear. "Yes."

∼

"When was the last time you visited your brother's grave?"

The question made Raven quake inside, and she put a hand

to her heart, though it didn't do any good to lessen the erratic thumping that started beneath her ribs.

"Raven?" Dr. Wheland asked, pushing his gold wire-rimmed glasses up his nose.

"It's difficult for me to visit him."

"Difficult as in, difficult for you to find transportation?"

"You know that's not what I'm talking about," she snapped, annoyed. This wasn't the time to be glib.

Her tone didn't render a reaction, he only sat back and regarded her with steady eyes. "You don't feel you owe it to yourself to . . . apologize to Levi?"

Raven parted her lips, but no sound came out.

"Apologize," Dr. Wheland repeated. "Apologize to your brother for being late." He tapped his pen against his palm. "Raven, when you do something to someone, like you claim it's your fault Levi was in the park because you were running late, you apologize. It would help you to move forward if you told your brother you're sorry. It's what you want to do. It's what you need to do."

"I haven't been to the cemetery since his funeral."

"That's a long time to go without paying respects to a loved one."

It was said softly, evenly, without a hint of reproach, and she took the comment for what it was. An observation.

"What would I say?"

"That you're sorry you were running late. That's it. That's all you have to say."

Raven rubbed her hands over her eyes.

Dr. Wheland put aside his notebook and pen and scooted to the edge of the loveseat's cushion. "Raven, I'm going to overstep my boundaries, just this once. We're trained, you know, to help people come to their own conclusions. It's why therapy can take such an ever-loving long time." He smiled. "People can't see what's right in front of their faces. They circle around, circle around, and it takes a tremendous amount of patience and willpower for us not to just blurt out what should be quite clear. Do you understand?"

Raven nodded.

"I'm going to tell you this because it seems no one else has: Your brother's death wasn't your fault. Your running late may have put Levi in the wrong place at the wrong time, but it wasn't your fault."

With a shaking hand, Raven picked up her coffee and took a long sip. Bless Mariah for making sure they had fresh coffee during these sessions.

"I don't know how you can say that. If I would have been home on time, Levi never would have left. My parents never would have asked him to look for me."

Dr. Wheland poked at his coffee mug. "There's more at play here than you running late. Levi cut through the park. He didn't need to do that. Your parents asked him to bring you home. They didn't need to do that, either. Chances are good you would have been fine on your own. Maybe the trigger-happy cop needed more training before patrolling the streets. Maybe Levi should have taken his car because after all, walking home with you in the middle of the night, it could have been both of you in that situation, not just Levi. There are so many variables to this whole god-awful mess. Yet you choose to blame only yourself. There's no blame here Raven, because there's no fault."

Raven buried her head in her hands as Dr. Wheland's words tried to penetrate through her denial. She hadn't *ever* thought of it that way. She'd never blamed her parents for asking Levi to fetch her home. She never thought for one second how silly Levi had been for not driving to pick her up.

And she never once blamed the cop.

Because cops face danger every second on the city streets, and she would never blame anyone who was trying to protect themselves. She, out of anyone, knew the cost of protecting herself on the street.

"As a therapist, I should have been skilled enough, patient

enough, to lead you to these conclusions on your own, but as things are, I don't foresee we have the months, maybe even years, it would have taken for you to come to these realizations. I hope you understand why I decided to stick my foot in it."

Raven twisted her engagement ring. She hadn't worn jewelry for years, and the weight on her finger felt foreign to her. "I appreciate that you did. You've given me a lot to think about."

Dr. Wheland discreetly slid his phone out of his pocket and checked the time. "We still have close to an hour, Raven. Let's talk about something . . . a little more pleasant. You're engaged to Jax."

"I . . . yes."

With shrewd eyes pinned on her, Dr. Wheland said, "You don't seem happy about it."

"I am. I am happy. But . . . look at this house, Dr. Wheland. Do I look like I fit in here? I've been to social gatherings. I know how those people act. I've gone shopping with Mrs. Brooks. I know the kinds of stores she likes, the money needed to shop at them. I know the expectations. I *know*. Our engagement will be in the papers. There will be parties. Never mind what people will say about Jax and his ex-fiancées."

"That's not it. You look a very refined young lady. You have no problem looking like you belong here. As for what's inside you, that will take time, but that's true for anyone who's adapting to a new situation. If Jax loves you, he'll be sensitive to your needs, and he'll assist you with the transition. No, there's something else. What is it?"

Raven reminded herself he was paid to pry. She bit her lip, trying to formulate into words the shaky feeling in her stomach when she thought about making her stay permanent. "I don't know Jax that well. When we met . . . he was so cold. Not even just toward me. Toward his parents, toward his brother."

"Why do you think that is?"

"His mother told me he shot someone in the line of duty. But that was a long time ago. Why wouldn't he have gotten over that by now?" She pressed her thumb against the diamond heart, the stone biting into her skin.

"Why haven't you?" Dr. Wheland asked, then picked up his mug. "You've blamed yourself for Levi's death for years. Close to seventeen to be exact."

Raven blushed. "Touché. He just seems so much stronger than that. And he's had so much support around him. He threw it all away."

"As did you. Your parents, they offered you help? Before going with the last resort and kicking you out?"

"Yes. They tried therapy, they tried family vacations. They tried everything to bring me around. But, they just . . . they were wounded, too, you know? And I shouldered that as well as Levi's death. It got to be too much for me."

"Do you love Jax? Are you willing to put in the amount of work a marriage to a man like him would require? Or are you only marrying him for what it will do for you?"

"What a horrible thing to say!"

Dr. Wheland spread his hands. "He was engaged to other women who thought the same. In fact, if you told him you were marrying him for his money, would he even blink?"

The thought made her sad. Sad for the man who turned so cold and heartless after a mistake he didn't think a woman would tolerate him unless he paid her. "That's not who I am."

"No, it's not. And he sees that."

"I'm willing to do the work. It's just a lot to take in."

"It is," Dr. Wheland agreed, closing his notebook. "But you're strong enough, Raven. You think you're weak for hiding on the streets. But the opposite is true. The time you spent on the streets made you stronger than you'll ever know."

Raven tried to smile. "Thank you. That's . . . a nice way to look at it."

"Nice, perhaps. But also true. I wouldn't lie to you. Have you set a date yet?"

"The date . . . is up in the air being we're already married."

"Understandable. Then make time to see me. I think couple's therapy could benefit both of you."

"I don't know if Jax would agree," Raven said.

"Try to convince him. You may feel uneasy because you haven't entirely come clean with him. You haven't told him the story of Levi's death, not like you've told me?"

"No. Only that I lost my brother when I was young, and I couldn't handle it. I don't know, Dr. Wheland, the details don't seem necessary. In my healing, yes, but not in regard to my relationship with him."

"Maybe. Maybe not. Revealing the details may bring you closer together. You could tell him here, or in my office. It may help if you felt you had someone in your corner, a buffer. Are you afraid he'll blame you for Levi's death the way you've blamed yourself?"

"I don't know. That's something I need to think about."

"We've all made mistakes, Raven. Forgive his, and he'll forgive yours."

Raven didn't have any trouble accepting Jax for who he was, or, to be more precise, who he turned into after the shooting.

But there was a gnawing in the pit of her stomach. Her life before Jax, and her life after Jax . . . black and white. Raven wished she could find a shade of gray. Only then would she know she found her place.

Jax stood outside the third police precinct.

He'd avoided the old stone building since the day he was cleared and he came back.

But before he told Raven the whole story, he needed to hear it, too.

There were so many details he'd didn't know, both because he closed himself off after the shooting and because his parents protected him.

If he wanted any kind of real chance with Raven, he needed to know and put this behind him once and for all.

Chief Morgan had been the chief of police when the shooting occurred, and Jax had an appointment with him in just a few minutes.

The police department smelled the same and felt the same, but they replaced old furniture and updated public service posters, replaced the ancient coffeemaker and dirt-stained carpet.

The chief's office was still located in the same place, and Jax found it with little problem, even after all these years.

"Jaxon Brooks," Chief Morgan greeted him, holding out his hand. Dressed in a gray suit with an American flag and the emblem of the precinct attached to his lapel, even at sixty plus years old, the man was still a formidable force to be reckoned with, and when he shook Jax's hand, his grip was firm and true. "It's been a long time."

"Chief Morgan."

"What can I do for you?"

Jax sat in front of Morgan's desk, and the chief shut his office door, drowning out the sounds of phones ringing and cops shouting.

Morgan regarded him with serious blue eyes before sitting behind his massive desk piled high with papers and a multi-line phone, all the lights ablaze.

"I have questions about the shooting, sir." Jax swallowed around a lump in his throat and wished he'd taken Erik up on his offer of moral support.

"All the information has been released. You didn't need to come by."

"I want to read the report, sir."

The chief leaned heavily in his office chair and blew out a sigh. "We're equals now, you can call me Preston. I figured that's why you made the appointment, and I asked for the file to be brought up from storage. You were cleared of any wrongdoing."

"I know that, sir . . . Preston," he corrected, finding it difficult to feel he was the chief's equal when time and experience had proven him anything but. "I never found out who the . . . victim . . . was. I need to know so I can properly make amends."

Morgan loosened his tie. "Are you sure that's a good idea? It's been sixteen years, and in my experience, that would be enough time to let sleeping dogs lie."

He shook his head. There would never be enough time gone by for him to do that. "I need a name to attach to the face. I want to visit his grave. I need to write a formal apology to any family that young man has left. Perhaps start some kind of foundation in his name. It will never make up for what happened, and his family may not care about anything I want to do, but I need to do this for me. I've been living in limbo for years because I couldn't face what I've done, and now it's time."

"How long were you on the force before it happened?"

"Just a few months, sir."

"And what have you done since then?"

Jax jiggled his leg, impatient to get this going. He didn't want to catch up Preston Morgan on what he'd done for the last sixteen years, and it didn't matter much, anyway. He'd made a fortune in security, and after finding out the name of the person whose life he stole, he could put some of that money toward the victim's family.

Gritting his teeth, he forced himself to be polite. The chief wouldn't give him what he wanted if he appeared ungrateful for the time and information.

"I started Titan after the accident. I had to channel my energy, my grief, into something, and I built my security firm from the ground up."

"What about your personal life?" Morgan pressed, thrumming his fingers along a beige envelope that Jax hadn't noticed until right then. He wanted to snatch the file, memorize the details, feel the desolation and fear woven between the words of those typewritten letters.

"I'm engaged, sir. Preston." He met he wizened eyes of his

superior and stuttered. He just wanted the goddamned file so he could leave. "But we're having a problem . . . connecting." It wasn't any of his business, and if he read the society pages, Morgan already knew of his two failed engagement attempts. Jax force the words out. "I need to put this behind me. I want to have a clear future with my bride."

"You've been engaged before."

Jax jerked his head in agreement. "And it didn't work out, for this very reason. I can't expect a woman to be happy with me if I can't be happy with myself."

There, that drivel should be enough to encourage his old boss to hand over the file.

Morgan nodded. "That's so. I've seen many unfortunate incidents ruin marriages, ruin lives. You were able to beat some of those odds, but not all. You've suffered, like many police officers who pull the trigger on the job. It's no easy feat, and the department shrink will be waiting to speak with you after we're done here."

Fair enough. Maybe it would be best to chat with someone before heading home, if even just for a moment, after finding out the victim's name. He could ask her what she thought of approaching his family, of the foundation he was planning. Maybe she'd have other ideas that would assist in finally putting this behind him once and for all.

Morgan's phone rang, and he answered it with a clipped, "Yeah?"

He listened for a moment and then, "Be right there."

Jax shifted in his chair. He hoped the call didn't mean he would need to wait to look at the file.

Morgan slammed the receiver onto the cradle and picked up the envelope. "I don't have to tell you not to take this out of my office. I'm needed downstairs, and I trust you'll find what you want to know then head straight to the shrink's office. She'll tell me if you don't show up, and I'll make your life miserable if you cross me."

"Yes, sir. I appreciate it."

Morgan handed Jax the file. "I expect a wedding invitation."

"Yes, sir."

The chief banged out of his office without a backward glance, and Jax let out a shaky breath.

He unwound the string holding the flap in place and pulled out the thick stack of pages his partner typed up.

It had taken Jax weeks to surface enough to report the details from that night. It had taken several days after that to be cleared of any wrongdoing.

He skimmed the details. They brought back that night in stark relief, not that any second had been forgotten. There wasn't a day that didn't go by where some part of that night didn't flit through his brain like wisps of a nightmare he couldn't quite shake.

If by any chance, any chance at all this would give him some peace . . .

The victim's name was on the top of the last page.

At first, the letters didn't make any sense.

Jax did the math, but he didn't need long to figure out what he already knew.

Sixteen years ago, Jax shot down a man in a park. He hadn't looked sketchy, but it was past midnight, dark. Jax was trained to be prepared. Trained to assume that when someone reached into their pocket for something, that something was usually a weapon. He didn't take a chance to find out, and he shot. Just one straight bullet to the heart.

The man with dark hair wearing a jean jacket fell to the ground in seconds.

Stunned, Jax dropped the handgun where it landed on the cement. The clatter echoed through the park.

A scream pierced the air, but Jax hadn't heard it over the screaming in his own brain.

His partner radioed in immediately. "Shots fired. Man down. Ambulance needed."

The moment the man had fallen, Jax knew he was dead.

He crumpled to the ground, his legs no longer able to sustain his weight. Clutching at his chest, he thought he was having a heart attack, but he'd had been told later, after a physical exam, it was a panic attack.

The pieces all clicked together as Jax sat there now, rivers of tears running down his cheeks, dripping onto the report, smearing the typewriter ink.

Raven, disappearing off the grid because she lost her brother.

Levi Grey.

There, in black type.

Victim: Levi Grey.

On one cool spring night, when the stars twinkled, and the breeze blew, when everything should have been right with the world, he shot Raven's brother.

Eleven

A million different scenarios ran through his mind. He wouldn't tell her. He could confess. He could write her a letter and hide while she read it. He could tell Erik, and his brother could tell her. He could tell his mother and let her tell Raven.

Everything he came up with turned him into one thing: a coward.

But the one thing he decided to do turned him into something even worse.

Jax sat in the back of the sedan, his every muscle tense with agony. With the way Justin would frequently flick his gaze to him in the rear-view mirror, his driver knew something had happened.

Before he left the city, he made two stops. One to an apartment building he owned. He reserved a two-bedroom apartment in the heart of downtown for five years. The other brought him to his bank where he shifted money and had a debit card made. He asked the teller for an envelope, and as Justin drove him out of the city, Jax hastily scribbled a note and shoved it inside with the leasing agreement, keys for the apartment, the debit card, and a balance sheet.

Then he used the rest of the drive home to prepare. To prepare for how he'd feel . . . after.

He didn't worry about her. She'd be taken care of. And she was smart and resourceful enough to make something of what he gave her.

Jax found Raven in her room, studying. She hadn't completely moved into his bedroom, and while that annoyed him, he thanked her for it now.

Her mark on his room would have been deeper than the others.

"Raven."

"Hey," she said, laying a pencil on an opened notebook. "You don't look so good. Did you have a rough day?"

He had to harden his heart to get through this, and he thought back to the way Gwen treated him, to the way Lucia used him.

"I want you to pack and leave."

She licked her lips, panic shooting through her eyes. "I don't understand."

Jax clutched the envelope, his palms' sweat soaking into the paper. "I've changed my mind about my proposal. I've changed my mind about a lot of things. When I said I loved you, I was . . . mistaken. I was caught up in the moment, and today I realized you just aren't . . . good enough for me. You wouldn't fit into my world. I need a Gwen or a Lucia. I need someone who won't embarrass me in public. I need someone I can bring to a gala and the guests won't think she's a whore."

With every word he spoke, her cheeks lost color, and bile rose in his throat. Nothing, nothing he'd ever said was further from the truth, yet, Raven nodded, even smiled.

"I . . . it's like you could read my mind," she said, twisting her fingers in her lap. "I spoke to Dr. Wheland about that very thing not long ago." She cleared her throat. "He said you loved me enough to help me fit in. I guess he doesn't know everything after all."

"I've taken good care of you." He forced himself to continue as if she hadn't spoken, stepping inside her room and holding out the envelope. "I gave you access to an apartment downtown. The leasing agreement is inside. It has two bedrooms. One for you and one for Elle. Decorate as you like. There's a debit card in your name, as well. I won't be adding to the balance, but I think you'll find it fair. I know you wanted to do for yourself, but I wanted to give you plenty of time to finish your GED, perhaps earn a degree at a university. Whatever you think is best."

Raven took the envelope, her hand trembling. "Thank you."

He wanted to reach out and touch her, had never wanted anything so badly in all his life. Just one touch to keep with him. Just one reminder of how soft her skin was, how much love she felt for him in her embrace, how much passion she possessed in the searing kiss of her lips.

They may have been on different wavelengths because of the secrets they kept from each other, but there was one simple thing Raven had done that no other woman had.

She'd believed in him.

That one thing was priceless.

"Feel free to take anything you want. My mother, as well as myself, purchased those things for you as gifts, and they belong to you."

She stared at her lap and whispered, "Thank you."

He had to get out of there before he took it all back. Before he dropped to her feet and confessed everything. Before he could beg her forgiveness.

This was what he had to do.

Do it first, before she found out and she left him.

There was power in that.

He twisted the knife he pushed into her back. "I've instructed Justin to take you wherever you want to go. Be out by dinnertime, please. I'll . . . need the house the way it was."

The bomb landed precisely where he intended.

She was brave, his little Raven. She was brave, and not one tear fell from her eyes.

"Of course."

It took every ounce of his strength to close the door quietly behind him and walk away.

He'd never felt so empty inside. Not even when he pulled that trigger.

~

Raven packed slowly, methodically. She would take everything Grace purchased for her. She would need the clothing as she finished school and took up a job. Looking the part was halfway there, Jax had been right about that.

She'd known all along, really, they weren't a good match. But it hurt more than she thought it would. She could blame herself, for keeping part of her heart from him, but in the end, she was glad now. She was glad now she had parts of herself she hadn't given him.

It made it easier to walk away.

Well, not walk away without feeling anything, but it did buy her a few minutes more before she fell apart.

She used the luggage Grace insisted on buying her, claiming she would never know if Jax would decide to whisk her off to Paris on a whim. Grace even made sure she had a passport, just in case.

She stuffed the suitcases full to bursting, and she worried how she would get it all outside, but Justin knocked on her door and said, "Mr. Jax said you would be needing assistance, miss."

Help her get out as fast as she could. She wouldn't thank Jax for it, but she wouldn't turn Justin down, either.

She gestured to the baggage. "Thank you, Justin. These suitcases are ready. I need to change and have a word with Mariah. I'll be out as quickly as possible."

My, didn't she sound refined?

"Very well, miss."

She changed into a dress and knee-high boots. After brushing her hair and fixing her makeup, she stuffed the last of her things into a satchel.

The room was almost empty but for the books she borrowed from Jax's library. She could take them, and maybe sell them online for a pretty penny, but even without looking in the envelope, she knew she had enough to last her and Elle for quite some time.

She'd leave the books.

She'd leave her heart behind, too.

The house was so quiet she could hear the grandfather clock ticking downstairs. She knocked on Jax's door.

He'd forgotten one very important thing.

The thing that had started it all.

When there wasn't an answer, she pushed the door open.

Her heart pounded, but it slowed just a little as she discovered the empty room. She refused to look at the bed, instead keeping the writing desk in her vision. The papers were right where she found them, and it took her only a second to find the signature line at the bottom of the last page.

Using his Mont Blanc, she scrawled her name.

There would be no reason for him to come find her again.

Nothing she did now was any of his business.

She could marry Axel.

She could go back to the streets.

She could do anything she damn well pleased.

It was too bad she wanted to stay married to Jax.

Raven kept the papers open to the last page and set her engagement ring on top of her signature.

He'd given her what she wanted, and now he could say she kept her end of the bargain.

She left the pen laying on his desk.

Raven would never see this room again.

Didn't want to see this room again.

There were too many ghosts.

Unwisely, she took a moment, and leaned against the door-jamb while she caught her breath. She needed to remain calm, cool. She needed to tell Mariah goodbye without breaking down.

Once she gained her composure, she found Mariah prepping dinner. Tonight's lesson plan would have been some kind of Mexican dish Mariah grew up cooking for her family.

Already spices floated through the air.

"Mariah, there's been—"

"Oh, Raven, Mr. Jax, he told me."

"H-he has?"

"*Sí, sí*. Your mama, she very ill, no? You go see her."

Mariah's dark brown eyes teared with worry, a frown creasing her smooth skin.

Of course Jax would have this figured out.

What to say.

A cover story he would tell everyone to absolve him of guilt.

Maybe he never changed after all.

He was still the same old Jax. Couldn't accept responsibility for anything he did.

Raven forced a smile. "Yes. I don't think I'll be back. I'll miss you, Mariah. Thank you for everything."

Mariah hugged her, and it was difficult to escape the cook's embrace.

She stepped toward the door. "Mariah, I need to make a phone call. Do you have Mr. Erik's number?"

"It is there, on the list by the phone," Mariah said, nodding to a landline telephone hanging on the wall next to the pantry.

"Thanks."

She dialed Erik's cell phone number, and he picked up on the second ring. "Mariah, are you all right?"

"Erik, it's me, Raven."

"Raven, you're in the kitchen? For your dinner lesson? Are you inviting me to dinner?"

She would miss Erik and his easy demeanor, but she didn't fool herself into thinking they could stay friends. Though she would need to depend on Jax's money for a little while, cutting herself out of his life as quickly as possible would be the only way to move on, the only way to try to keep the pain at bay.

Mariah stared at Raven with concern, and she turned her back so the poor cook wouldn't hear the truth. "I'm ummm, well. Ah." God. She didn't want to say anything horrible to Erik, not about Jax, not since they've been getting along so well.

"I was just on my way to Finn's, but I can turn around," Erik said, amused.

"No! No. I . . ." Suddenly tears clogged her throat, the last of her control slipping. Say it fast and hang up. "Jax, he, he broke it off with me. I'm leaving. Tonight. Now. I, ah, was calling to ummm, let you know and ask if you could stop by and check on him. He didn't look well." Deep breath. "Goodbye, Erik, I'll miss you."

She slammed the phone onto the cradle and ran out of the kitchen as fast as her high-heeled boots would allow her on the slippery waxed tiles. If she looked at Mariah again, she would become completely unglued.

Pausing in the foyer, she grabbed a jacket. She would only take one, and she slipped on a black trench coat that would match everything she owned.

She ran her fingers over the black cape, and she pushed the memory of her first dinner date with Jax aside.

Justin waited for her, leaning against the car. He took the satchel she remembered to bring with her from the kitchen.

"Where to, miss?"

She rattled off the address to her parents' house.

Raven prayed to God they'd be happy to see her.

Feeling unbelievably rude, she raised the divider between Justin and her and as he drove down the driveway, she pushed her face into the cushion of the seat to hopefully muffle the keening she could no longer keep inside.

～

"What the fuck is wrong with you?"

Jax slouched in a leather armchair in his library and tried to focus on his brother who stood just inside the door, his face red with anger, but it was no use. Too much whiskey. And scotch. Or was it bourbon?

"Should have known she'd call in the cavalry," he muttered.

Not that it would do any good. What was done was done.

"What the hell happened?"

"Nothin' to you."

"You told me you loved her," Erik accused, throwing his jacket onto a chair.

"It's why I did it."

"You're not making any fucking sense. You *love* her. What did you *do* to her?"

Jax knocked back another drink. The blame in his brother's voice grated on his nerves. "I didn't do anything to her. I did it *for* her."

"Like hell. Everything you've ever done since the shooting you've done for yourself. You never did anything for anybody, if you didn't get something out of it, too. So, what? What you had with Raven . . . you decided it wasn't worth it? You weren't going to get enough out of it? She loved you, but it just wasn't quite what you were looking for, so you cut her loose."

Jax's blood simmered out of control, and he took the crystal cut glass and flung it across the room where it shattered against the fireplace. "You want to fucking know? You want to fucking know what happened? I went to the police precinct today and talked with my former chief. That guy I shot? He was Raven's *brother*. Do you have any fucking idea what she would have done if I would've told her? She would have spit on me. She would have *despised* me. I did what I had to do. I would rather her hate me for anything, *anything*, than for killing her brother."

A sob cut him off, and he turned away. He didn't want his brother to see him like this. Erik had seen him at his worst, but this was a new kind of hell.

"I don't understand. Raven had a brother?"

Jax would have laughed at Erik's bewilderment if it hadn't been so infuriating. "Didn't she tell you when she was fifteen she lost her brother? It's all she told me, it's all I knew."

"That's why she was on the streets. Because she was mourning her brother," Erik murmured, the truth registering.

"Give the man a fucking cigar."

"But she knew you shot someone, that it had been an accident. Surely if she forgave you a stranger, she would forgive you her brother."

Jax rubbed his face.

The scream. The scream he hadn't thought he heard through his own, the scream that had sounded across the park.

"She saw it."

"No," Erik whispered.

"She was there. The investigative officer questioned her family, and she was there. Raven had been at a friend's house working on a school project. She cut through the park to go home, he cut through the park to pick her up. Every detail was in the report. Raven saw me shoot her brother down."

"She saw you? You, specifically?"

Jax grabbed a fresh glass from the bar and poured himself another drink. His reality was coming back.

"Not me, a blue uniform, but that's enough, don't you think? Do you think she would still want to be married to me after she found out? And she would—eventually. Do you think she could look me in the eye every day for the rest of her life and not see a murderer?"

"Then tell her," Erik begged, sinking onto the leather loveseat. "Tell her. Things can't get any worse than they already are."

He downed his drink, appreciating the warmth that once again slid through his belly. "No."

"Then I will." Erik grabbed his jacket and made for the door. "If you won't, I will."

"You never could stay out of my business, could you? You're

always shoving your nose where it doesn't belong." Jax paused, weighed his words carefully as they could never be taken back.

He knew, on some level, his relationship with his brother would change, would never be the same, but he didn't care. He just didn't care about any of it.

He said the words even as they shamed him. "Just like your dick."

Erik's face drained of any amount of color. "I hadn't realized you felt that way. Thank you for telling me. I'll tell Mom you need someone to check on you, and I won't bother you, ever again."

Jax was alone, just like he wanted to be. At least, he tried to tell himself that.

He drank more than he ever drank before to make himself believe it.

The car lights faded into the night as Justin drove away.

Raven's parents' house was lit up, but that didn't mean anyone would be there. That didn't mean they would let her in if they were. She'd be in trouble if they turned her away. They lived in a residential neighborhood, and it would be a few miles' walk to a hotel. And she wouldn't be able to carry most of her luggage. Perhaps she'd been unwise letting Justin go, but she didn't want to have to depend on Jax any more than she already had.

The mild evening did nothing to alleviate the feverish sweat dampening her face, and she smoothed her forehead as she waited for someone to answer the doorbell.

She stiffened when a figure appeared in silhouette behind the stained glass of the front door, and she pasted a smile onto her face.

Her father opened the door, and immediately tears filled his eyes. "Raven," he choked. "My little girl."

He opened his arms, and she fell into them. "Dad."

"Come in, come in. Your mother . . . Ever since that young man—"

"Slow down, Dad." Raven wanted to burst with joy. Never in her wildest dreams did she think she would receive this kind of welcome.

"Roz, look who's come home. See how pretty she looks."

Raven was once again pulled into a huge hug, this time by her mother, her mother's scent washing over her as comforting as a favorite blanket.

It'd been too long.

Much too long.

"You look so good, Raven," Roz gushed, framing Raven's face between her trembling hands.

She sat sandwiched between her parents and had never felt happier.

Well, maybe once.

"Thanks, Mom." She'd envisioned this reunion a million times. She had so much she wanted to say, but now she found herself tongue-tied and unable to lift her eyes from her hand clutched in her mother's.

Philip tried again, and the pressure in her chest to make conversation eased. "That young man . . . rich. He came by looking for you. It looks like he succeeded."

Raven listened for recrimination, but there was none, and she relaxed another degree. Maybe this time it would be different.

"Yes. We met . . . well, I was cleaning a church and . . ."

"We know, baby girl. He told us." Philip gently placed a hand on Raven's shoulder.

"I've always tried, Mom, Dad, to get back on my feet. Somehow. When Jax said he'd help me in exchange for a divorce, I took it. I hope you don't think poorly of me."

Roz squeezed her daughter's hand tighter. "No. If that man helped you, that's all that matters."

"I didn't have much time there, at his house, I mean, before he got tired of me."

She had to stop speaking then, because she didn't want to cry.

This visit was supposed to be happy.

"Raven," her mother whispered, "you fell in love with him, didn't you?"

She attempted a smile. "Things happen, but he made it clear when I left we were over. So, that's that."

"Your clothes, and your luggage, your hair and makeup. That was all him?" Philip asked.

"Yes, well, his mother. I'm almost ready to take my GED test, too. I was seeing a therapist. Jax knew I was trying my best to be a better person, so you would let me into your lives again. If you don't want me to stay with you, he gave me an apartment to use downtown and an allowance, too, until I can get a job."

"Raven—" Philip started.

"You'll do no such thing," Roz cried.

"Ever since that man came here looking for you, we waited for word. We prayed to God he would find you and let us know you were safe. When we didn't hear anything, we thought the worst. You're staying with us for as long as you like."

She pushed herself off the old couch and trailed a finger over the fireplace mantel. It saddened her there weren't any family photos in her parents' house anymore. She'd have to fix that.

"I would love to stay with you, but . . . I made a couple of friends while I lived . . . elsewhere. I need to check on them."

Her father opened his mouth to protest, but Raven lifted a finger to quiet him. "They're my friends, and I need to check on their wellbeing. That's all. I've come too far, worked too hard, to jeopardize what I have. I don't want to lose you again, either."

"We'll cross that bridge when we get to it," Roz said, waving a hand in the air as if to dissipate a sour odor. "God, look at you. You don't look like you belong in this little house."

Raven tried not to be hurt even while knowing what her mother said was true.

She needed to find her place. It wasn't on the streets. It wouldn't be at her parents' house. Not long-term, anyway.

It wasn't at Jax's.

She would do her best, one day at a time, until she found where she belonged.

"Grace Brooks spared no expense," she said, smoothing the skirt of her dress. "Mom, Dad, I need to go see Levi's grave. I haven't been there since his funeral."

"Your mom and I go every Sunday after church. He would like that, Raven." Philip cleared his throat. "We need you to know we never blamed you, honey."

"I know. I blamed myself. Jax paid for a good therapist. Dr. Wheland said I could keep seeing him, even without Jax paying for it, and I think I will. He made me see that it wasn't anyone's fault. Not mine for being late. Not yours for asking Levi to come find me. Not even the cop's for shooting him." Her voice broke on a sob. "People always say, 'they wouldn't want you to live that way,' but I think in Levi's case, it's really true. He would have hated my time on the streets, and he would be glad they're over."

"I think so, too." Roz stepped around the coffee table and wiped the tears off Raven's cheeks. "It's good to have you back, baby."

Philip wrapped his arms around her and his wife. "I agree," he said, pressing a kiss onto the top of Raven's head. "I agree."

Raven stayed with her parents for two weeks before she visited Elle.

She made herself have patience, and the time she spent with her parents was like a soothing balm. She cooked with her mother, showed her how to make some of the dishes Mariah taught her. She watched home movies with her dad, and sometimes he would take her out driving for practice. She had yet to take the test for her driver's license, but she looked forward to driving her own car.

During quiet evenings in front of the fireplace, she told them about her time with Jax, and Philip and Roz encouraged her to take up where Jax's help left off.

Raven signed up for GED classes. She called Dr. Wheland and explained the situation. He repeated his offer, and Raven gratefully accepted, scheduling an appointment.

She took her time in her parents' house, reveled in the seconds, minutes, and hours she spent with them. But after two weeks, she needed to see Elle. The haunted look on her friend's face wouldn't let her be.

She rode the bus as close to Z Avenue as it would go, and she walked the remaining blocks.

Spring melted all the snow, and the homeless came out of their winter hiding places.

Raven recognized many of them as she walked along the cracked and littered sidewalk.

No one recognized her.

She found Elle in her back room, shoving shampoo bottles into a shipping box.

"Elle," Raven said.

"Oh my God, Raven," Elle gasped, plopping onto her butt. "I never thought I'd see you again. I thought either Damien really got you this time, or you ran off with that rich guy."

Raven sat on the cot she used to crash on. "Neither, actually. Jax rescued me from Damien, didn't Axel tell you? But . . . Jax decided he'd had enough." Her face crumpled. If there was one person she could show her true feelings to, it was Elle.

"Oh, hon."

She waved a hand to ward off any sympathy. She didn't need it. "No, it's okay. He helped me, and I'll always be grateful. I've been at home. My parents were afraid coming back would tempt me to stay, but I'm ready to move on. I just . . . Elle. Come with me. There's nothing here."

Elle taped the box closed. She rested her elbows on top of the cardboard and rubbed her eyes. "You're right. There isn't. That's why I'm packing up. My sister-in-law in Ohio just had twin girls, and she needs help. She told me if I quit smoking she and my brother will put a roof over my head and help me find work at a salon in town while I help take care of the babies."

She sighed. "I'm happy for you. Do you need anything?"

A peace she hadn't seen before settled over Elle's features. "No. She paid for a plane ticket. Can you believe it? I've never flown once in my life. A damn plane. I told her I'd be happy on the bus, but she said the sooner the better. My brother works all the time, and she's exhausted. Imagine me, a nanny."

"You'll be an amazing aunt," Raven said. "What about this place?"

"I got a buyer for it. Luck was shining on me, that's for sure. Some hot shot developer's gonna try to fix up the block. I hope it works."

"When are you leaving?"

"You had perfect timing. I'm leaving tomorrow. Sending my stock UPS. I could leave it, but this place may not be a salon anymore. Wouldn't be surprised if they razed the entire avenue. Good riddance."

Raven knelt on the floor next to the woman who offered her shelter and a place to laid her head without ever asking for anything in return other than friendship. "I'll never forget how you helped me."

Elle wiped a tear off Raven's cheek. "We helped each other. Don't you go crying now." Elle sniffed. "This is all good news. Did you hear about Axel?"

"Not a word."

"You should have seen him at Club Nova—"

"Wait. *You* were at Club Nova?" Raven asked, her jaw dropping.

"Yeah. I left my shop and everything." Elle laughed.

Another surprise for Raven. She hadn't heard Elle laugh in a long time.

"Go on," she urged.

"I was standing on the sidewalk, talking to Axel, when this

long-assed fancy car pulls up and this hoity-toity driver was all, 'Axel Caldwell?' And good old Axel didn't even miss a beat. Acted like he ordered the car and everything. Your guy—"

"No—" Raven objected.

"Okay, not your guy, but the guy who looked for you here hired Axel to work for him. Sent his driver to pick him up. That was a couple of days ago."

"I'm happy for him," Raven said, meaning every word.

"You didn't know?"

"No. Jax and I parted ways a while ago. He gave me an allowance and keys to a downtown apartment. I came by to ask you to move in with me there. But if you're really leaving, I'll stay with my parents. I don't want anything more from him."

Elle ran a hand through Raven's hair. "You're so pretty, all done up, but I miss your streaks. Your parents, they forgave you?"

"For living on the streets? Yeah. They didn't want me to come back here, but I'm glad I'm able to say goodbye."

Raven buried her face in the crook of Elle's neck, breathing in the cheap perfume and permanent solution.

No cigarette smoke though.

Some things did change.

And for the better.

"I'll miss you," Raven murmured.

"Don't be like that. I'll keep my phone on me, you have the number, right? And get online. Do Facebook or something. Keep in touch."

"I promise."

Raven stepped into the sun, her heart light.

Elle wasn't staying on Z Avenue, and Raven thanked God for that.

Jax kept his promise and hired Axel. Axel was smart, and he would work hard. She hoped he didn't ruin the chance. Especially when he found out she wasn't with Jax anymore—in any capacity.

On her way to the bus stop, she paused and pressed a ten dollar bill into an old man's hand who was squatting in the shade of an overhang. The store was abandoned, and the empty window matched the look in the old man's eyes.

She couldn't fix the world, but she would do what she could for herself and her family.

That meant finally visiting Levi's grave.

It was a good day for it.

The cemetery and her memories of Levi's funeral didn't match, and she had to ask a groundskeeper where her brother was buried.

He sniffed in disapproval, and she couldn't blame him. What kind of sister was she, she hadn't taken the time to lay flowers on her brother's grave?

It shamed her more because in all the years Raven had been gone, her parents hadn't missed a Sunday.

Levi meant more to her than this, and she needed to start showing it.

As the groundskeeper called the cemetery offices, Raven adjusted the bouquet of flowers she purchased at a small corner grocery store near the bus stop. The light breeze blew hair into her face, and she brushed it aside as the old man tucked his cell phone into the back pocket of his olive work pants.

"Levi Grey's burial plot is over the hill close to the tree line. There will be two empty plots near him. Rozlyn and Philip Grey reserved their sites there. Are they your parents?"

"Yes. My brother passed away some time ago. I've been . . . out of town and was turned around. Thank you for the directions."

"I can give you a ride," he offered, jerking his thumb toward a utility cart.

Raven dismissed the cart filled with landscaping tools and an enormous water tank. "No, thank you. I'd prefer to walk. Thanks again and have a nice day."

Her heels sank into the soft soil, and she took them off, walking barefoot across the grass.

As she approached Levi's resting place, Raven's stomach began to churn, and the night of the shooting came back to her.

The quiet evening. The stars. The gunshot and clatter of metal on stone when the cop dropped his weapon.

She'd never gone into the park after that night, even though it was close to her parents' house.

If she wanted to heal, to . . . not necessarily put the past behind her, but confront what happened so she could finally live in peace, she needed to face her fears.

She had a lot to look forward to, and she couldn't let the horrific memory keep her from living her life anymore.

Raven topped the hill.

Her parents had chosen a grave marker with a large guardian angel atop it. She kept watch over Levi so nothing could ever hurt him again.

Raven sat for a long time on the lush grass, resting her hand on the smooth granite warmed by the sun. She told Levi stories about her time on the street, about Elle and Axel. She apologized for what she put their mom and dad through, and she promised to do better, live better.

"I love you, Levi. Thank you. Thank you for coming for me, for being such a wonderful big brother." Tears gushed down her cheeks, and her throat scratched raw. She forced out the words, because they were what she needed to say, what she needed to finish with, or this visit would have been for nothing. "I'm sorry I was late. I'm so sorry." Raven used the angel for solace and support as she released almost seventeen years of pain and misery. Her tears landed on the bright green grass and an assortment of flowers her mother planted into the ground.

Crows squawked in commiseration.

Raven cried like she'd never let herself cry before, finally grieving without guilt. It wasn't her fault Levi was dead. It wasn't her fault, but she'd more than paid the price.

She dried her eyes with the light blue skirt of her summer dress.

Taking one last moment to compose herself, she skimmed her

fingers over the clear cellophane of the bouquet. It crinkled under her touch.

This would be a new starting point for her.

Jax helped her begin, but she needed to finish on her own.

Her relationship with him brought a different kind of pain to her heart. She hadn't been enough for him. His wounds ran too deep. For that, she'd always be sorry.

She grabbed her shoes and stood, offering a prayer of thanks she could still draw in a breath, that she could still enjoy the sight of butterflies playing tag under a crisp, blue sky.

She could have killed herself with grief and guilt.

Jax had, shutting himself off from the world . . . from love.

A living thing couldn't live without love.

She hoped the cop who shot Levi found some kind of peace. It wouldn't be easy taking a life, even in self-defense.

So much tragedy.

But hers would stop today.

Raven took her time as she wandered to the bus stop, weaving between gravestones and markers, her heart breaking when she would happen upon a child or an infant, the time between dates impossibly short.

She stopped by a tree near the bottom of the hill to slip her shoes onto her feet.

With a brief glance toward Levi's grave, just to whisper another goodbye and a promise of return, Raven frowned. A man caught her eye, standing at her brother's grave, a bunch of flowers dangling from his hand.

It wasn't the man's presence that made her heart pound. It wasn't that he was laying his flowers near hers. It was his identity that made her vision swim as if she couldn't quite trust what she was seeing.

For the man wasn't a friend of Levi's, though he very well could have been. The man wearing a navy suit, with the jacket in place though the spring temperature neared seventy degrees, wasn't a co-worker of Levi's paying his respects.

No. The stiff posture, the unforgiving line of the man's spine, could only belong to Jaxon Brooks.

The sight of him made her body tremble, and she leaned against the tree, shielding herself, fearful he'd see her if he turned her way. She fought against the deluge of memories as they threatened to drown her. His hands on her skin, the gentle look on his face as he made love to her . . . She'd been so proud she was able to erase the pain that had been such a permanent emotion in his eyes.

Raven gritted her teeth. It had all been a game to him. He never meant to build a life with her. That had never been his intention.

How dare he, how dare he feel he had the right to pay respects to a man he'd never met after treating his sister like garbage to be put out onto the curb?

How did Jax know who her brother was? She hadn't said anything, though the information was public and he had enough resources to find out anything he wanted to know.

Surely, he couldn't be visiting Levi for her? Jax made sure all ties between them were broken.

Why would he care?

Her heart pounding, she sank to the base of the tree.

Grace said he shot someone in the line of duty.

Erik said Jax thought he saw something, but he hadn't.

Raven pressed her cheek against the tree, the bark cutting into her skin.

Levi reached into his jacket pocket, or tried to. He kept his cigarettes there.

Jax thought he'd seen something.

He thought Levi was reaching for a weapon.

She shoved the side of her fist into her mouth and bit, hoping the pain would anchor her.

Jax wasn't visiting Levi for her.

He was visiting Levi for himself.

Raven squeezed her eyes shut.

Now she knew. The cop who shot Levi hadn't found peace. Far from it.

And she couldn't help him, either.

Raven shredded her heart trying.

Staggering to her feet, she tried to gain composure. She couldn't go home ruffled or her mother would worry. As she sat in the dirty bus on her way to her parents' house, Raven breathed in, breathed out. Knowing who shot Levi didn't change anything.

Knowing Jax lied didn't change anything.

Everything was over and done.

It was a cruel twist of fate Jax had come into her life, but as with everything in life, she had to take the good with the bad. She could curse his name for killing Levi, but on the other side of the same coin, he'd saved her life.

By the time the bus let her off at her stop, Raven calmed herself and pasted a smile onto her face for her mother, determined not to let Jax hurt her anymore.

Twelve

Roz delighted in having her daughter back under her roof, and Raven thanked every god in the heavens her mother and father accepted her into their lives so easily. It helped Raven didn't look like the vagrant she used to be. She couldn't blame her mother for wanting to distance herself from the kind of life she used to live.

She tried not to let it bother her how grateful her mother was she returned from visiting Z Avenue unscathed.

Homelessness was a part of who she was, had shaped her into the compassionate woman she was today, at that moment, standing in her childhood foyer, accepting her mother's invitation to a late lunch.

"We have so much time to make up for," Roz said, fluffing her hair in the hallway's gold-framed mirror.

"Yes, we do," Raven agreed, pleased she could put some twinkle into her mother's eyes.

"You drive," her mother said, tossing her the car keys. "You need your time behind the wheel."

"Sure. Where do you want to go?" she asked following her mother to the car.

"Let's go to Hawthorne Place. Afterward, we can take a walk

in their gardens. You're so pretty, Raven. It will be a pleasure to show you off."

When the host asked them where they would like to be seated, her mother said, "Let's dine al fresco. It's beautiful outside."

They were shown to the garden and a table protected by a large umbrella.

Raven scanned the menu. If she hadn't gone out with Jax so many times, an outing like this so soon after leaving the streets would have made her nervous. Water-filled crystal goblets and three different kinds of forks were a far cry from pie and dirty spoons in a rundown diner with Dorothy for company.

Her mother took it for granted Raven would fit in, and she thanked Jax under her breath. It seemed superficial and trite, but the man knew what he'd been doing.

The picture he made kneeling on her brother's grave dried her mouth, and she sipped the champagne her mother ordered, declaring they were "celebrating" to the waiter, who stared with a bored look on his face, not caring what they were doing.

"I'm going to have the salmon," Roz said. "What do you think?"

"That sounds good, Mom," Raven said, setting her menu aside. She didn't care what she ordered. Seeing Jax still twisted her stomach.

Roz looked up from her menu and squeezed her hand. "I love hearing that. I've missed you so much. Did you have a good day?"

"I said goodbye to Elle. She's moving to Ohio. I was happy to hear that."

"She was a good friend to you." Her mother's eyes shuttered. Roz didn't want to talk about it, and that was fine. With Elle moving and Axel situated at Titan, there wasn't much use dwelling on the past.

"Mom," Raven said, changing the subject before her mother started talking about something else entirely, "Did you ever find out who shot Levi?"

Roz frowned but smiled immediately when a waiter appeared

to refill their champagne flutes and take their orders. "I don't know what you mean, dear. We always knew it was a policeman."

"I know." She ran a finger along the base of her flute. "But did you find out his name?"

Roz shook her head and looked over the garden. "The city was very hush-hush about the whole thing. It's not like how it is today, everything splashed all over social media. They swept it under the rug and paid us off so we wouldn't ask questions."

"You never told me that."

"There wasn't any point in saying anything, and you were beyond speaking to. You were inconsolable. When could we have told you? When would you have listened?"

Raven's cheeks heated. Her mother wasn't accusing her of anything, just simply stated the truth. "I'm sorry."

"It was a long time ago, and there's no point in knowing. What would we have done? I'm sure that young man . . . or woman . . . has dealt with enough. Killing someone by mistake," Roz *tsked*. "What hell he must have went through. Do you ever get over something like that?"

"What if I found out who shot Levi?"

Roz glared. "Don't even think about it. The information will do no good to anyone. Leave that poor person alone. I doubt anyone at the police station would tell you anyway, and that's how it should be. Now, here's the waiter with our meals." Roz sighed. "We loved your brother, but he's almost seventeen years gone. He'll always be with us, but we can't stop living. Now, can we speak of something more agreeable?"

Raven spent the rest of the time with her mother discussing her mother's friends, her new hobby—tennis—and a dance at the country club her mother wanted her to attend.

"Maybe there will be a match for you there," Roz speculated, a gleam in her eye.

The country club was something her parents picked up while she was living on the streets, and nothing could have interested her less.

Tennis, parties, luncheons, the whole thing seemed like a tremendous bore, not to mention completely frivolous after fending for herself for so many years.

Adjusting to her parents' lifestyle would take time, and insulting what they'd come to enjoy without Levi and her in their lives wouldn't be starting off her relationship with them on the right foot. If she wasn't going to move out—and how could she yet?—she'd need to play by her parents' rules. That meant making her mother happy. There wouldn't be harm in it, she would just have to figure out what was important to her and pay Jax's kindness forward in her own way.

"That sounds like fun."

Her mother rewarded her with a huge smile. "I know just the young man to introduce you to. He's a hedge fund manager."

Roz could introduce her to a million men, but it wouldn't matter. Though she'd given it back, she still glimpsed the diamond she used to wear on her left hand.

Rings were a symbol of continuity, of never-ending love.

Where one ended, the other began. Forever.

Jax saved her. In every way that mattered.

That had to count for something.

She'd given Jax her heart, and he'd given it back.

Raven had no desire to give it to anyone else.

She'd rather be alone.

"Sounds great, Mom."

Her mother waved to a friend and Raven gazed over the bright spring flowers of the garden to hide the tears that sprang to her eyes.

She missed Jax, and she could stop lying to herself any day now.

〜

Spring faded into summer, and summer melded into fall. As the weeks and months went by, Raven hoped she would feel better as time went on.

But while she waited for her wounds to heal, the opposite was true.

She thought about Jax all the time. Whether doing the activities her mother planned, or sitting in classes at the community college near her parents' house, Raven waited.

And waited.

She spoke to Dr. Wheland about her feelings, how empty she felt, how afraid she was Jax started dating another woman who wouldn't love him, just spend his money.

After a particular teary session, she sagged against the building, tears slipping down her cheeks.

There wasn't much he could tell her, of course.

There wasn't a cure for a broken heart.

"Raven, love. Are you all right?"

She wiped her cheeks and smiled in simple joy. She hadn't thought she'd see Erik Brooks ever again. "Erik! I'm okay." She sniffled. "I'm still seeing Dr. Wheland, and I just finished an emotional session with him. You're looking quite dapper, if I may say so."

Erik patted the pockets of his suit, keys jingling. "Keeping up appearances for the ladies," he said, winking, but a shadow crossed over his face for just a moment.

"Did something happen between you and Finn?" she asked, adjusting her purse. That had taken some getting used to, carrying a purse. Lipgloss, tampons (she didn't need birth control anymore), keys for her parents' house, and the car her father purchased so she could drive herself to classes.

Her new cell phone. Wallet. Money. The list was endless.

Things she hadn't had to think about in years.

"No, we're well, thank you for asking. Hey, are you free for a cup of coffee?" he asked as a woman walking several dogs narrowed her eyes at them. "We can find a quiet place to catch up."

Raven stifled a smile when Erik inched away from a Pekinese nosing his shoe.

It probably wasn't wise to spend time with Erik. They couldn't be friends. If Jax found out, Erik would pay. She didn't want to put him through that.

But an hour wouldn't hurt. Maybe it would give her the closure Dr. Wheland said she didn't have, what with Jax kicking her out without warning, making it more difficult for her to move on.

Maybe it would help if she heard Jax was doing okay.

"That would be nice. There's a café a block down that bakes chocolate chip croissants to die for."

"Lead the way," Erik said, holding out an arm.

She didn't try to speak until they were settled at a corner high top table near the window overlooking the busy sidewalk, and she hung her purse on the back of her stool as she asked, "How have you been?"

"Don't you mean, how's Jax?"

Raven breathed in the scent of gooey chocolate as the barista delivered their orders, but she didn't pick up her fork. "Jax made sure he's no longer a concern of mine. I asked about you."

Erik sipped his latte served in a mug the size of a bowl. It was another reason Raven loved the café.

"Jax and I don't speak. He decided he couldn't accept my . . . preferences."

"That doesn't sound like him," Raven said. "When we invited you and Finn for dinner, he had a good time."

Erik leaned against the wobbly table, his arms resting on the sticky surface. "He said what he said because he wanted to hurt me and cut off communication. I doubt he meant it, but his words caused the desired effect nonetheless. You haven't been in contact with him at all?"

"No. Why would I? I've been doing my best to keep going. I

have my driver's license now. I'm still seeing Dr. Wheland. He was kind enough to take me pro bono twice a week. I earned my GED, and I'm taking classes at a community college. My parents joined a country club while I was . . . gone . . . and my mother's been dragging me to various activities. She's pushing me to spend time with this guy. He's very nice, but . . ." She used both hands to steady her mug and sipped her coffee.

"Aren't you well, Raven?" Erik asked, touching her arm.

Smooth and soft, with manicured fingernails, his hands reminded her of Jax's touch, and she looked away.

"My mother, she pretends I wasn't living on the streets, that I was, I don't know, in Nevada or something. I talk about Z Avenue, and her eyes narrow at me like I'm talking about joining the KKK. I'm trying to fit in, and for the most part, well . . . let's just say I'm doing my best. I didn't fit in with Jax, or he wouldn't have gotten rid of me. I don't fit in with my parents and the life they started living without me and my brother. Dr. Wheland said it will take time to find my place. But the only place I felt like me was on the streets." *And in Jax's arms.*

"Love—" Erik started, tension pulling at his eyes.

"No, I know. I won't go back there. My friend's gone, and I heard Jax stole Axel from me."

"He didn't kick you out because you didn't fit in," Erik said. He sipped his latte. "He had other reasons."

"When you love someone, you're supposed to be able to work through anything. When Levi was shot, my parents got through that together. They didn't turn on each other. They love each other. Jax didn't love me. He said he did, but he didn't."

"He did. I truly believe he did. Does. But, he found out . . . something." Erik dabbed at his forehead with a handkerchief he pulled out of his pocket. "I'm not at liberty to say what."

"That he was the cop who shot Levi?" Raven asked, giving up trying to eat her croissant and poking her fork at it instead.

"You know?" Erik asked, his eyes wide. "Then why didn't you . . .?"

"Why didn't I what?"

"Go see him? Talk to him?"

"He kicked me out, Erik. I don't see you begging to talk to him after his derogatory comments."

Erik sighed.

"You caught me crying because yes, I love him. I miss him. Dr. Wheland said healing will take time, and God, even after all these months, it doesn't feel like anything will be enough to help me. But you have to understand. I can forgive him for shooting Levi. I never blamed the cop, I'd always blamed myself. And with therapy, I'm realizing that blame and guilt were misplaced. I'm trying. Is Jax? What has he done? He kicked me out instead of *talking* to me. Instead of sitting down and having a discussion with me. Why? He was scared to lose me? He was scared I'd leave him? The end result was the same. Jax is nothing but a coward."

People turned in their direction and she sucked in a breath.

Lowering her voice, she murmured, "He said I could always go back, but he lied. I can never go back there. He has to own up to what he did. He has to be brave enough to face the consequences. He came for me. Found me on Z Avenue twice because he thought he had to. I gave him his signature, Erik. Did he tell you that? I signed the papers before I left. Now I need him to come for me because he wants me. Because he loves me, because he can't breathe without me. But I don't see that happening, do you?"

Erik opened his mouth, then closed it, then opened it again to say, "I love my brother. I love him even after the nasty things he said to me. But in respect of your feelings and how hard you've worked, how far you've come, I owe you the truth. No. I don't believe he'll come for you. I'm sorry to say it. And I'm sorrier that I mean it."

"At least you can admit it. It's more than Jax was ever able to do. You'll have to excuse me. I have a dinner date with the man my parents introduced me to at their country club."

Raven slid off her stool, her heels snapping against the tile.

"He's a hedge fund manager. Even after asking him to explain, I still don't understand what it means, but my mother thinks it's pretty great."

Erik twisted on his stool. "I'm sorry for how it all turned out. You look magnificent, by the way."

"I'm not sorry. Jax helped me. I wouldn't have fit in as quickly without his help." She waved a hand from her head to her feet. "I thought he was being shallow, but little did I know my parents and everyone around them would value what I looked like on the outside more than the person I am on the inside. I was naïve—about a lot of things." She wrote her cell number on a beige napkin, the café's logo in the upper right-hand corner. "I didn't know Jax would be the same way. I thought maybe I changed him, just a little. But people don't change. He probably has a woman like Lucia living in his house, even as we speak. I need someone who has a heart. My hedge fund manager volunteers at an animal shelter. That's a start. Call me sometime, Erik. We'll get together and talk about happier things."

She kissed his cheek, and he rested his hand on the small of her back.

"Goodbye, Raven."

"Goodbye."

She walked out of the café without looking back.

She just said her final goodbye to the Brooks family.

And she allowed only one tear to escape the entire way home.

Thirteen

Raven hadn't moved into the apartment, and she hadn't used the card. Not even once.

Jax counted on being able to keep tabs on her, but every day he called the concierge of his apartment building and every day he was told that apartment 1102 remained empty.

The bank representatives insisted the card hadn't been used, and Jax discovered that for himself when he signed up for online banking and the entire balance was still available.

That meant either two things: she was back on the streets or she lived with her parents, possibly even working.

The thought of Raven on the streets made him sick. Not because of all the time and money he invested in her. No. He'd seen the way she lived and thinking about the woman he loved living that way worried him in a way he'd never worried for another human being before.

His heart made of ice melted.

Too little, too late.

He hadn't spoken to his brother since his disgusting remarks that still shamed him whenever he allowed himself to think about them.

To ensure he was entirely alone, he'd let Mariah go, much to her dismay. But she didn't need to cook for one, and when he smelled her cooking, it only reminded him of Raven and the joy and accomplishment she took in her emerging skills in the kitchen.

His mother cried whenever she came to check on him, which was too often for his liking.

Jax remedied that situation by spending more time at work than what was usual for even him.

Axel said little about Jax and Raven's split and concentrated on learning Titan inside out. As he suspected, Axel had taken Erik's place quite easily, if he didn't count the drug deals he had to break up in the lavatory.

Despite those small transgressions, Jax prophesied Axel would be ready to leave Titan in five years to start his own company.

He would need to prepare for the competition.

The lonely evenings loomed in front of him before he opened his eyes to the sunrise, and he began to spend his evenings at his club downtown. More often than not, he sat in a corner of the plush bar sipping scotch, his demons eased because he wasn't alone.

This night, while a storm raged outside, a thin blonde waif writhed in his lap.

They sat hidden in the shadows, his hand discreetly up her skirt, though nothing would have been said even if it had been evident what they were doing.

He twisted his fingers, and the woman moaned, her head resting on his shoulder, her minty alcoholic breath fanning against his neck.

Wetness trickled down his wrist, his thumb pressing against her clit. He'd been at it for longer than he liked, that last mojito she drank before crawling into his lap doing her in.

He violently jabbed at her, hoping the pain would finally get her off. "Come now," he growled into her ear.

It did the trick, and she shuddered, grasping at his jacket, nipping his jaw with her teeth.

His skin crawled.

Jax pulled his fingers from between her legs and nudged her away.

Straightening the silver skirt of her dress, she giggled. She stumbled away smelling of sex and booze.

Jax cleaned his hand off using the damp cocktail napkin beneath his drink, and he drained the dregs as the woman stumbled into another man who put his arm around her, pegging her as an easy lay.

"Some things never change."

Jax always ran the risk of running into people he didn't want to see when he spent time at the dinner club. Yet he preferred his club over dining elsewhere, getting his money's worth out of the exorbitant membership fee.

Ensuring he could be alone but not alone was a perfect antidote for his misery.

Usually.

"Why mess with a good thing?" he mused.

"You would say that," Lucia DuBois said, sliding into a seat in the winged-back chair near Jax's.

A waiter appeared at her elbow, a pink, frothy, fruity drink already on a tray.

He replaced Jax's scotch on the rocks as well.

Jax silently thanked the man. He was too sober to deal with Lucia now.

Scowling, he asked, "Was there something you wanted? Did you come to exact your revenge? I'm afraid you're a little too late."

Lucia set her drink on a cocktail napkin and tucked her evening purse beside her. "I've come over to apologize."

Jax blinked. "You what?"

"I said I want to apologize," Lucia repeated, twisting her fingers in her lap. "For the way I behaved while we were engaged."

"Yes, I'm sure you feel absolutely terrible."

"No, I do. I introduced myself to you for the wrong reasons. I accepted your proposal because I wanted . . . well, not anything you're supposed to marry anyone for."

"What's wrong with you?" Jax barked, annoyed the hussy's scent still lingered on his fingers, catching a trace every time he took a sip of his drink. He hated the reminder of what he'd done. He needed to wash his hands.

His heart heaved.

He missed Raven so much. Her sweet touch. The gentle look in her eyes.

Her spine of steel forcing him to be kind while he made love to her.

Lucia placed a hand on his knee. "Jax."

He needed to see her. Just for a moment. He kept himself from looking for her. He convinced himself what she was doing without him wasn't any of his business.

But he wanted to see her just one more time.

To put it away for good.

"Jax."

He focused on Lucia's face. She looked different. Softer. She looked how he wished she'd looked when they'd been engaged.

"What?"

"I met someone. He loves me, and I . . . love him, too. I didn't know love should feel this way. I talked to him about how I felt, and he suggested I apologize. So, when I saw you sitting here, I took the chance. I'm ashamed of how I behaved. How I treated you . . . and Raven. God, I've never let my jealousy get out of control like that. You may think I'm a bitch, but I swear, I've never hurt anyone, before, or since. I deserved that broken wrist, and more than that."

Jax sagged into the leather chair. He was tired. So tired of the games. Maybe a vacation. Some time alone would do him some good. Only, he couldn't escape himself. The things he said, the things he'd done.

He'd carry his regret everywhere.

It didn't matter where he went.

Waving Lucia off, he said, "Don't think about it anymore. I was just as bad, if not worse. We're lucky we didn't kill each other."

He closed his eyes hoping she'd take the opportunity to slip away and they could both pretend the exchange didn't happen, but she didn't, and when he opened his eyes, she still sat, chewing her lip.

"Did you want me to say congratulations? If you get married, send me an invitation. I'll buy you a gift."

"Jax, there's something else."

"No, I think that covers it. Unless you're pregnant?" He said it off the cuff because she was rail thin and most assuredly not pregnant. At least, not with *his* child.

Lucia laughed and placed a hand on her concave belly. "No. I mean, we're trying, but, no. Not yet. I just . . . well . . ." She pulled her purse into her lap and withdrew a newspaper clipping no bigger than two inches across and three inches long. "I was paging through the paper—"

Jax lifted an eyebrow. "Not your usual reading fare."

Her cheeks pinked. "I'm trying to care about more than the latest shoe sale. I want to get involved in the community."

"Good for you," he said, uninterested. He didn't care what Lucia had been doing since he'd kicked her out for hurting Raven.

"Anyway, I saw this. I didn't know you and Raven broke up. I was sorry to hear it. I'd heard for years you were incapable of falling in love. I hoped you finally had."

Jax took the clipping.

The photo was grainy, but there was no mistaking Raven on the arm of a man wearing a tux. She looked perfect dressed in a black low-cut dress, diamonds at her throat.

He skimmed the article, something about a benefit for an animal shelter.

Jax thrust the clipping into Lucia's face, not wanting to see it a moment longer. "Did you want to gloat?"

The weight he carried was suddenly too much.

He lost Raven. He'd done so much damage to his relationship with his brother.

Erik would never talk to him again.

Mariah cried when he let her go and his mother worried about him being alone in his huge house. She couldn't leave him alone and avoiding her made his guilt worse.

Respect for Raven thrummed through him. No matter how bad things had gotten for her, she never gave up.

Not like he had.

"No," Lucia said, bringing him back to the club. "I wanted to show you because, I mean, I don't know why you two aren't together anymore, but if you still love her . . . look at her again, Jax. Look. She might be with him, but she doesn't love him. She should be smiling, but she's not. If I had to guess, I would bet she doesn't even like him much."

She held out the clipping once more, but he turned away. He didn't need to see it again.

Lucia dropped her hand. "Everyone knows what happened, why you treat people the way you do. You closed yourself off. I tried to use that, and I'm sorry. I didn't deserve how you treated me, either. I finally learned that when I fell in love. When you love someone, you're supposed to be a better person. You were, Jax. No, you were," she insisted when he scowled. "You kicked me out to protect her. You *loved* her. You still do. I don't care how many blondes you finger in the dark."

"Lucia—"

"No, listen. Try one last time. Please."

"Lucy, there you are!"

"Hi, Bradley. I was just finishing up with Jax."

"Brooks," Bradley said, greeting Jax and shoving out his hand for a handshake. "Thanks for letting Lucia go and giving someone like me a chance."

"Bradley," Lucia said, giggling as she swatted him on the arm.

Jax shook the older man's hand, amazed *this* was the man with whom Lucia had fallen in love. Balding, a paunch besides, Bradley was far from the type of man a woman like Lucia would look at, much less fall in love with. But her smile was sincere, the look in her eyes too sparkly to fake.

"Have a nice evening," Jax said as Lucia stood and tucked herself into the crook of Bradley's arm.

"You do the same," Lucia said over her shoulder. "Think about what I said."

Jax huffed at the unlikely pair. There was indeed someone for everyone.

Glancing at his watch, he decided to call it a night.

He stepped away and the newspaper clipping caught his eye, half hidden under Lucia's seat.

Settling on his haunches, he picked up the small, crumpled piece of paper.

Lucia was right. Raven didn't appear to like the guy, her body language giving her away. The stiffness of her shoulders, the pull of her mouth. But one day, she would find someone she liked. Someone she would love. And then he would lose his chance forever.

Raven's hair glimmered, even in the gritty photo. Her skin gleamed luminescent. The photographer had taken a three-quarter body shot, treating Jax to a view of Raven's cleavage and the sexy curve of her hips.

The gnawing hunger of missing her brought him farther than his knees, and he sagged onto his ass, leaning heavily against the chair.

"Jax, are you all right, dear?" an alarmed older woman exclaimed, rushing to him in a clanking of beads.

"No," he croaked, pushing her away, the cloying scent of her honeysuckle perfume churning his stomach.

"Can I call anyone for you?"

"No," he said again. "No one can help me." He could only help himself.

He needed to now, before it was too late.

~

First, he had to make other amends.

He called Mariah who was more than happy to come back, and immediately began cleaning the neglected rooms.

"I'm putting it on the market, Mariah."

"*Sí*," Mariah agreed. "Something more for . . . family."

"*Sí*," Jax said. "For family."

He wanted a drink before he made his next call, but forced himself to refrain. Drinking hadn't helped before, and it wouldn't help now.

Jax breathed a sigh of relief and sent a thankful prayer when Erik answered his call and agreed to allow him to stop by.

Driving to his brother's he thought to bring some kind of peace offering, but in the end, he stood in Erik's hallway waiting for him to answer the door with nothing but his heart in his hands.

"Jax," Erik said. "Don't worry, Finn isn't here. You won't be forced to deal with him or my lifestyle choices."

"I came to apologize."

Stiff with anger, Erik strode to the refrigerator and grabbed two bottles of beer.

Jax took one, but set it aside without comment.

"You're going to have to do better than that this time. Behaving like an asshole and then saying you're sorry is getting old. I've looked out for you since the shooting. I gave you the bulk of my time for sixteen years. I worked at Titan when I would have been happier sucking shit out of portable toilets. I supported you through your crazy-ass schemes to marry whoever would take you. Then Raven came along, and I went with your stupid plan to fake marry her because God forbid you tell the truth to anyone. But her helping you just wasn't enough. You brought her into your house and abused her, and allowed Lucia to abuse her, too. *Then* when things didn't go your way, you kicked her out without even a 'good luck.'"

"I know. You're right about everything. There's nothing I can say in my defense and I'm getting what I deserve. Someone gave this to me the other night."

Erik flicked the photo. "Huh. This must be her hedge fund manager."

Jax tore the paper from Erik's fingers. "You know him?"

"No. She told me about him."

He sank onto Erik's couch. "You've seen her? And you didn't tell me?"

Erik growled. "Why in the *hell* would I tell you? We weren't speaking, and you kicked her out. What she was doing, or whom she was seeing, wasn't any of your fucking business, and to be perfectly honest, I didn't give one thought to telling you."

Jax rubbed his jaw. "How did she look?"

Sitting on the arm of a chair near Jax, Erik said, "She was crying."

He stiffened.

"She'd just come out of a session with Dr. Wheland, but besides that, she looked good. She said she was having problems fitting in, finding her place. Can't say I blame her after all that's happened."

"Her place is with me."

"Is it? Because it sure as hell doesn't seem like it."

"You're right. *My* place is with *her*."

Erik flung out his arms. "Then what are you doing here?"

"What if she doesn't want me, Erik?" Jax voiced his worst fear. After everything he'd done, could she look him in the face and say she loved him?

"Then you accept it and move on. You think you'll be the only man on this earth rejected by a woman? I'm tired of coddling you. I'm tired of being your accomplice in bad behavior. If this thing with Raven doesn't work out . . . Mom and I won't be targets for your anger. You didn't face up to killing an innocent bystander in the park. Knowing his name did nothing or you wouldn't have thrown Raven out on her ass. You *need* to face this,

Jax. Apologize, and if she accepts it, then she does. If she doesn't, let it go. Then it's the end. *The end.* I will never again let you say things to me like what you said the night you made Raven leave. How do you think I even knew to stop by? She called me to look after you. Kind until the end, our Raven." Erik guzzled his beer. He wiped his mouth with the back of his hand. "Figure this out or leave her be."

"I can't live without her."

"For fuck's sake. Then be a man and go get her."

At the door, Jax hugged his brother. A rush of love swamped his heart. "I'm sorry," he choked. "I'm sorry for what I said. I didn't mean it. You're my brother, and I love you, no matter what."

"I love you, too. Raven's a good woman. Start treating her like one."

Sitting in his car, Jax programmed the address of Raven's parents' house into his phone.

He hoped Lucia wasn't wrong.

Jax prayed he hadn't lost Raven to another man.

It was nothing less than what he deserved.

Jax shoved his car into Park and tried to steady his shaking hands.

Philip and Roz's house looked just the same, only now decorated for fall with hay bales and pumpkins.

A car sat in their driveway.

Someone was home.

He smoothed the tie of his navy suit. His armor. Raven softened him for a little while, but he'd gone back to wearing them. He always used his suits as protection, but he never realized it until now.

As the leaves blew across their yard of withering grass, Jax pushed the doorbell, steeling himself to see Raven.

He sagged in relief as well as disappointment when her father answered the door.

"Mr. Grey. I'm here to see Raven." Jax shook the man's hand.

"It's Philip, if I can call you Jax. Raven has told us so much about you, we feel like we know you. Roz, you'll never guess who's here."

Jax followed Philip into the living room. The house looked different from the last time he was there, searching for Raven. There were pictures on the walls, on the fireplace mantel. Colored throws and pillows brought touches of brightness to the previous drab and dreary space.

Raven brought joy back into her parents' lives.

"Oh, my God," Roz exclaimed. "We never thought we'd get the chance to thank you. When you were looking for her all those months ago . . . we had no idea you'd actually find her."

Roz wrapped Jax in her arms and gave him a hug that rivaled Mariah's.

Tentatively, Jax returned the embrace.

"Sit, sit," Philip urged. "Raven isn't here, but she should be back soon. She's in the park. She's come such a long way, and we have you to thank."

Jax tried to deny it, but Roz cut in with excited chatter. "Her hair, her clothing. Your mother has exquisite taste. And her schooling, Mr. Brooks, we appreciate that so much. When she came home, it was no time at all before she took her GED test. She's taking classes at the community college now. And she's writing a memoir about her time on the streets. She told you . . . about her brother, Levi?"

Jax shifted on the couch. The air was stuffy, and he suddenly found it hard to breathe. Talking to Raven about shooting Levi was one thing. He had to, or he'd lose her forever. Telling her parents he'd shot their only son would be a different matter.

But, again, he had to. If he hoped to marry Raven, he would be part of the Grey family, and he would never be able to keep it a secret.

The time for keeping secrets was well past.

"She told me what happened," Jax said, bile rising in his throat.

"We've finally been able to put it behind us," Philip said.

"I haven't," Jax murmured.

"What do you mean?" Roz asked, casting a worried glance at her husband.

"I didn't start in security," Jax began, standing to his feet, adrenaline beginning to pump through his veins.

Fight or flight.

He had to stop running.

"I started as a rookie on the city's police force. I was twenty-two. Idealistic. Wanted to save the world as most people who graduate from the police academy are wont to do. I was paired with an officer who had some time on me, showing me the ropes. We were doing a midnight walk through the park along Cherry Blossom Boulevard."

Roz covered her mouth.

"Jax," Philip rasped.

"You don't need me to go on, but I have to. I've been running from this for over sixteen years."

"You knew, when you came here, looking for Raven?" Roz accused. "And you never said one word to us?"

"No. What I told you that day was true. I hired Raven to be my fiancée's stand-in. That's all. I spent days looking for her, after you alluded she was homeless, Mr. Grey. I tried to bribe a lot of people for information they didn't have or wouldn't give me. Until I happened upon a little kid. I paid him two hundred dollars, and he told me about Elle. You know about her friend?"

Roz nodded.

"Elle told me where Raven could be, and I searched an abandoned apartment building on Pike for hours. I finally found her, burning up with fever. The doctor who examined her told me I saved her life, but really, she saved mine."

Jax picked up a framed photo of a young man and a little girl.

The little girl wore Raven's face. The almost-man looked like his father.

"I carried a lot of guilt from that night, the night of the shooting, but when I fell in love with your daughter, and I do love Raven, Mr. and Mrs. Grey, what I did kept me from doing anything about it. I told her I loved her, but it wasn't enough. I couldn't show her."

"You didn't know the connection?" Philip asked, tilting his head in skepticism. "You didn't know all this time you killed her brother? Our Levi?"

"The police shrink thought it best I didn't know the truth, and Levi's identity was kept secret to protect my mental health. That worked for a long time. It would have made it all too real to know. I was happy to live in ignorance. Until Raven."

"Then what are you doing here?" Philip demanded. "What do you want from us? You took our son away. We've lived without our daughter for thirteen years." He pulled off his glasses and angrily swiped at his eyes.

"Raven didn't talk much about Levi. She only told me she lost a brother when she was younger. Her time was spent with her tutors and other lessons."

Making love with me.

He didn't volunteer that information.

"It was several weeks before we started spending time together on a personal level. It was then I knew I loved her, and if I wanted a life with her, I needed to face up to what I'd done. I went to the police station and asked to see the file. I wanted to make amends. Offer scholarships, start a foundation in the victim's name."

Roz flinched.

Jax understood. Levi was more than a victim. He was her son.

"When I saw Levi's name on that police report, my world imploded. Raven would never love me if she knew I killed her brother. How could she look me in the eye every morning over coffee and be happy? So I kicked her out. But it was my own brother who made me see knowing Levi's name wasn't enough.

I'm here to apologize. To you. To Raven. I'm hoping once she knows, she'll forgive me. I've treated her horribly, and I won't be surprised if she tells me she never wants to see me again."

"She may not," Roz said. "I think she already knows."

Jax swallowed. "What do you mean?"

"One day we were at lunch, and she asked me if we knew who had taken Levi's life, and I said no. She hinted at finding out, but I told her to leave it alone. Now, looking back, I think she knew. There was something in the way she said it, that if I had said yes, I wanted to know, she could have told me. It's just a feeling I have."

Jax bowed his head. That would explain it. That would explain why she never moved into the apartment or used the debit card he'd given her.

She'd severed all ties because she knew.

"You could leave it alone. You could let her be. She met someone at our country club and I know he proposed. Just leave it alone and let her be," Roz said.

Jax's heart sank. His worst nightmares were coming true, but he needed to see her, just one last time. Even if it meant saying goodbye.

"I love her. I never told her, never really showed her. I could walk out of your house now and nothing would be different for me. I can't do that. For once in my life, I need to do the right thing."

Philip grasped Jax's shoulder, and he prepared to be thrown out of the house. Instead, Philip hugged him.

"Go to her. Tell her what you told us. She's doing okay, taking classes, living her life off the streets. But we're her parents, and we're not stupid. She's not happy. When she smiles, she smiles with her mouth but not her eyes."

"Mr. and Mrs. Grey, I want to marry her. I'm asking for your blessing, even after everything I've done to your family. I've learned enough to know I can't be happy without her. But I'll understand if you don't think I deserve her."

"We all deserve a second chance. You gave Raven hers. Now

take yours. Good luck, and welcome to the family." Roz kissed his cheek.

~

Jax drove to the park where he shot Levi Grey that fateful night, changing the lives of five people forever. He included Levi in his count, and said a prayer for the young man whose life he robbed under a moon and a sky full of spring stars.

Though he hadn't been to the park since that night, he found the square without a problem.

Raven sat where Levi had stood, sobbing into her hands.

It'd been months since he last saw her, and the sight of her stopped his heart.

He missed her so much.

"I was standing right here when I pulled the trigger," he said, his voice raised to carry to her.

He planted his feet in the same exact spot he stood when he shakily yanked his gun out of his holster and shot a man his age, who was only reaching for a pack of smokes. Levi's crime? Being in a dark park at midnight to fetch his sister who was at a friend's house.

Raven jerked her head toward him, and she wiped her eyes. "What are you doing here?"

He waited until he was closer to her before he responded. "I just came from your parents' house. They told me where I could find you. They know, Raven. I told them."

~

She didn't need to ask what he told them. It was evident in his pallor he referred to only one thing.

"How did they take it?" She winced. What a stupid thing to ask. There were a million other things she wanted to know instead. *Why are you here? Why do you want to see me? Do you still love me? Did you ever?*

But the sight of him rendered her to a stuttering idiot, her mind blank except for the fact he stood before her in his usual navy suit, shadows haunting his eyes.

"As well as I could expect, I guess. They didn't throw me out. They could have. Perhaps they should have. How have you been? You look good."

She ran a hand over her hair, messy from the wind that would sporadically burst through the trees. "I've been . . . okay." *Missing you. Craving your touch. Wishing things had turned out differently.*

Jax took another step forward. "Your mother tells me you're engaged."

Raven slipped her left hand under her skirt. "How are you? You look tired."

He did, too, the poor baby. She wanted to hug him to her, kiss away his pain. Only, she'd tried that before, and it hadn't worked so well.

"I am. I'm tired of running. I'm tired of living my life without you. Can I?" he asked, gesturing to the concrete.

She nodded.

Jaxon Brooks sitting on the ground in a suit. It would have made her speechless if his presence hadn't already done so.

"The night I kicked you out, earlier that day I saw my old police chief. I wanted to be able to start fresh, a clean slate with you. Stop running once and for all. When he handed me that report . . . I knew the moment I saw Levi's name we were over. How could you love the man who killed your brother?"

Tears welled in his eyes, and he looked away as they dripped down his cheeks.

Raven opened her arms, and after the briefest of hesitations, he fell into them.

She cradled him as he cried against her breast.

His keening shook his entire body, and Raven held him to her, rocking back and forth, running her fingers through his hair.

"Shh, shh. I would have still loved you because that's what love is. It's standing by someone when they've lost their way. I let you push me away because I didn't feel like I belonged with you. I felt so out of place in your life. I'd been on the streets, you saw the kind of life I lived. I thought maybe it was all for the best. You said I could always go back, and maybe you would have taken me back had I begged. But nothing would have changed."

Jax lifted his head, and the pain in his eyes tore her heart in two.

"Now it's too late," he choked. "You found someone else."

He tried to stand, but Raven held on. She couldn't let him go just yet. The warmth of his body, the touch of his skin. Just another second.

Rubbing the pad of his thumb over her cheek, he said, "I'll file the papers. I saw you signed them."

Raven clutched the lapel of his jacket. "Isn't that what you wanted?"

Jax pulled the ring she left behind from the inside of his suit pocket. "Since the moment I saw you in the church, you're all I've wanted, Raven. It just took this fool too long to see it."

She held out her bare left hand, and he slipped the ring onto her finger.

Kissing her palm, he murmured, "You're not engaged."

"No," she said and cradled his face between her hands. "I love you. You're the only man I want to be married to. You came for me. I lost my faith in you, in us. But you came for me."

He rested his forehead against hers. "Always."

She pressed her lips to his. Salty with tears, but firm and warm.

He wrapped his arms around her, and leaning against his chest, she sighed against his mouth.

When she looked into his eyes, she finally found peace there.

And love.

"Are we still married, then?" she asked.

"Yes. I didn't have the heart to file the paperwork." Jax rubbed his nose against hers.

Raven brushed her thumb over his lips. "Good. Let's keep it that way. I love you, Jaxon Brooks. Never will I see the man who took Levi's life, but the father of my children, the man who rescued me. And always, always, the man who will search for me until he finds me."

Jax smiled. "Let's go home."

Raven let Jax pull her to her feet. It didn't matter where he took her. In his arms, she was already there.

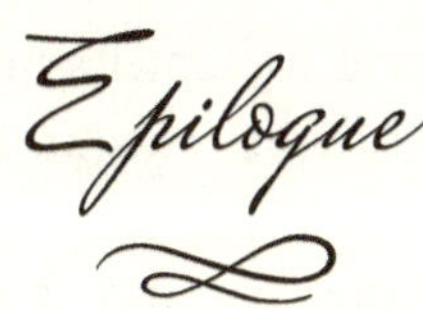

Epilogue

re you okay?" Jax asked, sinking into a chair beside his wife. He loved thinking about Raven that way. Though she'd been his wife since the day they met, they lived it now, and nothing suited him better.

"I'm fine, but the baby must be doing somersaults in there." Raven patted her belly.

At eight months along, Raven said she felt like a house, but Jax had never seen her look lovelier. He leaned over and kissed her bump, grinning like a madman when the baby kicked under his lips.

"Erik looks so happy," Raven said, placing a hand against Jax's cheek.

"He and Finn make a fine pair," Jax agreed, straightening the tux he wore as Erik's best man.

The four years since Jax found Raven in the park had gone by in a whirlwind. They sold the house, leaving behind the worst memories and determined to make new ones, happier ones.

They found a house in a lovely part of the city near the river and good schools, which proved lucky when two years later Raven announced she was pregnant.

"You look like the cat who ate the canary," Raven said as Axel strode up to them, and Jax laughed at the accurate description.

After Axel graduated with his business degree, Jax put him in charge of the foundation he founded in Levi's name. The foundation awarded funds and resources to at-risk young men and women bound on the path to homelessness. Axel's knowledge of the streets, and how easy it was to end up there, became invaluable.

Raven finished her memoir, and though sales were slow at first, they snowballed. All the royalties she earned went to Levi's foundation.

She was in constant contact with Elle, who wrote in long letters she was doing great, and she'd come to visit once, too. That made Raven very happy.

And there was nothing Jax wanted more than to make his wife happy. That included a renewal of their vows, combined with a belated honeymoon, after their daughter was born.

Raven's parents accepted him into their family and they held fundraising events at their country club for the foundation. Not to mention, they were thrilled with the idea of becoming grandparents.

"Jax, will you dance with me?" his mother asked.

"I—"

"Go," Raven said, pushing on his shoulder. "Axel will keep me company while I put my feet up."

He gave Raven a kiss and led his mother onto the dance floor.

"Your father and I are so happy for you," Grace said, pausing their dancing to give her son a fierce hug.

"Thanks, but I owe it all to Raven. She could have hated me for what I did, but she never said one word against me."

"Have you told her yet?"

"About turning Z Avenue into housing and places of employment to help the homeless get off the streets for good? Not yet. I'm waiting until after our wedding. Our real one. It's my gift to her."

Grace squeezed Jax's arm. "That's a huge wedding gift. Do you know what she's giving you?"

Jax watched Raven laugh with Erik and Finn who joined her and Axel, distributing thick wedges of wedding cake. "She doesn't need to give me anything. She's already given me everything I could ever want."

Also by Vania Rheault

On the Corner of 1700 Hamilton

Summer Secrets Novellas 1-3

Summer Secrets Novellas 4-6

Don't Run Away (Tower City Trilogy Book One)

Chasing You (Tower City Trilogy Book Two)

Running Scared (Tower City Trilogy Book Three)

Wherever He Goes

All of Nothing

The Years Between Us

His Frozen Heart (A Rocky Point Wedding Book One)

His Frozen Dreams (A Rocky Point Wedding Book Two)

Her Frozen Memories (A Rocky Point Wedding Book Three)

Her Frozen Promises (A Rocky Point Wedding Book Four)

As VM Rheault

Captivated by Her (Cedar Hill Duet Book One)

Addicted to Her (Cedar Hill Duet Book Two)

Rescue Me

Give & Take (The Lost & Found Trilogy Book One)

Lost & Found (The Lost & Found Trilogy Book Two)

Safe & Sound (The Lost & Found Trilogy Book Three)

Faking Forever

Twisted Alibis (Ghost Town Trilogy Book One)

Twisted Lullabies (Ghost Town Trilogy Book Two)

Twisted Lies (Ghost Town Trilogy Book Three)

A Heartache for Christmas

Cruel Fate (King's Crossing Book One)

Cruel Hearts (King's Crossing Book Two)

Cruel Dreams (King's Crossing Book Three)

Shattered Fate (King's Crossing Book Four)

Shattered Hearts (King's Crossing Book Five)

Shattered Dreams (King's Crossing Book Six)

Vania Rheault writes contemporary romance and billionaire romance under VM Rheault.

She lives in Minnesota with her two children. When she's not writing, she's working her day job, sleeping, or enjoying the four seasons with a hot cup of coffee in hand.

Find her at vmrheault.com.